Turncoat

Turncoat

A MARC EDWARDS MYSTERY

DON GUTTERIDGE

M&S

National Library of Canada Cataloguing in Publication

Gutteridge, Don, 1937-
Turncoat / Don Gutteridge.

"A Mark Edwards Mystery".
ISBN 0-7710-3677-9

I. Title.

PS8513.U85T87 2003   C813'.54   C2002-905542-3
PR9199.3.G84T87 2003

We acknowledge the financial support of the Government of
Canada through the Book Publishing Industry Development
Program and that of the Government of Ontario through the
Ontario Media Development Corporation's Ontario Book
Initiative. We further acknowledge the support of the Canada
Council for the Arts and the Ontario Arts Council for our
publishing program.

Typeset in Sabon by M&S, Toronto
Printed and bound in Canada

McClelland & Stewart Ltd.
The Canadian Publishers
481 University Avenue
Toronto, Ontario
M5G 2E9
www.mcclelland.com

1 2 3 4 5   07 06 05 04 03

For Kate, who loves a mystery,
and for John, my Right Reader

Author's Note

Turncoat is wholly a work of fiction, but I have endeavoured to convey in it the spirit of the period and the political tensions that led to the Upper Canada Rebellion of 1837. The statements, actions, and character traits attributed to actual historical personages referred to in the novel – Sir John Colborne, William Lyon Mackenzie, Peter Perry, and Ogle Gowan – are fictitious, and readers will have to make up their own minds as to whether such characterizations are consistent with the historical record. All other characters are the invention of the author, and any resemblance to persons living or dead is coincidental.

Toronto and Cobourg, of course, were and are real towns. Although Crawford's Corners is imaginary, many hamlets or postal drops like it could be found along the Kingston Road in 1835–36. The political issues raised in the story – the Clergy Reserves and the question of rights accorded to American immigrants – are presented as they would have appeared to those adversely affected by them. The Hunters' Lodges were an actual underground movement for the liberation of Upper Canada, but I have moved their activities up two years to facilitate the plot. Many such "secret societies" existed or were perceived to exist during the stress and paranoia of this turbulent period of Ontario's history.

A number of books provided useful background information and serendipitously suggested ideas that made their way into the story. Edwin C. Guillet's *Early Life in Upper Canada*, E.C. Kyte's *Old Toronto*, Frank Walker's *Sketches of Old Toronto*, and Percy Climo's *Early Cobourg* provided specific geographical and sociological detail; Sam Welch's *Recollections of Buffalo* was, among other things, an inexhaustible source of interesting names; G.C. Moore-Smith's *The Life of John Colborne* and Charles Lindsey's *The Life and Times of Wm. Lyon Mackenzie* offered close-up, contemporary accounts of the 1830s; and Gerald M. Craig's *Upper Canada: 1784–1841* brought some bracing scholarly balance to the task of interpretation. Any errors of fact in the novel, deliberate or naive, are exclusively my own.

ACKNOWLEDGEMENTS

I would like to thank the following for their encouragement and advice: Bob Clark, Gerry Parker, Stan Atherton, John Gutteridge, George Martell, Graham Brown, Terry Leeder, Beverley Slopen, and Dinah Forbes.

CHAPTER ONE

Toronto, Upper Canada: January 1836

The message that was to change Ensign Marc Edwards's life forever was simple enough. It was relayed to him by a chubby-cheeked corporal as Marc came out of the Cock and Bull, a tavern frequented by officers of His Majesty's 24th Regiment of Foot.

"You are to report to Government House immediately, sir," the corporal said nervously.

"But I'm due back at Fort York within the hour," Marc said. "Colonel Margison is expecting me."

"It's the Governor, sir. He wants to see you, personally. I've got a sleigh waiting around the corner."

"Very well, then." Marc tried not to let his excitement show, but after eight long months of barracks life and daily military routine in this far-flung colony of the British Empire, the possibility of something – anything – out of the ordinary was enough to set a young man's heart racing.

Government House had once been the country residence of a local grandee, a rambling wooden structure sporting several ornate verandas and sprouting a dozen chimney pots above its dozen wings and belvederes. It was set in a six-acre park at the corner of King and Simcoe streets, well out of view of those who might be envious of its splendour. As Marc was driven through the park and down a winding, snow-packed lane at breakneck speed, he tried to guess what was so urgent that an ordinary ensign like himself had to be summoned into the august presence of Sir John Colborne. But he had come up with no answer by the time he was ushered through the foyer into an office on the left-hand side of the carpeted hallway.

The lieutenant-governor's office was not the luxuriously appointed room Marc had expected. It was small, with a single window and a plain desk, upon which several neatly stacked piles of papers were strategically arrayed, like figures on a model battlefield. Beside it sat a simple table, cluttered with notes and binders – the secretary's desk, now unoccupied.

Behind the larger desk, in a wooden captain's chair, sat the man himself. Sir John was a veteran of the Peninsular War and the decades-long fight against Napoleon, culminating in Waterloo, where he had been instrumental in securing the allied victory. As Marc was shown in by the duty corporal, Sir John rose and offered a brief, tight smile – of recognition and welcome. For a moment his tall, austere figure and intelligent, appraising gaze left Marc speechless. He had, of course, chatted with Sir John several times at various galas in the fall, and most recently at the New Year's levee, where the Governor had gone on at some length about Marc's Uncle Frederick, who had served under him during half a dozen campaigns on the Continent. But Marc knew he had not been summoned here for polite chit-chat about his uncle.

"Come in, Marc – I'm going to call you that, Ensign, if you don't mind – and take a seat. We have much to discuss and too little time in which to do it."

Sir John began without further ceremony.

"I will tell you as much as I know and am able to reveal to you at this time. As you may be aware, having been abroad in the countryside on several occasions last year, I have numerous agents and correspondents in the districts who keep me informed on a regular basis of matters pertinent to His Majesty's interests in Upper Canada. Joshua Smallman was one such man."

"The chap who used to run the dry goods store on King Street?"

Sir John smiled, as if some portion of his unerring judgment had been duly confirmed. "Yes. He packed up and moved off to Crawford's Corners, a hamlet near Cobourg about seventy miles from here, after his son died, to assist his daughter-in-law and her crippled brother in the operation of their farm. A Christian gentleman and a loyalist through and through. For the past twelve months he has been sending me sealed letters that have provided me and His Majesty with invaluable information regarding agitators and would-be insurrectionists in the Cobourg region – men who would have us yoked with the United States and its insidious republicanism."

It was little wonder, Marc thought, that Britain was hypersensitive to the threat of democracy from the south and the passions it stirred among the disaffected in Upper Canada. She had lost her Thirteen Colonies in the Revolutionary War, and then had barely hung on to the remaining ones up here during the American invasions of 1812 and 1813.

"And I needn't remind you that that area is Perry terrain," Sir John continued.

Peter Perry, Marc recalled, was a leading light among the radicals in the Legislative Assembly (called "Reformers" out here) and an outspoken critic of the Governor and his conservative administration.

"You think, sir, that Mr. Perry may have gone over to the annexationists or the Mackenzie republicans?"

"He's been conspiring with Willy Mackenzie on this latest so-called *Report on Grievances* cooked up by the Legislative Assembly. But no, it is not Perry or Reformers like Rolph or Bidwell or Baldwin I am concerned about – troublesome though they may be. In fact, it is precisely the inability of old conservatives and Tories like Allan MacNab or Orange fanatics like Ogle Gowan to discriminate between a loyal dissenter and a committed seditionist that has caused so much of the present confusion and discontent. Even Mackenzie does not concern me: he abides and caterwauls not half a mile from this office. His movements and nefarious doings are reported to me before they occur, and quite often when they don't." Sir John, whose military bearing dominated any room he chose to grace, glanced up from the papers on his desk to see what effect his modest ironic sally might have had on the youthful ensign.

"Joshua Smallman was not among the fanatics," he said emphatically. "He was a humble citizen of the Empire endowed with common sense and a strict but not strident adherence to duty."

"Was?"

"He died just before New Year's Day. And I have good reason to suspect that he was murdered."

Marc's surprise registered clearly on his face.

"As you may already know," Sir John said, in the same straight-ahead, matter-of-fact tone, "I have been unavoidably busy with packing my books and belongings in the past week."

"Then it *is* true that you are leaving for Montreal," Marc said.

"I am. Simply put, I am needed more urgently in Quebec, where open rebellion may be nearing. My sovereign has called me there, and the long and short of it is that all of us, major general or drummer boy, must do his duty."

The manner in which Sir John first looked down and then glanced furtively back up alerted Marc to the sudden change in his own fortunes about to be announced, and the necessity of an unwavering obedience.

"I have here," Sir John continued, picking up a letter from his desk, "the last report that Joshua Smallman sent me. It is dated December 28, almost two weeks ago. It came into my hands after New Year's Day, but I must confess to you – and upbraid myself yet again – that I let it idle amongst more trivial messages and petitions until yesterday evening."

"He wrote you, then, three days before his . . . death?"

"That's right. Naturally I was informed of that tragic event within the day by courier. The district magistrate, who is a staunch supporter of the government, sent me the news, and three days later I received from him and from the sheriff of Northumberland County a summary of their findings and the results of the inquest."

"Murder?"

"Death by misadventure."

"I don't follow, sir."

"According to Sheriff MacLachlan's report and the minutes of the inquest, Smallman, for reasons undeterminable, set out on horseback from his daughter-in-law's house on New Year's Eve. He told her that he was doing so in response to a message, but she doesn't remember seeing any note and swears no one came directly to the house that evening, other than neighbours invited in for a quiet celebration. Nor would he tell her where he was going, despite her earnest entreaty and her expression of fear for his safety." Before Marc could interrupt, Sir John said, "The weather was inclement in the extreme: below zero with squalls of snow and a strong wind off the lake. But off he went."

"Worried? Anxious?"

"One would assume so," Sir John said with a rueful smile, "but apparently not. He was described as rather excited, eager even, with not the least suspicion of danger. In fact, his last words to the young woman – Bathsheba – were: 'When I return I may have some news that could change our lives forever.'"

"How, then, did he die?"

"Presumably he headed east along the Kingston Road, turned off on one of the newly surveyed concessions – he was seen to do so by a reliable witness – and kept going towards the lake. Fortunately the snow stopped completely before midnight and the wind soon died down, so when a search party was organized the next morning by Philander Child, the magistrate, and the supernumerary constable for Crawford's Corners, one Erastus Hatch, the trail left by Smallman's horse was still traceable. They soon heard the wretched beast whinnying like a sick child from the woods nearby. They found it tethered and near death, and a few yards farther on they came across the frozen corpse of Smallman himself."

"Surely he couldn't merely have lost his way. Not with a horse to lead him out."

"True. But he had donned snowshoes and trod straight into a deadfall trap set years ago by the Mississauga Indians and long since abandoned."

"Could it have been re-rigged more recently? For other ends?"

With each question or comment from Marc, Sir John grew more assured that, despite the beardless and callow countenance of the youth sitting in near-solemn attentiveness before him, he had chosen the right man for the task he had in view.

"No," Sir John said. "The entire area was thoroughly scrutinized by Sheriff MacLachlan and Constable Hatch. However, I expect you'll want to see for yourself."

"But what can I hope to discover that they have not?" Marc said, genuinely puzzled.

"Why I am suspicious of murder, you mean?" Sir John said dryly. "Well, I wasn't, not until I read Smallman's report last night." He held the paper up as if he needed to consult its contents, whose import and detail he had committed to memory. "Among other things, not relevant to our concerns here, he hinted near the end that he had grown weary of playing secret agent, that he had started to have doubts about his own sentiments in regard to the grievances so recently raised by the Reformers in the Assembly."

"He doubted his own loyalty?"

"Not at all. That he could never do, whatever the provocation. That is the very reason I trusted him. Even the frank expression of such fleeting doubts endeared him the more to me and further validated his probity in my eyes. When you have commanded men in battle as I have, or attempted to administer justice among colonial grandees driven by deceit and self-serving ambition, then perhaps you will better understand what I mean. No, I doubted not, nor do I now doubt, Joshua Smallman's loyalty. But he did go on to inform me that he felt that his role as a 'spy' – his characterization, not mine – was close to being exposed, that his daughter-in-law's increasing sympathy for left-wing causes was becoming public knowledge and threatening to compromise him. He was beginning to feel torn between his patriotic duty to His Majesty and his Christian duty to his son's widow and her family. Finally, he said that while he had no firm evidence yet, he felt matters were coming to a head on several fronts."

"Did he suggest he was in any physical danger?"

"Yes. Not directly, mind you. I'll read you what he wrote: 'There are men in these parts who are growing more desperate by the week. Many of them I have mentioned in previous reports, all of whom, until quite recently, I would swear still held to legislative and lawful means to achieve their purposes. At this moment, I don't know whether there is more danger in my being thought to be a true-blue member of the Family

Compact or a Tory-turned-Reformer under the influence of his son's wife. In either case, I fear my usefulness to you is at an end. I do not lack courage, but I must admit that I was shaken last week when a young lad from a radical family on one of the back concessions was found tarred and feathered and bearing a sign that read "turncoat."'"

"Upsetting, but, as he says, not evidence of a threat against him personally," Marc said.

Finally Sir John said, with some of the steeliness that had earned him such respect on the Spanish Peninsula and later at Waterloo: "Joshua Smallman would not have left his home in the midst of a New Year's celebration and ventured out into a blizzard upon a fool's errand. He was born and raised along that portion of the lake, he knew every brook and ravine. His horse was found tethered, not roaming frantically on its own. He was going somewhere in particular and in earnest. And even though the surgeon testifies that he died in the manner suggested by the circumstances in which he was found, neither he nor the constables knew that Joshua was my agent, and friend. Nor *will* they." He held Marc's eye long enough to settle that point, then said, "They have no reason to suspect that he may have had some clandestine and possibly life-threatening motive for being out alone on the last day of one of the saddest years of his life."

"But *I* do," Marc said.

"Precisely." Sir John shuffled several papers on his desk, then looked up. "Please send your report directly to me in Quebec."

Marc nodded. "When do you want me to leave for Crawford's Corners?"

"In half an hour." Sir John kept his appraising gaze on the nephew of Frederick Edwards.

Marc gave him the answer he was looking for: "Yes, sir."

There had been little more to say, then, except to sort out in their brusque, soldierly way the mundane details of Marc's departure and, as it were, his marching orders. Sir John went over the contents of the warrant that would allow him to interview witnesses and otherwise use the Governor's authority to investigate the suspicious death of Joshua Smallman. Marc was given a bundle of notes and papers that might be pertinent to his efforts and told to read them over before he reached his destination. Colonel Margison, his commanding officer, had provided a swift horse and was to concoct a suitable story to account for Marc's absence from Fort York.

So it was just before three in the afternoon that Ensign Edwards set off down King Street on a secret and possibly dangerous mission into the troubled countryside of Upper Canada. He still had no idea why he had been chosen.

As Marc trotted along the main thoroughfare of the province's capital – past its self-important little strip of shops, offices, and taverns – he was pleased that the sun was shining and highlighting the scarlet and grey of his regimental uniform, most of it dazzlingly visible through his unbuttoned and wind-buffeted greatcoat. But his initial sense of excitement soon gave way to consideration of what faced him seventy miles east on the Kingston Road. Even if murder had actually occurred – and there was no guarantee that Smallman's death had not been a bizarre accident – his chances of resolving the matter were slim. First, he knew no one who might be involved in the affair or was in a position to provide useful information. But then he would not be known to them, a factor that he might be able to exploit, even though he had already made the decision not to investigate incognito. His good looks and aristocratic manners, he reasoned, belied the keen intelligence that his favourite tutor, Dr. Crabbe, insisted he possessed. Perhaps a studied disingenuousness, combined with the secret information supplied by Sir John, would be his best hope.

Someone waved a mittened hand at him from the doorway of Miss Adeline's dress shop, and a feminine cry sallied up. Marc kept his eyes front so that his quick smile went unappreciated. The brisk winter breeze chilled and stirred him. He felt physically alive, acute, like some exotic woodland creature that was both hunter and hunted.

Only one discordant note threatened to disturb the pleasure he was feeling, and he fought hard to suppress it. By the time he got back to Toronto – even if he were to be spectacularly successful in Crawford's Corners – his role model and benefactor would be in Quebec. Sir John's replacement, he had learned, was already on his way from England: Sir Francis Bond Head, a man with not a single battle under his belt or laurel to his name, a scribbler of travel books and sonnets for the titillation of ladies-in-waiting among the petty gentry of Toronto and York County.

As he crossed Simcoe Street, Marc's eye was drawn to the red-brick silhouette of the two-storeyed parliament buildings a block to the south. Their glittering glass windows and cut-stone pilasters gave them an air of permanence and pertinence. Like their counterparts along the Thames in London, these legislative halls were mere houses of words, monuments to bombast and hyperbole. He had seen the originals at Westminster, at first in awe as a child at the side of Uncle Jabez (as he called his adoptive father, Jabez Edwards), and later as a law student at the Inns of Court when he was old enough to judge for himself. Even now, even here, a thousand leagues from all that mattered in the world, men slung epithets as if they were weapons: to sting, incite, confuse, and corrupt. But in the end it was the soldier who had to set things right, risking body and soul.

Marc was so deep in thought that he didn't notice crossing Yonge Street or seeing the Court House or St. James' Church farther east. Before he realized it, he was easing Colonel Margison's second-best horse back to a walk as they began a slow descent to the Don River. The few sporadic clearings on either side of the road indicated that the industry and mercantile zest of the capital city was reaching well beyond its civic borders. He breathed in the yeast-sweet odour of Enoch Turner's brewery before he spotted its outbuildings and brewing stacks. Just below it lay Scaddings Bridge, as it was still called by the locals, even though Scaddings and the original structure were long gone to grass. Ignoring the bridge, Marc tugged the horse down the slope and onto the frozen surface of the river itself. The recent snowfall allowed him to spur his steed into a lusty gallop, and together they charged across the wind-swept, treeless expanse as if it were the perilous space separating the armies of Wellington and the Corsican usurper. As he plunged through knee-deep drifts up the far bank, a fur-capped trapper stood up to take notice, then waved enthusiastic approval. Marc tipped his plumed shako cap with elaborate politeness.

At the top of the rise he paused to rest the horse and check that he had not overheated it. The trapper held up one of his trophies as if to say, 'Both of us are having a good day, eh?' It looked to Marc as if the drowned creature (missing one leg) was what the locals called ermine, which in truth was merely a fancy word for stoat or common weasel, a canny predator who could, like a turncoat, adjust the hue of his skin with the fickle swing of the seasons. Even the hares in this alien landscape went white with the snows.

And it *was* alien territory that Ensign Edwards – late of the shire of Kent and the Royal Military School – was heading into. He had no reason to believe that affairs in Crawford's Corners or the nearby town of Cobourg would be much different from the querulous, mongrel politics he had done his best to ignore here in Toronto: with its raving and moderate Tories, rabid Reformers and ordinary Grits, annexationists like John Rolph and William Lyon Mackenzie, out-and-out Yankee republicans recently arrived from Detroit or Lewiston, and Loco Foco Democrats insinuated from Buffalo or Oswego. His own brief dalliance with the study of law had taught him to be logical and analytic, though he hadn't persevered there long enough to learn the trick of deviousness. His subsequent career as a soldier, so much more to his liking and talent, had taught him to be direct and ever poised for precipitate action. How far would such qualities take him in the ambiguous hinterland of Upper Canadian politics? He would soon find out.

Marc emerged from the woods and once again headed east along the Kingston Road. The sun was well past the high point of its daily arc but still shone bravely in a cloudless sky. The weather would hold. He would take his time, he would savour the liberal air and pleasing sensation of his body moving with the rhythm of the horse's stride.

When Sir John had suggested that he go directly to Crawford's Corners, where he felt the answers, if any, to the puzzle of Smallman's death lay, he had assured Marc that he would find ready allies there to assist him, should he have need: in particular Magistrate Philander Child; Major Charles Barnaby, an ex-army surgeon; and James Durfee, local postmaster and innkeeper – sensible gentlemen and true Tories all. Moreover, the supernumerary township constable, Erastus Hatch, was also the miller for the region and a man whose honesty and bluff friendliness should prove invaluable. It seemed he always had a spare room for allies in the cause and a not-unhandsome daughter inexplicably unattached. And, most conveniently, Hatch's hostel was situated right next to the Smallman farm.

Marc's plan was to arrive unannounced at the miller's place sometime the following afternoon (after a satisfying supper and a feather bed at the Port Hope Hotel), discreetly explore the site of the "murder" with Constable Hatch's assistance, and then interview the members of the victim's household before his presence in the area became generally known and speculated upon. He would then pronounce himself satisfied that everything connected with the death was just as it had been reported. From that point he would fabricate some plausible excuse for remaining in Crawford's Corners (the handsome, unengaged daughter of miller Hatch?) and then, using leads generated by Magistrate Child or other loyalists, he would keep his ears pricked for the undertones of sedition he was certain would provide him with the motive and, if God were a monarchist, deliver up the treacherous assassins themselves.

It seemed like a sound strategy. However, his wide reading in military history had left him with the disconcerting conclusion that most generals were astonished to discover their impeccable schemes for battle starting to unravel at the opening volley. With such thoughts still contending in his head, Marc sighed with relief when, late in the afternoon, he spotted in the near distance the square-log building he knew would be the popular wayside hostelry of Polonius Mitchum.

As he rode up to the primitive log structure, he found himself whistling.

CHAPTER TWO

"We don't get too many of your kind this far out." The tavern-keeper chuckled as he dipped a tin cup into the barrel under the counter and poured the contents into a mug that had seen happier and kinder days. "Least not in the daylight." His whiskers quivered to highlight the wit of the remark.

Marc dropped a threepenny piece on the unvarnished pine board and stared straight ahead. "I'm on the King's service," he said. "I'd be grateful if you'd have your lad see to my horse. It'll be getting dark in an hour or so, and we've got a ways to go yet."

"Indeed, sir, it's always a pleasure for Polonius Mitchum to serve a servant of His Majesty. Even though I ain't had the honour of shakin' his hand, I'm told the King's a decent sort of German gentleman."

Marc lifted his mug and took a man-sized swallow of the liquor.

Mitchum swivelled his heavy body to the right and yelled towards the curtained alcove behind him: "Caleb! Drag your lazy arse outside an' see to this gentleman's horse. *Now!* Before I tan the hide off ya!"

A lazy scrabbling sound was heard from the murky recesses, and a moment later a door opened somewhere and the winter wind whipped gaily through the premises. "Jesus Murphy," Mitchum roared. He seemed about to bend his entire bulk around, then changed his mind and, instead, swept the coin off the counter and fetched up a fearsome grin. "That ain't *my* lad, thank Christ, though he calls my wife 'Mother.'"

"And this isn't whisky," Marc said, peering up and fixing Mitchum with a quizzical eye.

"Thought you'd never notice," Mitchum said. "I don't serve Gooderham's rotgut to gentlemen of quality, and I can see plainly you are that, sir, if nothin' else." He reached across and laid the grubby stub of a finger on the sleeve of Marc's tunic. "Now that's real quality, sir, even if it do make you look as temptin' as a guinea hen in a coopful of foxes."

"This tastes very much like rum from the garrison stores," Marc said quietly.

"Upon my word, young sir, you wouldn't be accusin' Polonius Mitchum, Esquire, of breakin' the law or encouragin' others less fortunate to do so?" Mitchum's eyes bristled with friendly menace.

"I merely remarked upon a suspicious coincidence," Marc said.

"As indeed have many of your fellow officers who are wont to frequent this establishment to quench their thirst – and other appetites."

The rambling outhouses behind the tavern itself were reputed to be places where a libidinous bachelor with an instinct for gambling could indulge both vices with a minimum of inconvenience. Marc's repeated refusal to join his comrades-in-arms on their nighttime excursions, out here or closer to home, was a source of wonder to them and, for a few, a cause for resentment. Marc himself could scarcely find reasons for his reserve in such matters, though the scars of a youthful romance cruelly broken up had not perhaps healed as fully as he had hoped.

"Even so," Marc said to Mitchum after finishing off his draught, "the importation of Jamaican rum into the province, directly or surreptitiously through the United States, without paying the excise on it, constitutes a crime under the statutes, as does the purveying of bootlegged army rations."

"*Smugglin'*?" Mitchum said, as if the very utterance of the word was horror enough for any respectable citizen.

"Aye."

Mitchum refilled Marc's mug. "On the house," he said.

Marc dropped a shilling on the counter. "That'll cover the drinks and the ostling," he said.

"I ain't had truck with any smugglers," Mitchum said. "But there's plenty of 'em about for them that's inclined to be unlawful. Most of them Yankee peddlers up from Buffalo or across the ice from Oswego are rum-runners, or worse."

Marc sipped the rum, grateful for the warmth it imparted.

"Why, I seen a pair of 'em earlier today, headin', they claimed, for the bright lights of Cobourg. And if they was tinkers, I'm the Pope's bum-boy."

"You tell that news to the sheriff of York," Marc said, reaching over and grasping the bib of Mitchum's apron. "I'm on serious business, and the Governor's warrant."

Mitchum mustered an ingratiating grin. "No need to do that, now, is there, sir? Gentleman soldiers need their little bit of fun an' relaxation, don't they?"

Marc released his hold. "How far is it to the next hamlet?"

"That'd be Perry's Corners: eight miles, give or take a furlong. You can make it before dark, if the weather holds."

Mitchum dropped his grin. "'Course, there ain't an inn with a decent bed between here an' Port Hope."

Marc pulled his greatcoat back on. "Tell your *wife's* boy to bring my horse around to the road."

"I'll do that, sir. And I'll remember you to your mates this evenin', shall I?"

The weather didn't hold. Marc hadn't gone half a mile when the prevailing northwesterly abruptly died, replaced seconds later by a southeasterly pouring in from the cold expanse of Lake Ontario. Huge nimbus clouds gathered in the wake of the wind. Marc took off his stiff-brimmed shako with its green officer's tuft, pushed it into his saddle-roll next to his French pistol, and pulled on – with more urgency than ceremony – the beaver cap so prized by Canadian voyageurs and woodsmen. He wound his scarf several times around his throat and collar and leaned forward as far as he could over the horse's withers.

He had not long to wait. The wind-driven snow struck horse and rider like a loose flail. The road vanished, and the treeline, no more than twenty feet away on either side, fluttered and swam. Marc felt the horse's panic and heard with alarm the stunted wheeze of its breathing. In a minute it would rear and bolt – somewhere. Marc leapt off into the packed snow of the road without releasing his grip on the reins. The startled horse shied and then spat the bit. But Marc, whose own fear was approaching panic, wrenched the frenzied animal sideways, then hauled it, step by stubborn step, into the sheltering pines on the lake side of the Kingston Road. They halted under a tall Jack pine, itself shielded by a hedge-like ring of cedars. Marc laid his cheek against the beast's shoulder and stroked its neck. After a while they both stopped shivering.

When the wind eased, they got back on the road. It was covered with a foot of fresh snow, and no track or rut was visible, either to the east or the west. The wind had eased off and only decorative little eddies of snow spun intermittently at the horse's hooves. Less than half an hour of light remained. It would be pitch dark before he could reach even the unwelcoming hamlet of Perry's Corners. Port Hope itself, and a hearty fire, was at least twenty miles farther on.

Suddenly, from a bend just ahead of him came the sound of horses pounding and snorting, accompanied by cries of human merriment. Marc drew to the side just in time to avoid collision with a four-horse team and a massive sleigh whistling along behind it. The driver waved a friendly mitt in Marc's direction and clamped a smile around his pipe, but did not slow down. Weller's thrice-weekly mail coach sailed past, leaving its fur-wrapped passengers only a moment to cheer his presence and admire his perseverance. One of them, apparently female, stood up, swung around, and held up a silver flask, as if offering a toast to the ensign. Such was social nicety among the self-professed gentry of the Upper Canadian bush.

Marc felt a pang of disappointment that the coach had not stopped, even though he knew the storm meant that both it and he had to get to their destinations as soon as possible. Marc had been quick to observe how the Upper Canadians went about preparing themselves for comfort and survival during winter. Snug in his saddle-roll were extra blankets and underclothing, a large square of sailcloth, and three-days' rations, in addition to his army kit and pistol. Colonel Margison, who had arrived in person with the horse for Marc, had persuaded him at the last minute to include his sabre. It lay in its scabbard, which was attached to the saddle, not his belt, where it would have been handy but too conspicuous. His Brown Bess musket, however, stood in its rack in the officers' quarters at Fort York.

A short time later, one of the landmarks that had been mapped out for him came into view. Here the roadway veered so close to the lake that its icy expanse could be glimpsed through a screen of leafless birch and alder trees. He was three miles or so from Perry's Corners, where, if he was lucky, he would find a cold meal and space by the postmaster's fire. A steady canter would put him there in less than half an hour, despite the deep snow, the rapidly descending darkness, and a weary mount. He looked up in time to see the single star in the southern sky swallowed by cloud. The east wind, bringing no good, was cranking up for another run.

Not a person to repeat his mistakes, Marc cajoled his horse into the woods on the right, knowing that the cliff above the lake would deflect some of the fury of the approaching squall and send it screeching over the trees. He soon found a suitable spot, tethered the horse, spread the canvas out at the base of a stout pine, covered this with a wool blanket, and sat down to wait out the worst.

It was an hour later when, with no sign of the storm abating, Marc made the decision to camp somewhere in the shelter of the woods. The snow was not deep enough yet for him to have to strap on his Indian snowshoes (if he did, it would be his maiden excursion on them), but he couldn't walk far. His feet were nearly frozen: he needed a fire and some boiling tea – soon. He had noticed earlier, just to the south of him towards the lake, a small rise in the land that had kept the drifts from accumulating on its leeward side. He thought he might erect a makeshift lean-to there.

After giving the horse a shrivelled apple and a reassuring pat, he trudged through the snow towards the ridge. Within a few minutes he had reconnoitred a sort of den formed by the ridge and the exposed roots of a large tree. With the sailcloth for a roof and a ground sheet from his army kit under him, he would be as snug as a hibernating bear, with plenty of brushwood for a smudge fire. He was in the midst of congratulating himself when he saw the smoke.

He stood stock-still, cursing himself silently for having trod so noisily into an unknown area with no thought for his personal safety. He was unarmed: his pistol was in his saddle-roll, his sabre in its scabbard. He spoke no aboriginal tongue. He was shivering and, to his consternation, found himself nearer exhaustion than he had been willing to admit. But his mind remained alert: he listened for the slightest sound and was certain now that he could hear voices. The smoke itself continued to pour upward in thick whorls not twenty yards to his left, its source hidden by a knoll and several squat cedars. This was no campfire smoke, or if it was, it was of no kind Marc had ever seen.

He had two choices: he could return to the horse and risk being heard (one nicker from the animal would ring like a rifle shot through the silence of these woods) or get close enough to the murmuring voices to discern if it would be safe to approach whomever it was and ask for a warm place by their fire. He chose the latter strategy.

Taking one slow, muffled step at a time, he edged towards the knoll and the coils of woodsmoke. When he was within a few yards, he eased himself up the slope of the ridge. Then he crawled along its height until he was at last able to look into the wintry glade below him. What he saw was a log hut, no more than ten by ten, windowless (on the two sides he could see), but sporting a lime-and-straw chimney – in active service. A trapper's cabin.

"Well, sir, don't just sit up there like a frozen cod, come on down and join us." A face poked out from behind the chimney. "You look like you could do with a wee drop of the *craychur*."

"Ninian T. Connors at your service," said the big Irishman with the Yankee-accented brogue and the ready smile. He handed Marc a cup of whisky and urged him to move his feet (unbooted, with much effort and more pain) closer to the fire. "My associate, Mr. Ferris O'Hurley, and I are always pleased to oblige a gentleman of the officers' fraternity, whether his coat be blue or scarlet."

"And I'm the fella to second that," added the other one, as dark and wiry and toughened as his partner was florid and generously fleshed. When he drank his grog, he gulped the cupful entire, squeezed his eyes shut as his whiskered cheeks bulged, and then blinked the rotgut down his gullet like a toad with a stubborn fly.

"I am most grateful for your kindness," Marc said, sipping at his drink and wishing it were hot tea. His horse stood at ease outside the cabin, keeping a donkey company and sharing its feed. When Marc had offered to pay, Connors had taken exaggerated umbrage: "The laws of hospitality in this savage land are as strict as the ones in ancient Greece, and necessarily so. It is we, sir, who are obliged to you for honouring us with your unexpected but worthy presence."

"You headin' for Cobourg?" O'Hurley said between gulps.

"In that direction," Marc said, taking the slice of bread and cheese held out to him by Connors.

"What my associate means," Connors said, with an impish twinkle in his blue eyes, "is that we seldom see an officer of His Majesty's regiments travelling alone on the Kingston Road."

"You know it well, then?"

"Indeed we do, though you have no doubt surmised that we are citizens of a neighbouring state."

"We're up from Buffalo," O'Hurley said.

"Peddling your wares," Marc said evenly.

"We don't do nothin' illegal," O'Hurley said, then he glanced at Connors as quick as a cat.

"What my confederate means is that we are not mere Yankee peddlers, as noble as that profession might be. Mr. O'Hurley here, whose father was as Irish as mine, is a *bona fidee* tinker, a tinsmith and *artiste* of the first rank. You, good sir, are drinking from a recent product of his craft."

The tin cup held by Marc looked as if the donkey had tried to bathe in it, but he refrained from comment. His toes had thawed out, the crude meal and whisky were sitting comfortably on his stomach, and the mere thought of curling up in his own bedroll next to a fire was beginning to warm him all over.

"Mr. O'Hurley here travels these parts – highway and back road alike – several times a year. He not only sells a grateful citizenry household items unattainable in the British half of America, though commonplace in the great Republic to the south, but he repairs anything constructed of metal, and where repair will not suffice, he fashions original works with the touch of a true master – an impresario, you might say, of tin and copper."

"You have an established itinerary, then?" Marc lit his pipe with a tinder stick and puffed peaceably.

"Well, not what you'd really call regular-like," O'Hurley said.

"Which is to say, we improvise," Connors said, leaning over to allow Marc to light his clay calumet with a fresh tinder, "as occasion dictates." He sucked his tobacco into life and continued. "As a man of the world, I'm sure you know there are people in this distant dominion of King William who, notwithstanding the intent and principle of His Majesty's law so recently and justly amended –"

"You are referring to the repeal of the Alien Act, which

means that naturalized citizens from the United States can now keep their property and participate fully in political life?"

Connors squinted – part frown and part smile – then grinned and said, "But, alas, many of your countrymen persist in believing that any resident of this province who hails from the United States of America – however long ago and however naturalized since – is a *primee fashia* blackguard and potential seditionist. A Yankee spy under every rock, to use the vernacular."

"So you move about . . . judiciously," Marc offered.

"How well put. You seem uncommonly schooled for a soldier, sir."

Marc acknowledged the compliment with a nod. "And are you a smithy as well?"

O'Hurley coughed and spluttered into his cup.

"I, sir," Connors declaimed, "am a smithy of words and subordinate clauses, of tracts and contracts – monetary, fiduciary, and commercial. I draw up bills of sale and bills of lading, deeds of property and dunnings of debt. I drum and I stake and I capitalize; I minister and mollify."

"A solicitor, then."

Connors reeled back as if struck by a blow as cowardly as it was mortal. "You jest, sir. If I am to be vilified by that name, it can only be in the generic sense. I do what lawyers in my country do, but without the handicap of education or licence. In brief, young sir, I am what the Republic hails as its quintessential citizen: an entrepreneur." He leaned back, laid his gloved hands across his mustard waistcoat, and smiled without a trace of guile.

"He does the thinkin'," O'Hurley said, "and I do the craftin'."

"The perfect partnership, you might say," Connors added.

"And you travel together, then? Both of you on a single donkey?"

"Not literally, of course, like Yankee Doodle or our Good Lord on Palm Sunday. I come up by myself to scout out new territory and solicit orders, and once in a blue moon I get the urge to hit the open road for a spell. Then Ferris and I set out in tandem."

Assuming he had been tossed a cue, Ferris blinked sleepily and said, "Ninian's got a sister up here he likes to visit."

"And where does she live?"

"Now you've gone and done it, Ferris old friend," Connors sighed. "You've flat out embarrassed me." He turned to Marc and slowly raised his downcast, abashed eyes. "The visits to my dear sister are, sir, acts of kindness towards that poor impoverished soul and her wretched children, and Ferris knows full well I do not wish to have broadcast those acts of Christian charity that should be executed privily for their own sake and not for the public aggrandizement of the perpetrator."

"I think it's time for me to turn in," Marc said.

"You'll not have one more drink, then?"

Marc yawned and shook his head.

"Surely one toast to His Majesty."

"Just two fingers, then," Marc said.

"Why don't you give him a swig from the canteen?" O'Hurley suggested.

Connors shot him a look that was part reproval, part resignation, then managed to attach his smile to it in time to say, "Splendid thought! We keep a modest dram of superior spirits to mix up a syllabub now and then." He drew what appeared to be a regulation army canteen from under his jacket and poured each of them a toddy.

"To King William the Fourth!"

They drank to the fount and guardian of the British Empire.

"*Your* toast, good sir."

"To honest men everywhere!" Marc said.

The liquor slid silkily down Marc's throat: overproof Jamaican rum.

As soon as horse and donkey had been made as comfortable as possible, the three men set about arranging their bedrolls around the last glow of the fire. When Marc went back out to relieve himself, he slipped his sabre from its scabbard and tiptoed back inside. All was dark and quiet.

For a long while, Marc lay awake, despite the demands of his body for sleep, waiting for the telltale snoring of the peddlers, who, graciously enough, had given him pride of place next to the fire. While checking his horse earlier, Marc had given the donkey and its packs a searching look and decided that these men carried no weapons of any size. Nor did he see anything that resembled contraband goods among the pots and pans of their tradesmen's gear.

Some time later he opened his eyes wide. How long he had slept he did not know, but he soon knew what had wakened him. Connors and O'Hurley were both upright, huddled against the door and fumbling for the latch.

"Jasus, it's cold. We shoulda stayed in Buffalo."

"Well, I gotta take a piss and I'm not fouling my own nest."

"Me too, dammit." O'Hurley was jerking at the latch in the dark.

Then Connors whispered, "Sorry to wake you, Ensign. Ferris and I have got to answer a pre-emptive call of nature."

The door opened, colder air drifted in from outside, and the peddlers vanished. Seconds later the air hissed with their exertions, but they did not return. Marc reached over and felt for the saddlebags, his own and his hosts'. Both were still there. Once again he fought against sleep – thinking hard.

O'Hurley had his ear against the door. "I don't hear no snorin'."

"Let me have a gander, before my balls freeze solid and drop off." Connors eased the door open a crack. The unexpected onset of moonlight allowed him a partial but clear view of the Ensign wrapped in his bedroll, his fur cap pulled down over his face against the biting cold of a midwinter night.

"Edwards," Connors said in a low, amiable voice. "You awake?" No reply. "We're just gonna move the animals to the other side of the cabin."

"He's out for the night," O'Hurley said nervously.

"The rum did the trick."

"We gonna go through with this?"

"Of course we are. We can't take any chances."

"He seemed like an okay fella to me."

"You wouldn't last a week on your own," Connors said without rancour.

The decision had been made after they had relieved themselves in the brush at the foot of the knoll, though not without several minutes of furiously whispered argument.

"I bet that horse's worth fifty bucks," O'Hurley said, warming to the task at hand.

"It may be too risky to take," Connors said.

"If only the bugger'd not asked so many questions."

"Here," Connors said, and he held out a stout log frozen as hard as an iron bar. "Get on with it."

"Why me?"

"Your turn, old boy," Connors said, smiling. "Besides, it was you that blabbed about the rum and my sister."

With the weapon shaking in his grasp, O'Hurley inched the door farther open, shuddering at every creak it made. But exhaustion seemed to have claimed the redcoat utterly. He would never see the blow that killed him. Perhaps there would even be no pain: he would simply not wake up.

O'Hurley stood over the silent, unsuspecting sleeper, his eyes riveted on the ornate haft of the officer's sabre just peeping above the army blanket. He could sense Connors watching in the open doorway behind him. He raised the log, hesitated, shut his eyes, and brought it down upon the fur cap. He opened his eyes just in time to see the entire bedroll spasm and grow still. There wasn't even a moan. Thank God.

"Jasus Christ and a saint's arse!" Connors yelled. "You can't kill a man with a fly-swat like that!" He ripped the club from O'Hurley's grasp and slammed it down on the rumpled cloth. "And may you rot in Hell like every other English bastard!"

"Go ahead and hit him again, if it makes you feel better."

The assassins wheeled about in confusion, then dismay. Ensign Edwards stood in the doorway – bareheaded, coatless, unshod – with a loaded and primed pistol in his right hand. "I can only shoot the liver out of one of you, but I assure you I will kill the other with my bare hands."

Even the smithy of words could find none suited to the occasion.

"I followed you out when you went to take a leak," Marc said by way of helpful explanation, "and heard everything. You've gone and made a mess of my hat."

"What're you gonna do?" Connors was able to say at last.

"I want you to hop on that donkey and hee-haw your Irish arses out of this province."

"Now? In the middle of the night?"

"Now. You're lucky I don't haul you into Fort York and have you hanged before sun-up. Get going before I change my mind."

The peddlers tripped over one another scrambling out the door. Connors fell into a drift and lost a glove, but he didn't stop to retrieve it. They skedadelled to the donkey as if expecting at any moment to feel a lead ball between their shoulder blades. The tinkling of copper and ironware and sundry animal grunts were loud enough to rouse every wintering creature within ten miles.

"Hey," Connors called back from his precarious perch on the donkey's rump, "what about our saddlebag?"

"You can pick it up sometime at the Crawford's Corners post office, if you've got the courage to show up there!"

"You bastard! Our life savings are –" The sentence went unfinished as the donkey foundered in the snow and Connors tumbled off.

"If I see or hear of you two anywhere in this province, you won't have a life worth saving!"

Remounted, cold, wet, and dishevelled, the tinker and his financial adviser cursed the donkey forward.

Marc took one step in their direction, raised his right arm, and fired the pistol. The ball went where it was aimed, into a thick branch just above the fleeing duo.

"Giddy-up, ya jackass! We got a maniac behind us!"

The donkey, true to the breed, slowed down.

That felt good, Marc thought, damn good.

Marc judged it to be about four o'clock in the morning. The three-quarter moon was shining in the windless, star-filled sky. He saddled up the horse, packed his gear, tossed the peddlers' money-pouch across the withers, and led his mount back to the Kingston Road. He would ride steadily until he reached Port Hope, rest a few hours, and proceed to his destination early the next afternoon.

He knew he should have taken half a day to escort the would-be murderers to Toronto, but Sir John's warrant and instructions outweighed all competing considerations. Nor could he ride into Crawford's Corners with his pistol primed and a pair of cuffed miscreants clanking the news of his arrival everywhere. Instead, he would have to be content with giving their names and a description to Constable Hatch, who would forward the information east and west by the first available coach or courier. Besides, two bumblers who connived to clobber you with a makeshift club in the middle of the night were dangerous only if you allowed them to be. Still, he would like to have known what their motive was.

As he veered onto King William's high road and let the horse settle into a canter, it occurred to Ensign Edwards that, in a very real sense, he had just experienced his first skirmish in the field, fired his first shot in the heat of battle, and lived to tell the tale.

CHAPTER THREE

"Up here, about a hundred yards," Erastus Hatch hollered back to Marc, pointing to a trail of sorts.

"You'd have to know it was here to find it," Marc said, catching up and drawing his horse to a halt beside the miller's.

"Joshua Smallman was born and raised in these parts. He knew where he was going all right." Both men nudged their horses forward into the drifts between the trees.

"Then you don't accept the story that he became disoriented in the blizzard and wandered into the deadfall in a fit of panic?"

"You've been reading the Magistrate's report," Hatch grinned. They had met less than an hour before, but Marc was beginning to like him already and, prematurely perhaps, to trust him. "I don't think Child himself believed what he wrote there. But it was the only conclusion that made sense."

"You think he met with foul play, then?"

Hatch waited until Marc was abreast of him and they had paused to let the horses rest. He turned to look directly at him before answering. "To be frank, I don't. Major Barnaby, the surgeon, came out here with Child and me on New Year's Day after the alarm was raised. Barnaby's an ex-army man and a good tracker. We were able to pick up Joshua's trail despite a little overnight snow, and it led us where we're headed right now. The three of us found the body. Charles looked him over real careful here at the scene and later at his surgery in Cobourg."

"He died when the deadfall struck him?"

"Possibly, but more likely some time afterwards. His neck wasn't broken. Poor bugger probably froze to death."

"But why was he out here?"

"I said I didn't think there was foul play, but I also figure he didn't trot out to this old Indian trail to enjoy the scenery on New Year's Eve, leaving his daughter-in-law and guests to fend for themselves."

"So you do believe he was coming to meet someone. A secret rendezvous, of some kind."

The horses plunged forward again, wheezing and protesting.

"Or he was out here in search of something."

"It would have to have been bigger than a moose to be seen in this stuff."

Hatch laughed, as he had often since their meeting at his house earlier in the afternoon. By temperament and build, the man had been destined to become a miller or smithy. He had a broad, wind-burnished face with a raw, unfinished look to it. That was true of so many of the native-born out here, Marc thought, even though their parents most probably had been undersized, underfed émigrés fleeing famine and persecution. Even their accents vanished, it seemed, in a single generation.

"Don't make sense, does it?" he said.

They dismounted and, with some difficulty (most of it on Marc's part), laced on their snowshoes. The horses had done all they could.

"This is where we found Joshua's big roan," Hatch said. "Despite last night's blow, you can still see where the poor beast thrashed about."

"Nothing had been taken or tampered with?"

"Nothing. And Joshua was carrying no money, according to his daughter-in-law."

"Bathsheba Smallman."

"Everybody around here calls her Beth. You'll get a chance to ask her yourself. The Smallman farm's right next to the mill. What she told the inquest, though, was that Joshua told her he'd got a message and had to go out. Nothing more."

"You found no note or letter on him?"

"No. And neither Beth nor any of the neighbour guests at the party remember any note being delivered."

Marc took his first giant steps on the raquettes, amazed to find himself on top of the snow. He felt the same light-headed exhilaration that might have come from waltzing on cloud or striding over a Cumbrian lake – that is, until he tipped sideways into a drift and had to be hauled out by the grinning Hatch.

"You can't tell a snowshoe how to behave," he said, not unkindly. "Let it take you with it and you'll be fine."

"You could still follow Smallman's trail this far on that morning?" Marc said once he was upright and moving once more.

"Just faintly, but clear enough. Till we came round this cedar."

They stopped. A few feet ahead the massive boles of several trees formed a natural aisle that any hunter or wayfarer would be foolish not to enter. Even now the scene before them was peaceful and innocent under the fresh snow: except for the huge log that stuck up odd-angled out of the drift at the base of the arch. They moved cautiously towards it, as if its murderous power were still somehow extant.

"Was there any sign that the contraption had been recently re-rigged?" Marc said, staring down at the brute log and the tangle of rawhide rigging that had provided the trigger for its lethal drop.

"None. As you can see, it's the kind of trap the Mississauga Indians used to make when these were their prime hunting grounds. The rawhide is old and quite dried out. Joshua was just unlucky, I figure. Nine times out of ten this rope'll snap when it's hit and leave the deadfall in place. Still, the log is designed to fall when the shim is given the slightest shock."

"You searched the area all around here for other footprints or signs of human disturbance?"

"Yes – once we'd recovered from the shock of seeing one of our dearest friends lying there dead and stiff."

"I'm sorry," Marc said. "I must remember he was no stranger to you."

"As soon as he came back to help out on the farm after his son's death last year, we took him into our company. He was one of us. He joined us every Wednesday evening he could."

"Us?"

"The Magistrate, the Major, me, and Durfee, the postmaster. He was supposed to be with us on New Year's Eve over at Child's. It's a sort of gentleman's club, made up of like-minded citizens, you might say."

"Loyal Tory gentlemen," Marc said with a slight smile.

"That's right," Hatch said, taking no offence.

"You were all there, then?" Marc said, more abruptly than he'd intended.

"Could one of us have been floundering about out here, you mean? Lurking in the shadows like Madame Guillotine?"

"As you said, nobody else had been out here anyway. Anyone else would have had to have come in along the same route that Smallman did, and that means tracks – deep hoof marks or snowshoe tracks." He was staring back at the turbulence his own raquettes had left in the snow. "And you found no tracks beyond the trap?"

"We went carefully on ahead for a good twenty yards or more. Then we fanned out in a circle twice as wide. Nothing. Not even a rabbit track. Our friend died out here alone, looking for some*one* or some*thing*. Even so, who could have known or predicted that he would take this particular route? Or that the damnable device would work, if someone were obliging enough to blunder into it? It hadn't been touched for years."

After a pause Marc said, "What's beyond that ridge up there?"

"That's the rim of the cliff before it drops down to the lake," Hatch said, suddenly more alert.

"The *frozen* lake," Marc said.

The two men stood on the ridge and stared out at the endless, ice-covered stretch of Lake Ontario, more vast than most of the Earth's seas. A little farther to the east, it would be frozen completely across its thirty-mile breadth, and on any Sunday afternoon you would be able to see cutters and sleighs and homemade sleds sliding merrily in both directions between the American republic and the British province. Families pulled apart by borders and politics and memories of the War of 1812 reconvened as soon as the lake froze, as if humanity was meant to be without division or dissent.

"You figure somebody may have come up here from the ice?" Hatch said.

"It's thick enough to hold a horse, even a sleigh. And the highway at Crawford's Corners can't be more than a quarter of a mile from the shoreline, can it?"

"True enough. That would explain why we only found Joshua's tracks coming in here. But how would anybody coming up along the lakeshore know exactly where he was? You'd have to be an Indian or a wolf."

"What's that down there? To your right. Looks like an inlet or a little bay to me."

Hatch's eyes lit up. "That's Bass Cove, a favourite fishing spot in the spring."

Marc began to move along the ridge in that direction, raquettes in hand. Then he stood straight up and didn't move until Hatch had joined him. He pointed to a shadowy indentation in the escarpment just below them on the wooded side of the ridge. "I think we've found our rendezvous," he said.

Together they scrabbled down to a ledge that was invisible from above but easily seen from the woods just below. They pushed through a dark entranceway into a low, cramped, but otherwise habitable cave. They waited until their eyes had adjusted to the murky, late-afternoon light before commenting.

"We aren't the first visitors here besides the bears," Marc said.

"These ashes were made by more than one fire," Hatch added, holding up a tin cup and a blackened soup spoon.

"And something's been stored here at some time or other," Marc said from his crouching position at the far side of the cave. "I can see the ridge-lines in the dirt: crates or barrels, I'd say."

Outside again, Hatch said, almost to himself, "Still, we don't have the foggiest idea of whether anybody was waiting here for Joshua Smallman two weeks ago. And if they were, they might just've been as friendly as hostile. Until we know *why* he came out here, we're just spittin' in the wind."

But Marc was already edging along away from the mouth of the cave, bent low like a hound on the spoor. Hatch was tempted to chuckle at the Ensign's antics but didn't.

"Come over here, Constable Hatch."

"Only if you call me Erastus, or just plain Hatch. I'm only a part-time, supernumerary constable, and under duress to boot."

From their vantage point they had an unimpeded view through the evergreens to a spot somewhere on the trail they themselves had made: their tracks were clearly visible.

"That's the trail all right," Hatch said, puzzled. "But the deadfall's farther down."

"On the other side of that patch of evergreens. You can just see the limbs of the big oak it was attached to."

"But if someone *was* standing here that night – in his snowshoes! – looking down and waving Joshua on, he would've come straight up this open stretch and missed the trap."

"Look at the size of the drifts down there," Marc said. "They're deep, but not deep enough to cover the trees that've been knocked down by storms or something. See how they're blocking the way?"

"Knocked down by lightning," Hatch said, spotting the telltale blackened branches and stark, splintered trunks poking through the snow. "You figure somebody stood here and encouraged Joshua? Maybe even pointed to the left, knowing the Indian trail went that way and –"

"Knowing that the deadfall was just ahead at the next bend."

"Possible," Hatch said slowly. "Still, it sounds a bit farfetched. Two *maybe*s don't make a certainty."

"Could a person who was really expert on snowshoes have gone down to the trap from here, come back up again, and then whisked away all signs of his tracks?"

"Oh, I think so, 'specially if there'd been some additional snow to cover the brush marks. But you're forgetting one important thing: anybody meeting Joshua here that night might just as easily have been a friend or someone with information to sell or whatever."

"Then why didn't he walk down to the trap to help the

man? He couldn't have been sure that Smallman was killed outright. And that horse of his would have been making a hell of a racket. They can smell death, I've been told."

"That's so, but we're still guessing that somebody was actually here."

"Not now we aren't," Marc said. He was hunched over a place where the ledge broadened slightly. Hatch leaned over his shoulder. The webbed signature of a pair of raquettes stared up at them as clean-edged as a palm print. The sheltering rock had kept it almost free of drifting snow and untouched by the recent squall driving off the lake.

"And look at this," Hatch said. "A stem broken off a clay pipe, right beside it."

He handed it to Marc, who gazed at it thoughtfully, then tucked it into his tunic.

"Every man and most boys in the township've got a pipe like that."

Marc was still thinking. "What are the odds of any two residents of this county being out in such a godforsaken place in the dead of winter on separate and unrelated errands?" he said.

"You know what all this means, then," Hatch said solemnly.

"I do," Marc said. "We've got a murder on our hands, or something damn close to it."

They made a more thorough search of the cave with the aid of an improvised torch but found nothing more of interest. The place seemed to have been used over an extended period of time, months perhaps, as a temporary storage depot for whatever it was that needed to be hidden, guns perhaps, or rum. Access to it would have been via the ice-bound lake, where the slope, being exposed to frequent snow squalls, would leave no trace of the traffic over it. Marc himself scrutinized the deadfall trap, but there was not a piece of bark bared or twig snapped off to indicate any tampering had been done to ensure its working on cue.

"I have to believe you're right," Hatch sighed as they turned west onto the Kingston Road and headed back towards Crawford's Corners. "Someone, a smuggler or an insurrectionist, was standing up there when poor, unsuspecting Joshua came up the Indian trail. There doesn't seem to be any other reason for a man to stand on that exposed ledge and puff on a pipe except to get a view of the trail and anybody on it. And if he didn't intend to kill Joshua, then he left him in the snow to die, which amounts to the same thing in my book."

"And God's," Marc said.

"How do you plan to proceed with this?" Hatch said, alluding to the Lieutenant-Governor's warrant that Marc had shown him. "I gather you don't intend to involve the sheriff in Cobourg?"

"Not right away," Marc said. "Now that we're almost certain we have a crime of some sort here, wouldn't it be wiser to let people think everything's all right as is, especially those with something to hide?"

"But you'll have to question folks, won't you?"

"When I know a lot more than I do now."

"You'll have to tell Beth Smallman," Hatch said, in a tone halfway between command and entreaty.

"Probably. I'll work that out when I see her."

"You can walk over there in the morning, if you like. And tomorrow being Wednesday, I can just cart you along to the weekly meeting of the Georgian Club, as we call it. You'll get all the background information you need there. In the meantime, it's getting late, and a man of my girth and wit requires a regular intake of his daughter's cooking."

"Better than army rations?"

"What isn't?" Hatch laughed. "And you'll be wanting to meet my Winnifred. She'll be back from the quilting bee by now and wondering where the hell I've gotten to."

The not-unhandsome daughter, Marc mused. Would she prove handsome enough to account for the prolonged stay of a visiting ensign – perhaps one of her dead mother's distant cousins from the Old Country?

On their right as they passed the intersection of the highway and the Pringle Sideroad, Hatch pointed to a quarry-stone house just visible through a screen of trees. "That's Philander Child's establishment. He's a county magistrate, but most folks just call him the Squire. We'll be going up there tomorrow night."

"And that must be the local tavern." Marc indicated a square-log cabin of considerable size, gabled like a true inn. Nearby were several semi-detached sheds and one rambling livery stable.

"One of them. The respectable one. Run by James Durfee and his wife. You'll meet James tomorrow night."

"He's the postmaster?"

"That's right."

"Then I'll need to meet him now," Marc said.

After introducing Marc to Durfee simply as a visiting gentleman from the garrison and a protégé of Sir John Colborne's, Constable Hatch took his leave and rode across the intersection, or "corners," towards the mill and his house next to it. If James Durfee was meant to be impressed by Hatch's remarks, he restrained himself admirably. He was a plain-speaking man, born in Upper Canada but of Scots extraction, with a ready smile qualified only by a pair of watchful dark eyes.

"We don't get many soldiers on furlough this far from Muddy York, as we used to call Toronto before she took on

39

those citified airs," he said. "Despite the obvious attractions hereabouts."

Marc smiled as he was expected to. "I'm here on official business," he said, accepting with a nod the wee dram offered and seating himself on one of the wooden chairs scattered about the outer room, which no doubt served as the principal drinking quarters of the inn. A plank bar and tapped keg of beer stood nearby. At this moment, Marc was the only customer.

"Business of a pleasant sort, I trust," Durfee said.

"I'm not at liberty to say much about it at the moment, but Hatch is bringing me to your club meeting tomorrow night. I'll have a lot more to say then."

"Ah," Durfee said, downing his whisky. "You'll be most welcome. But it's not been the same club without Joshua Smallman."

"You knew him well?" When Durfee gave him a quizzical look, Marc said quickly, "Hatch told me about the tragic accident."

"I see. And tragic it was. Joshua an' me grew up in the Cobourg area, you know. Joshua went off to York when he was twenty, married, an' did well in the dry goods trade. Then when his son, his only child, turned his back on the business, there was a falling out of sorts. Jesse, poor bugger, came here when this township was first opened up – to become a farmer an' show his father he could make it on his own."

"Hatch mentioned that the young Mrs. Smallman is a widow."

Durfee again seemed puzzled by how much information this casual visitor had managed to cajole out of the usually discreet miller. But there was an openness, naïveté even, about the beardless lad before him that begged his confidence and trust.

"Jesse died a year ago December," Durfee said. "That's why

Joshua came back. An' why we done all we could for him an' Beth these past months."

Marc waited quietly until Durfee whispered, "He hung himself. In the barn. His wife found him."

Emma Durfee insisted that Marc stay for supper, but he assured her that Winnifred Hatch was expecting him to dine at the mill within the hour. Mrs. Durfee, as round and plump as her husband was spare and gnarled, smiled as if she were privy to some mutual conspiracy. "Ahh," was all she said, but it was meaning enough. When Marc failed to take the bait, she added with feigned reluctance, "Well, there ain't a man in the district brave or foolhardy enough to ignore the wishes of the handsome Miss Hatch."

Marc was beginning to wonder if "handsome" was part of Miss Hatch's Christian name, in the manner of the pilgrims' "Goody."

When Emma Durfee left the room to tend to her own cooking, her husband leaned forward and said to Marc, "You must've had some other reason for droppin' by than to say hello an' sample my finest."

"Hatch tells me you have a safe."

Which turned out to be an understatement, for the iron box that governed the otherwise modest space of Durfee's office (itself adjoined to the taproom by a sturdy oak door) was roomy enough to have housed a successful brood of chickens and intimidating enough to have kept them safe from a regiment of foxes.

"It's been in the wife's family for years. We sledded it over the lake last February." Durfee fiddled with the dial and then drew the door open slowly, like a proud jailer who has no doubt about his dungeon's impregnability. "What've you got that needs protectin'?"

Marc dropped the leather pouch he had taken from the Yankees onto Durfee's rolltop desk. Then he gave the innkeeper the same abbreviated and carefully edited version of his encounter with Connors and O'Hurley he had given Hatch.

"I'm surprised to hear that," Durfee said, letting his breath whistle through the pair of wooden teeth on the left side of his jaw to emphasize his point. "Them two've been sidlin' about the province for several years now, an' they're like most Yankee peddlers we get here – quick with the lip and about as trustworthy as a bull in a field of heifers. But they've never been known to do violence to anyone: all bluster an' no delivery."

"I kept their saddlebag as security," Marc said. "As an agent of the Crown, I'd like you to witness my opening it, and then keep it in your safe until I can deliver it personally to Government House or the sheriff of York. I'm going to write up a description of the two renegades and have you send it off to Toronto tomorrow."

"I'll put it on the special courier comin' out of Cobourg at noon," Durfee said, and he stood beside Marc while he unbuckled the pouch and shook its contents onto the desktop. A wad of papers secured by a lady's pink garter fell out.

"A souvenir of the peddlin' wars," Durfee said dryly, giving the garter a playful snap. "But this ain't the profits from tinkerin'," he added.

"It's money of some sort," Marc said, riffling through the two-inch wad.

"American banknotes," Durfee said, taking them from Marc and counting them.

"They look brand new."

Durfee finished counting before he replied, "They are new. One hundred one-dollar notes of the Second Bank of the United States."

Marc made certain the pouch contained nothing else, then

nodded to Durfee to place the confiscated money and the pouch in the safe.

"Guns or grog, I'd say," Durfee said as he gave the dial a spin.

"I'll let the sheriff know about it," Marc said. "I've done all I can for now."

"That you have," Durfee said, but his watchful eye suggested otherwise. "Now you best be trottin' across to the miller's. The handsome Miss Hatch don't like to be kept waitin'."

As Miss Winnifred Hatch poured her guest his second cup of tea, she watched the hot liquid flow into the china cup as if it might, unfettered from her strict supervision, dash off towards some other, illicit cup. The tea settled obediently where it was directed. Miss Hatch had, of course, asked the table if it would prefer another round – "You'll have another cup, then?" – but it was only nominally a question.

Thomas Goodall – the angular young man who, Marc learned, assisted in the milling during the season and managed the modest farm as a sharecropper – swallowed his second cup in two gulps and said, "Well, I'll be off, then. Got three cows to milk."

The chatelaine of the house stopped the progress of her own teacup several inches below her thin, unrouged lip.

"If you please, ma'am." Thomas dropped his eyes and slid noisily off his chair.

"For God's sake, man, go to your cows." Hatch laughed. "They'll be popping their udders."

Mary Huggan, the Irish serving girl who had, in the strange custom of the country, joined them after her initial duties, giggled into her apron, blushed mightily, then sneezed to compound her embarrassment.

"As you can see, Ensign Edwards, we don't often have ladies or gentlemen in to dine," Winnifred said.

"One lady in the house is more than enough," Hatch said with a grin.

"That was as fine a meal as I've had since I arrived in York," Marc said.

Winnifred Hatch accepted the compliment with a curt but not ungracious nod. Either she had not bothered to change her clothes following her return from the quilting bee near Port Hope, or she always dressed in a manner designed to display her widely acknowledged handsomeness. Her magenta blouse, of silk or some such frilly fluff, hugged her tall, Tudor neck almost to the chin, flaring downward around long and elegant arms and outward to suggest subtly the curving of a robust bosom. Her purple, fluted skirt was pleasingly cinched at the waist by a lavender sash that might have seemed overly bold, tartish even, were it not for her regal bearing.

"And just how long have you been with us?" she said in a voice that a Milanese contralto might have envied.

"About eight months," Marc said. "I arrived at Fort York last May."

"And you have been discovering some of our quainter customs, I trust?"

The miller's eyes were dancing delightedly at this turn in the conversation. His daughter, meantime, let her considerable gaze linger on their guest, expecting, it appeared, something more than a polite reply but giving no intimation on which side of the question she herself was situated.

Marc smiled in what he took to be his most winning manner (the one that had such a volcanic effect on the female gentry of Toronto) and said, "I am a soldier, ma'am. A man of action. We have little time to concern ourselves overly much with the manners and deportment of His Majesty's subjects, scattered as they be over the whole of the globe."

Hatch chortled, but he was brought up short by a glance

from his daughter. The quickened anger in her reproof, followed immediately by a softening look that bespoke daughterly indulgence and forbearance, roused in Marc another sort of quickening. An image of the handsome Winnifred – her burnished mahogany hair loosed from its coiled bun, her Spode-white flesh gleaming in the moonlight – popped lasciviously into his head and made him feel foolish and abashed.

"We are doubtless a source of constant chagrin – and some sport, I suspect – for those raised within calling distance of the Throne."

"I was raised in the countryside," Marc said, as evenly as he could manage.

"Is that a boast or a whinge?" The onset of a smile trembled on her upper lip, and stilled.

"I have found much to delight me in Canada and little that has been discomfiting."

"Well said, lad." Hatch laughed. "Now let's go in to the fire and have a wee toddy so Mary can clean up the mess we've made."

Marc was only moderately surprised when, several minutes later, Winnifred joined them in the parlour, taking her place in one of the leather chairs arrayed around the blazing hearth. And he tried not to look too "discomfited" when she drew a clay pipe from under her shawl and clamped it like a sailor between her flawless white teeth. He recovered sufficiently to realize that she was waiting, ladylike, for him to reach across with his lit tinder and assist her in igniting the plug she had just tamped down. The look she gave him as he did so was inscrutable, though mockery, raillery, and mischievous glee all came to mind.

As Marc removed the warming pan from under the quilts on his bed and slipped on his nightshirt, he tried to stave off exhaustion long enough to reflect on what had been accomplished in the thirty hours or so since his departure from Government House and Toronto. While congratulating himself on having so expeditiously and discreetly confirmed the existence of a crime only suspected by Sir John, and having set in train at Durfee's the means of dealing with the peddlers, he tried not to think of Commander-in-Chief Colborne preparing for what would surely be a war in Quebec before the year was out, leaving behind his favoured ensign. However, a speedy and successful resolution of the matter at hand would, if the world were just, guarantee his promotion and, more importantly, a place somewhere in the thick of the coming battle. This cheering thought was interrupted by the more mundane recollection that he had brought with him only two changes of linen and one additional blouse. A speedy resolution might well be a necessity.

More happily, the mattress was a feather tick and the quilts thick and soft. Erastus Hatch, who seemed to have enjoyed every aspect of Marc's company, had given him the best bedroom, the one he himself had used when his wife was still alive. The miller now slept in a smaller room at the front of the house next to the dining area. Some time earlier, Marc had heard the two women, mistress of the manor and scullery maid, enter the room across the hallway from his, chatting in low but amiable voices. He found this amusing to recall, but before he could summon a smile, he was asleep.

He woke with a start, suffered a moment of disorientation, then rolled over onto his side and listened hard. A door had just closed. He heard the soft tread of bare feet on the pine boards of the hall – moving away towards the square-log cabin attached at the back of the stone building. This, Hatch had told him, had once been his parents' home – the first building on the property. There was a summer kitchen back there and several cubicles where, apparently, Thomas Goodall kept house.

Marc pulled his door open in time to hear a stifled giggle from one of the shadowy recesses beyond the hall. Young Mary doing a little night riding in the hired man's bed? Well, some needs changed little from one country to another.

Would that notion please the handsome Miss Hatch, or dismay her?

Chapter Four

Any euphoria generated by Tuesday's events had evaporated by morning. Even a hearty country breakfast did little to revive Ensign Edwards, whose spirits seemed more benumbed than depressed.

Winnifred Hatch arrived at the table moments after Marc, swathed in a taffeta kimono that flattered the shapely figure beneath it. Still, Mistress Hatch carried herself with such confidence that she could have come clothed in diaphanous veils and still retained an air of rigid respectability. Winnifred Hatch had not learned to blush. In a straightforward manner she asked Marc if he had slept well and refilled his cup with coffee. This kindness was interrupted by the arrival of Thomas and Erastus from the barn. The whiff of manure, muted somewhat by the winter chill, blended uneasily with the aroma of coffee and the tang of fried pork.

"How is the Guernsey doing?" Winnifred asked Thomas. He mumbled something positive but kept his eyes on his plate. Behind them, Mary Huggan sang softly over her stove.

"We'll take our coffee into the parlour and talk," Erastus announced.

"First of all," the miller said, "we need to dream up an excuse for you poking your nose about Crawford's Corners. Then, whatever else we find out between now and Saturday, when I've got a meeting with Sheriff MacLachlan, has to be made official. After that, you and the Sheriff can decide between you how to execute the Governor's warrant. Fair enough?"

"Agreed," Marc said. The hot food, the coffee, and the bracing sight of the two young women were working wonders on his mood. Excitement was mounting in him at the prospect of facing the challenges of the day. However, he realized, somewhat reluctantly, that the ruse of his courting the miller's daughter would not do to explain his continued presence.

"I've got a suggestion on the first score," Hatch said. "Every year about this time your quartermaster comes through the county looking to buy surplus wheat or fodder. We can tell folks you're one of his advance men reconnoitring the region. I've got a silo full of grain, my own and others', that will most likely end up at the garrison in any event. Once I drop the hint to Thomas or Mary, the news'll be all over the district by nightfall."

"I've already accompanied him on a similar foray, in December," Marc said, brightening perceptibly. "We're buying extra grain against the coming of troubles in Quebec."

"Splendid," Hatch said, restoking his pipe.

"I know what to ask. And it'll give me an excuse to visit the local farmers and snoop about without raising suspicion. I've got more than a hunch that the man we're looking for will be found amongst the left-wing zealots and Reform fanatics along the back roads." Marc knew that Hatch was waiting for elaboration, but he was not prepared to tell anyone, yet, about

Smallman's role as Sir John's secret agent in Crawford's Corners. After all, this was the trump card that would give him the edge he required to sift and assess every tidbit of information that might come his way in the days ahead.

"Well, then," Hatch said, getting up, "I guess it's time for you to meet Beth Smallman."

"Don't bother Thomas about getting my horse ready," Marc said. "I'll just walk across to her place."

"You going to tell her what we think we know?"

"I haven't really made up my mind," Marc said truthfully. "I need to talk to her first."

"That's a good idea," Hatch said with unabashed admiration for this tunicked officer half his age. Then he grinned and added, "Beth Smallman is no ordinary woman." It was as ambiguous a remark as Hatch was likely to make.

The Smallman farm, which had witnessed much tragedy in the space of twelve months, lay adjacent to the mill on the north side. Taking Hatch's advice, Marc followed a trodden path towards Crawford Creek that took him past the outbuildings of the mill, where Thomas and a stableboy no taller than the fork he wielded were mucking out the cattle stalls. The Colonel's horse whinnied at Marc, but he kept on walking until he came abreast of the mammoth gristmill itself, its water wheel stilled by the ice of the creek. Two impressive silos made out of the same quarry stone as the main house stood as testament to the growing prosperity of the young province. Land was the catalyst here, Marc thought, and the great leveller.

Beyond the silos he found a well-trampled path that meandered along beside the creek. So this was how the locals travelled by foot when the roads grew impassable – to spread all the news worth embroidering. Marc pictured a network of spidering filaments from house to barn to neighbouring house, indifferent to woods, weather, and other natural impediments. He went north on the path a hundred yards or so, enjoying the briskness of the early-morning air, until he spied through an opening in the evergreens on the riverbank the pitched roof of a clapboard barn, and above it, a little farther on, wisps of woodsmoke.

Next to the barn, a log hut with a plank door and single window sat hip-deep in drifts. The meagre smoke from its stovepipe slumped and frayed along the roofline. The door below it opened with a jerk.

"Got yourself lost, mister?"

Marc stopped, hid his surprise, and said, "Ah, good morning. My name is Marc Edwards. I've come from Constable Hatch's place – to see Mrs. Smallman, should she be at home."

"*Constable* Hatch, is it?" The old man, for he seemed indisputably old even by the gnarled norms of Upper Canada, glared fixedly at the interloper, blocking the footpath.

"I'm here on official business."

"Are ye now?" The old fellow gave no ground.

Marc met his stare, then for a moment he almost laughed as the impudent oaf stooped into what was meant to be a fearsome crouch but resembled nothing so much as a petulant crayfish, for he was all bony angles, his ungloved fingers were stiffened into arthritic claws, and the beady peppercorns of his eyes wobbled in rage.

"On Governor Colborne's warrant," Marc snapped. He had already said more than he had planned, and he held his tongue now with mounting impatience.

"The Governor that was, you mean?"

"Is Mrs. Smallman home or not?"

"Where else would an honest woman be?" There was a rasping, spittled quality to the voice that skewed whatever outrage might have been intended.

"I demand that you give me your name, sir, and then stand out of my way!" Marc reached down for the familiar haft of his sword and came up empty.

"No need to lose your temper, lad. There's plenty of daylight left." And he scuttled sideways into the corral beside the barn, where he appeared to execute a crab-like jig.

Marc walked with a dignified pace towards the house twenty yards ahead. The old fart was still jabbering to himself, or to some animal willing to grant him equal status.

Up ahead, the Smallman house was more typical of Canadian rural residences than was the stone structure of the miller Hatch: a notched, squared-timber block, caulked with limestone cement, small windows of murky "local" glass that let in an impoverished glow, a pitched roof over a cramped second storey, and a snow-covered stoop. Marc strode past the windows along the north side, one of which was draped with a swath of black crêpe, put one boot on the porch, and raised his fist to knock. The door swung inward and fully open.

"Nobody knocks in these parts," a light, feminine voice said from the shadows within. "I been expectin' you, Mr. –"

"Edwards," Marc said. "Ensign Edwards."

"I take it you've met Elijah," Bathsheba Smallman, known everywhere as Beth, said to Marc. They were sitting opposite one another in the parlour area – marked off only by a braided rug and an apt arrangement of hand-hewn chairs made welcoming by quilted seat pads – balancing cup and saucer with accompanying bread and jam (the bread fresh out of the iron pot over the fire, the jam homemade).

"Yes, but I'm afraid he wasn't overly helpful," Marc said just as a spurt of jam struck his chin. He rubbed at the offending blob, then licked it off his finger.

"Huckleberry," Beth said. "Grows like a weed in these parts."

"It's delicious."

"Elijah's harmless," Beth said. "He's very protective of me and Aaron."

"Your brother?"

"That's right. You'll meet him when he gets in from collectin' the eggs, if he don't get lost first."

When Marc looked concerned, she smiled reassuringly and said, "Sometimes he gathers more wool than eggs."

Marc could not take his eyes off Beth Smallman, even though he was aware of her discomfort as she glanced away and back again only to find him helplessly staring. As she did, sunlight pouring through the window behind her lit the russet tints of her unbound hair and framed her figure. She was as small and trim and wholesome as Winnifred Hatch was tall and hot-tempered and daunting.

"You're in the district to look at buyin' grain for the garrison, you say?"

Marc blinked, took a sip of his tea, and forced his gaze past her to the petit point figure of Christ on the wall beside the window. "That's correct. I'm merely lining up possible sites for the quartermaster's inspection later this month."

"Elijah tells me we've taken in more Indian corn than our cows can eat."

"I'll take a look before I go, then." The tea was consumed, and the bread and jam with it.

"I'm sure Elijah will oblige you." Beth smiled, blushing slightly. She was wearing a plain blouse and heavy skirt with a knitted cardigan tied across her shoulders. A white apron and cap lay on the pine table near the fire, waiting.

"There's somethin' else on your mind, isn't there, Ensign Edwards?"

"Yes, there is, ma'am. And I apologize for being so roundabout in approaching it."

53

She caught the sudden seriousness of his tone and looked intently towards him, willing him to speak.

"I have some disturbing news," he began.

"I can think of no news that could be more disturbin' than what I've had to bear these past weeks." She steadied her voice. He turned away briefly, but she had quietly composed herself, except for a slight glistening at the edge of her blue, unblinking eyes.

"And December last as well," he said softly.

Now he had her full attention and more: something sharp and suspecting entered her look – at once vulnerable and hardened by necessity.

"Why have you come?" she said. "Who *are* you?"

"I have been ordered here by the Lieutenant-Governor to investigate your father-in-law's death."

"Investigate?"

"Yes. And I have already reached the conclusion that Joshua Smallman was in all likelihood murdered."

A thump and a scraping clatter from the kitchen area forestalled any immediate reaction to Marc's news. Beth rose to her feet, a look of concern flashing across her face. "It's Aaron," she said.

Into the centre of the room came a tall, thin young man with an unkempt mane of reddish hair. He dragged one foot along behind him and, with a lurching effort, swung a basket of warm eggs up and onto a sideboard. As he did so, the left half of his face stretched. "I d-d-didn't break e-e-neee," he said with a lopsided grin. Then he spotted the visitor and froze.

"I didn't expect you would," Beth said. "Say hello to Ensign Edwards."

Marc rose.

"Mr. Edwards, this is my brother, Aaron McCrae."

Aaron simply stared, not in fright but in fascination at the scarlet frock coat, many-buttoned tunic, and glittering buckles so abruptly and magically set before him. "Where's your s-s-s-swooord?" he said.

"I am pleased to meet you," Marc said, "and my sword's tucked safely in my saddle-roll."

"Aaron's goin' to be sixteen next month," Beth said. "Aren't you?"

The lad nodded but seemed more interested in shuffling an inch or two closer to this mirage in his parlour.

Beth touched him on the arm. "Mr. Edwards and I have some important business to talk over. Go out an' help Elijah with the feed, would you?"

Reluctantly the youth shuffled himself out the back door.

"He was born like that. With the palsy. He's not really simple, but it's a strain for him to talk. With us, though, there isn't much need."

They sat down again.

A log rolled off its andiron, spraying sparks into the air, and the brief flare flung a wave of heat to the far side of the large room where they were seated, reminding them how cold it had become. Beth pulled her cardigan on with a shy, self-conscious gesture, but Marc had already averted his eyes.

"Murder is a terrible word, Mr. Edwards," she said at last.

"Does it surprise you to hear it used in association with your father-in-law?"

She did not answer right away. "I didn't believe the Magistrate's findin' for one minute," she said slowly. "Father wouldn't have got himself lost out there, even in a blizzard."

"More experienced woodsmen have," Marc said. "Or so I've been told," he felt constrained to add.

"The horse he was ridin' was the only one we've ever owned."

"Your . . . husband's?"

She nodded. "All he had to do was drop the reins an' Belgium would've carried him home safe an' sound."

"You told this to the inquest?"

She smiled wanly. "I did."

"Mrs. Smallman, I'm certain you are right."

If she found this remark unexpected or patronizing, she gave no sign. "He went out there for a reason, that much I do know," she said.

"And I believe that that reason, when we discover it, will lead me to his murderer."

"You forget that he walked into a bear-trap," she said. "That was . . . tragic, but not murder." She swallowed hard, fighting off tears, and suddenly Marc wished he were any place but here.

As quickly and tactfully as he could, Marc told her what he and Hatch had found the previous afternoon out near Bass Cove.

"You're sayin' someone just stood up there an' watched him die?"

"Yes. And that is tantamount to murder, especially if your father-in-law was deliberately lured out there."

She turned and looked closely at him. "Joshua Smallman was a lovable man. He could not bring himself to tell a lie. He had no enemies. He gave up his business in town to come back here an' help me run the farm." Her voice thickened. "He was the finest man I've ever known." The pause and the candidness of her glance confirmed that she was including her husband in the appraisal. "If he was called out on New Year's Eve, it was to assist a friend or someone in need."

Marc hesitated long enough for Beth to discern that he had absorbed and appreciated the reasonableness of this claim. After all, it coincided with everything he had heard so far about Joshua Smallman. Still, someone seemed to have wished him harm, or at the very least colluded in his death. He pushed ahead, gently. "Would you tell me as much as you can remember about that evening? If it's too painful, I could return another time."

"I'll make some more tea," she said.

"We were plannin' to have a little celebration here to mark the end of the year, it bein' also a year to the day since Father'd arrived. You understand, though, it couldn't've been entirely a celebration."

"Yes. Your . . . husband must have been uppermost in your thoughts."

"Still, we were preparin' a small party, with the Huggan girls, Emma Durfee, Thomas Goodall. We'd even asked Elijah to join us, but he'd already dashed off to visit Ruby the cook up at the Squire's."

"Philander Child's servant?"

"Yes. Father felt strongly that we had an obligation to these kind people, whatever our own sorrows might be. About six o'clock, right after milkin' an' supper, one of Mr. Child's servants comes to the door an' says they're expectin' Father at the gatherin' of the Georgian Club –"

"I know about that," Marc said. "Had your father forgotten about the New Year's celebration up at Child's?"

"He said – rather mysteriously, I thought – that he was through with all that frivolousness. I know he'd missed a few meetin's of late, an' he seemed to be growin' a bit weary of their whist games an' political chatter, but I was still surprised when he suggested that we plan our own celebration. Anyway, he sent the servant back with a polite refusal, an' we started to get ready for some mulled wine and a few treats Father'd brought us from Cobourg."

"Did he seem upset or agitated?"

"No. I could see he was sad, of course, as I was, but we were both tryin' very hard not to be. Mary Huggan an' her sisters were due to come over at seven. Father'd even hauled his violin out of the trunk."

"What happened, then, to call him so suddenly away from all this?"

"I can't say for sure. Just before seven, he went out to check on the animals for the night."

"A regular routine?"

"Yes. Once in a blue moon Elijah gets into the liquor an' so Father always checked the barn with him, or on his own, before comin' in for the evenin'."

"As he did that night."

"I can only assume so. Father was gone a little longer than usual, I think, but the girls'd come in the front door gigglin' an' carryin' on, so I can't say for sure. But when he did come in, he was a changed man."

"Describe him, please, as precisely as you can."

"As I told the Magistrate, he was excited. Not pretendin' to be happy as he'd been before. 'I've got go out, Beth, dear,' he said. 'Just for half an hour or so.' When I looked amazed, he smiled an' told me there was nothin' to worry about . . ."

Despising himself, and beginning to feel more than a little resentment at the predicament in which Sir John had so cavalierly placed him, Marc forced himself to say, "Did he have a note or letter or paper of any kind in his hand or on his person?"

"No. But he said he'd gotten a message, an important one, that could change all our lives for the better."

"Those were his exact words?"

"Yes," she said. "I've been unable to forget them."

Marc pressed on lest his nerve fail him utterly. "But you saw no letter, and he never said or hinted who had sent this 'message' to him?"

"I told the inquest that I heard what could've been paper rustlin' inside his coat. But he'd been doin' the year-end accounts earlier in the day an' so there was nothin' surprisin' about that."

"The surgeon says no papers of any kind were found on him."

"I know. I could've been wrong. I was so shocked to hear him say he was headin' out into that awful weather an' just abandonin' his guests, I wasn't thinkin' too straight." She sipped at her tea, found it unconsoling, and said, "But he seemed genuinely excited. Happy, even. When I heard him ride out on Belgium twenty minutes later, I was not in the least concerned . . ."

"If there *was* a note, with instructions about a rendezvous and some bait to lure him to Bass Cove, could anyone else here have read it?"

Beth Smallman peered up at Marc with a look of puzzlement, pity, and the beginnings of anger. "I'm pleased you are takin' such an interest in Father, and I would like some questions about that night to have better answers, but my husband's father was an' honest an' well-loved gentleman. If somebody deliberately killed him, then you're gonna have to come up with somethin' less fanciful than notions about secret notes an' mysterious footprints in the snow. You've gotta hate or fear somebody with a passion before you can kill them. If there was a note, *I* was the only person here that night *capable* of readin' it. Unless you suspect Emma Durfee."

Marc got up and made a stiff bow. Beth's features softened, and in other circumstances he was confident she would have smiled. "I have inconvenienced you long enough and imposed unconscionably on your hospitality," he said, wrestling his way into his greatcoat.

Beth took an elbow and helped him complete the task.

At the door she said, "You will let me know what you find?"

"I can do no less, ma'am."

"Call me Beth, *please*."

He touched the peak of his cap and left.

Marc was grateful for the slow walk back to the mill, one that didn't include a further encounter with the misanthropic Elijah. He needed a few quiet moments to mull over what he had learned before rehashing it with Erastus Hatch.

He was convinced that a note *had* been delivered. Joshua's decision to leave the house had been made sometime in the half hour or so in which he was checking out the barn. Most likely as he was returning to the house, someone gave it to him – a servant or stableboy on foot or someone who had ridden in from farther afield specifically for the purpose. The need for detailed instructions and some elaborate "hook" strongly suggested a written message, but a personally delivered oral one, though riskier, was not out of the question.

At some point he realized he was going to have to interrogate Elijah about when he had left for the Child estate and whether he had seen his master beforehand. But deep down he was certain that, until some motive became clear, little beyond informed speculation was possible. Nevertheless, he was still in possession of a salient fact known only to him: Joshua Smallman was an informer for Sir John. No one in the region, not even a friend like Hatch, was aware of this. But had someone somehow discovered or guessed at the truth? Some rabid annexationist or firebrand among the apostles of the rabble-rousing Mackenzie and his seditious newspaper? Even so, the area was already crawling with Tories and loyalists, any one of whom could be (and likely was) viewed as a spy with a direct link to the powerful Family Compact in Toronto or the government itself. You'd have to arrange for the deaths of a lot of locals to assuage that particular fever, Marc thought. At the moment, the most plausible premise was that Smallman had discovered some critical information, the revelation of which presented a real danger to some one or some cause. Such information may have been revealed already (Sir John would not be above withholding "politically sensitive" material from his investigating officer), prompting a revenge killing.

It was far too early to tell anyone what he knew about Joshua's relationship with Sir John. That he must, at some time, tell Beth Smallman that particular news filled him with dread: she obviously worshipped the father-in-law who in less than a year had become "Father." Any suggestion that he might have been leading a secret life and had perhaps used her political activities to gather information on her associates might prove devastating. Then again, Beth Smallman did not appear to be a woman easily devastated.

At the mill, Thomas Goodall informed Marc that Constable Hatch had been summoned to Durfee's inn to settle a dispute between two patrons over a bar debt. At the house he found no one in the parlour or dining area. Hearing voices from the summer kitchen, he walked down the hall and opened the door at the end of it.

Mary Huggan and Winnifred Hatch were bent over a washboard, their faces as steamed as a Christmas pudding. Winnifred's attire was more serviceable than it had been yesterday, a shirtwaist and voluminous skirt, but still she looked more like a lady-in-waiting who has discovered she must do her own laundry and has decided simply to get down to it without complaint. On a clothes horse set up beside an iron stove throbbing with heat, Marc saw the linens and stockings he had abandoned on his bed – scrubbed white now. Just beyond it, where a curtain had been pulled back and fastened, he noticed that the quilts on what had to be Thomas Goodall's bed were rumpled from recent sleep and other nocturnal activity.

Edging backwards, Marc eased the door shut.

CHAPTER FIVE

The evening being clear, cold, and still, Marc and Erastus Hatch decided to walk the quarter mile to the Deer Park estate of Magistrate Philander Child. They could have taken the route south along the Miller Sideroad to the highway, then east past Durfee's inn and Dr. Barnaby's house to the stone gates Marc had observed from horseback the previous day. However, since no snow had fallen to blur the "gossip trail," as Hatch called it, they ambled along its meandering, well-travelled way through a pleasant winter wood, most of which, Marc learned, was the property of the wealthiest man in the township. As they walked, and between puffs on their pipes, they found ample opportunity to exchange the news of the day.

Marc summarized his interview with Beth Smallman, omitting only his subsequent speculations. Then he recounted his successful subterfuge of the afternoon when, to establish his cover story, he had ridden east along the second concession to the farm of Jonas Robertson, a loyal Tory whose grandfather had once represented a rotten borough in Shropshire before the family's fortunes had declined. Ensign Edwards had gone through the motions of examining the surplus bags of the finest maize in the county and confirming their producer's own assessment. During this exchange of mutually flattering pleasantries (even now, Marc marvelled at his guile and the ease with which he had been able to prevaricate), Robertson had disembowelled the reputations of several "republican" farmers along the Farley Sideroad, whose seditious behaviours apparently threatened the political stability of the province and even the health of the local grains. Marc had begun to realize why Sir John had placed so much trust in level-headed men of goodwill like Joshua Smallman. Could such qualities, as valuable as they were rare, provide motive for murder in and of themselves?

Hatch had spent the afternoon in Cobourg, where he had given Sheriff MacLachlan the names and description of the Yankee peddlers. As agreed beforehand, he had mentioned Marc's presence without revealing the real purpose of his visit, as, after all, the Sheriff had supported the Magistrate's finding of death by misadventure. Hatch told Marc that no one had admitted seeing the Irishmen since the autumn. Hatch himself, on his way home, had stopped at several of the taverns that Connors was known to frequent on his sojourns in the district and had learned nothing of importance.

"I think it's safe to say that your assumption about Connors and O'Hurley hightailing it across the nearest ice to the home state was the right one," Hatch said as they swung a little to the north towards several columns of smoke visible above the tree-tops. Marc had raised a chuckle earlier when he'd described the pot-rattling donkey skittering up the Kingston Road towards Toronto. "That pair of weasels won't linger a minute longer on the King's ground than they have to," Hatch continued. "The roll of banknotes, though – that may be of real interest to Sir John or his successor. I don't like the smell of foreign money."

"At the moment I consider it merely a distraction," Marc

said. "It's hard to make any connection between a couple of scoundrels like that and Smallman's misadventure."

When Marc finally felt constrained to mention his *tête-à-tête* with Elijah, Hatch found the episode more amusing than the facts seemed to warrant.

"Don't worry," he said, "you won't have to put the screws to him. I questioned him very carefully myself, and MacLachlan had a run at him as well. After a lot of coaxing and a little threatening, he admitted that he had not been with his employer to do the rounds that evening, nor had he seen him since supper at six, because right after he'd eaten he'd beetled off to raise a glass with Ruby Marsden, the Squire's cook. Ruby backs him up. And, of course, everybody in the township knows the old codger slips up there every chance he can get. Why do you think this path is so easy on the feet?"

"So Smallman was out of the house and alone for at least half an hour before he came back in with the news that he had been called out, as it were?"

"I'm afraid so, with no way for anyone to find out who he might've seen or talked to."

"None of the guests coming to the New Year's gathering saw or heard anything?"

"We questioned them all before the inquest. Nothing. And Emma Durfee didn't arrive until well after he'd ridden off."

"Well, we know for certain he got a message from someone," Marc said, with an effort to hide his disappointment.

Hatch stopped. He placed an avuncular hand on Marc's shoulder. "You have to remember, lad, we've only got Beth's word on that."

Marc had seen nothing to match the opulence of Deer Park – not at Government House itself, or even in his illicit glimpses, from anterooms and vestibules, of Family Compact residences in Toronto like Beverley House, Osgoode Hall, or the Grange. Dozens of trees had been hacked down to allow those entering the estate by carriage to appreciate the Georgian proportions and Italianate façade of the manor house itself. Even now, in midwinter, the terraced gardens and housebroken shrubberies undulated elegantly beneath the snowdrifts. In the foyer, lit by an ornate candelabrum, Marc thought, for a sinking moment, that he was back in the entrance hall of Hartfield Downs in Kent, or that he had merely dreamed his secondment to North America and was just now waking up. When a pretty parlour-maid took his hat and curtsied, another, more stabbing memory intruded. He quickly suppressed it.

"Maybe you should've stuck to the law," Hatch said, chuckling at Marc's open-mouthed amazement, just as Philander Child, King's Counsel, trundled forward to greet them with a great welcoming guffaw.

Hatch had prepped his new, young friend for the evening at hand. Only charter members of the Georgian Club would be present on this occasion, at Hatch's request: he and Marc would be joined by their host, Philander Child, and by Major Charles Barnaby and James Durfee. Joshua Smallman had been among this number, though, understandably, his attendance had been irregular during the harvest season. Occasionally associate members or invitees were added to make up two whist tables or, when ladies were included, to enliven the card games and provide a pretext for music and dancing.

Winnifred Hatch, brushing Marc's freshly steamed frock coat earlier that evening, had winced at her father's reference to lancers and galops, prompting Hatch to add, "You'd think you'd never kicked up a heel or hopped to a jig, girl, but I know better, don't I?" Then he'd winked at Marc.

"You spend too much time living in the past," Winnifred had snapped with more impatience than anger.

"Well, all I know is a person shouldn't spend all their days doing good deeds."

"Like taking care of them who can't help themselves?" She paused, then shot him a telling look.

When she pulled Marc's coattails down, it was with a brusque, dismissive gesture: he felt the steel in her touch, the merest tremor of contempt.

"She'll never find a husband," Hatch had said as soon as they'd left the house. "God knows there've been many who've tried."

"I'm surprised," Marc said graciously. "Your daughter is a handsome and . . . *efficient* young woman."

Hatch glanced warily, hopefully, at Marc. "That she is," he said.

That hers was also a cold beauty did not need to be uttered.

"You'd be alone, would you not, if she were to marry?" Marc said, probing gently.

"I'm afraid that's how *she* looks at the matter." Hatch sighed. "But then, I've been alone since Isobel died."

Philander Child, Esquire, was an Englishman who had arrived in Upper Canada as a youth of eighteen, and in his subsequent thirty years in the colony had not permitted a whit of his God-given Englishness to be weathered away. His prosperity was evident in the layers and folds of his corpulence, and though he had grown fat upon the land, his mind had not forgone its lean and hungry motive. Having reaped a modest but irritatingly slow profit from farming (more accurately, from instructing others how to farm for him), he had turned to the law. The reliable flow of conveyancing fees bestowed by grateful associates and confederates of the ruling clique and the magic of compound interest had made him rich. Finally, appointment to the Legislative Council by the former lieutenant-governor, Sir

Peregrine Maitland, yeoman's service to the fledgling Bank of Upper Canada, and eventual retirement to Deer Park as magistrate for Northumberland County and superintendent of its quarter sessions had secured him a well-deserved and affluent old age.

This much Marc had concluded by the time the ceremonial cigars had been smoked, the first snifter of brandy consumed, and the blaze in the magnificent fieldstone fireplace had died down to a warm, conspiratorial glow. Coggins, the footman-cum-butler, poured each of the guests a second glass from a crystal decanter, bowed in the direction of a portrait of Squire Child in his hungrier days, and discreetly left the room.

"So, young man, Sir John was not entirely impressed with my report of the inquest into dear Joshua's death?" Child said, still *en rôle* as the affable Georgian gentleman, the epitome of good breeding, exemplary manners, and moral probity. And not, Marc thought, unlike his guardian Uncle Jabez, or their more illustrious neighbour in Kent, Sir Joseph Trelawney of Hartfield Downs.

"He asked me merely to double-check the evidence," Marc said diplomatically. "Smallman was a man he knew well and admired much."

"Certainly, certainly," Child said. "A gentleman could do no less, and Sir John Colborne is every inch a gentleman."

"The Governor intends to leave you here in the province, then?" said Major Barnaby, retired army surgeon, who had sawed the limbs off many a brave man on the killing grounds of the Spanish Peninsula. His Scots burr was a faint echo of the speech he had heard but little since leaving home at age eleven. His big-boned ruggedness was somewhat offset by deep-browed eyes that twinkled with humour yet gave away little of the thought and feeling stored up behind them.

"Like most young men," Marc said, "I joined the military to fight under the Union Jack."

"You think there will be insurrection in Quebec, then?" Child said.

"I have been led to believe so."

"Sir John's experience under the Duke of Wellington has not gone unnoticed by the colonial secretary, at any rate," Charles Barnaby said. "We've just heard of his promotion to commander-in-chief."

"And what is your assessment of the situation in *this* province?" Child asked Marc, opening a silver snuffbox.

"I don't really know, sir. I'm just a junior officer."

"Surely in the seven or eight months you've been here – in the confidence of Sir John himself, Hatch tells me – you've formed some opinion of the hurly-burly of our politics?"

"I was hoping to learn more about that this evening," Marc said, waving off the offer of snuff.

"It looks as though Sir John thinks there may be a political motive behind Joshua's . . . death," Hatch said helpfully.

Child smiled indulgently at Marc. "All three of us were there," he said. "No one preceded us. Charles examined the body carefully, on the scene and back in his surgery."

"Died of a massive skull fracture," Barnaby said. "Knocked insensible, but could've lingered for some while, alas. Rigor had just passed off, delayed by the cold. My best guess is he died sometime between nine and midnight."

"Which jibes with Beth's account," Hatch said, looking at Marc.

"There were no other injuries, no torn clothing, and no note or paper was found among his effects," Child said.

"And with no witness to corroborate Mrs. Smallman's suspicion that he had received a message sometime after seven o'clock, and no sign around the scene itself of any other disturbance or presence, we had no other choice than to make the finding we did." The Magistrate spoke without the least note of defensiveness. His was the kind of dispassion Marc had come to respect among the barristers and judges of the Old Bailey, whose precincts he had haunted as a twenty-year-old articling clerk playing truant from his firm of lowly London solicitors.

"However," Barnaby said in his more humoured, laconic style, "Durfee here informs me you have a detail or two to add to our investigation."

James Durfee, who had followed the dialogue closely with an encouraging nod from time to time (while managing to devote a good deal of attention to his brandy and cigar), smiled sagely.

"Erastus gave me a quick account of your trip out there yesterday afternoon," Child said, "but we'd all appreciate hearing you yourself describe it for us."

Marc could detect nothing but curiosity in the faces of the four men whose attention was now fully focused upon him. He sensed that the next few minutes were critical to any success he might have in his mission. Without the wholehearted co-operation of these influential men, he had no hope of proceeding one step farther. Moreover, to complicate matters, Sir John would not condone any unnecessary ruffling of feathers among the friends of the government. Why, then, had he – novice and interloper – been chosen? Suppressing any inadequacies he might feel, Marc plunged ahead. As he related the events in the exact sequence in which they had occurred, Marc found the excitement he'd experienced the previous day returning, and with it the confidence – arrogance even – he had felt in winning Hatch over to his own convictions.

"And so you see, sir, one is compelled to face the incredible coincidence of two men being in that peculiar vicinity on discrete errands, along with the cogent question of why a respectable gentleman like Joshua Smallman would, on a whim as it were, ride out there in a snowstorm while the New Year's Eve party he was hosting was about to start."

For a full minute no one spoke.

It was Barnaby who broke the silence. "Well, in the least you've added to the number of questions we haven't been able to answer," he said dryly.

"Ensign Edwards thinks that we must try to discover the motive for any possible foul play, and work backwards from there," Hatch said.

Durfee turned a concerned and pained face to Marc. "We four have spent a good deal of the past two weeks goin' over and over that question in our minds. Joshua was a generous, likeable man. He had no enemies. He was a loyalist more than he was a dyed-in-the-wool conservative like us. I've heard many a professed Reformer in my pub speak respectfully of him when they would rather have cursed him for his views."

"It was suggested a while ago, Mr. Edwards, that Sir John thought politics might be at issue here," Child said. "Joshua Smallman was not directly involved in politics. That he voted Tory puts him in league with hundreds of others in the county, many of whom have been more vociferous and a lot less tolerant. Why was it not one of *us* lured out there in his stead?"

"Sir John does feel politics might be involved," Marc said. "He told me he had good reason for thinking so, but, alas, he was not at liberty to give me chapter and verse."

"What did he think you could discover here on your own, then?" Barnaby asked, not unkindly.

"I guess he thought *we* could help," Hatch said, without a lot of conviction.

Marc paused, then spoke with some confidence. "I didn't press Mrs. Smallman on the matter, but I understand that her father-in-law accompanied her to a number of Reform rallies following his return here."

"Mrs. Smallman, I am sorry to say, having produced no children in three years of marriage, seemed unable to find anything else useful to occupy her time," Child said. "She spouted the contemptible opinions of Willy Mackenzie in public places in the most unseemly manner."

"And she was a Congregationalist to boot," Barnaby added.

"Never set foot in St. Peter's after the nuptials," the Squire huffed. "The poor devil of a husband would drop her off at that tumbledown hutch they call holy and then drive alone to his father's church."

"Well, I blame him in a way," Durfee said, ignoring the glare of his fellow Georgians. "I don't like to speak ill of the dead, but Jesse Smallman was dabblin' in dangerous waters near the end, if you ask me."

"That was a year ago," Hatch said. "As far as I can tell, Beth was involved in trying to get redress for the same grievances her husband and a thousand other farmers are pressing for – through the appropriate channels."

Child turned to Marc, adjusted his girth into its most magisterial posture, and said, "You've no doubt heard all the nonsense about these so-called grievances: the Clergy Reserves, the Alien Act, the evil monopoly of the Bank of Upper Canada, the general unresponsiveness of the Legislative Council and the Executive, who rightly refuse to yield to the demands of the mob. And so on."

"I'm hoping to learn more about them as I go," Marc said.

"Well, son, the first thing to remember is that 90 per cent of what you hear, on both sides, is hot air, bombast, and rabble-rousing rhetoric. As long as the levers of power and the will to rule remain safely entrenched, as they are now, we can tolerate a great deal of invective and vituperation. I've been here for thirty years and have an intimate knowledge of Northumberland County and the province as a whole. Most of the populace is British to the core, and now that Sir John has almost doubled the population with needy immigrants from the Motherland, the brief threat of American outcasts overwhelming us has abated. We are confident also that the next election will see a Tory majority in the Assembly."

"You'll get a chance to hear some of the rant for yourself," Durfee said.

"That's right," Hatch added. "Mackenzie and Peter Perry and all that gang will be in Cobourg for a Reform rally on Saturday afternoon."

"We're expectin' fireworks," Durfee said with a boyish grin.

"Only if the Orangemen arrive with them," Hatch said.

Looking mischievously at Barnaby, Durfee said, "Fanatic monarchists of the likes of Ogle Gowan an' his anti-Catholic Orange Lodge make Mackenzie's lot look like schoolboy debaters."

Barnaby snorted. "I let go of that monarchist nonsense years ago. It doesn't sit well on a Scot's stomach, even though they do claim to defend the Crown and the indissolubility of the Empire." He paused and added, "I defended them in my own way."

"These are men, I've been told, who will resort to violence to further their cause," Marc said.

"Head-bashing in a donnybrook, tar-and-feathering a Papist or two," Hatch said, "but not, I think, a cold-blooded assassination."

"Quite so," Child said. "Though that gang is quite capable of leaving a man to die in the snow – if it served their purpose."

"What do you know about the Hunters' Lodges?" Marc said.

Again, the room went unnaturally quiet, and one by one the members of the Georgian Club scrutinized the young officer, as if they might have overlooked something critical.

Child answered for his associates. "They are a secret society, organized very recently in New York and Pennsylvania, whose members, we presume from the little hard evidence we possess, swear an oath that they will help overthrow the British government of Upper Canada and link up with resident dissidents, republicans, and annexationists, with a view to forming a new, liberated republic. Most of them appear to be malcontents from the Loco Foco Democrats of Buffalo, with a few Irish incendiaries tossed in for leavening."

"I'm told that Mr. Mackenzie has for some years now promoted republican and annexationist doctrines in the *Colonial Advocate*," Marc said.

"Indeed he has," Child said. "Yet he was elected the first mayor of your city, takes his seat in the Assembly, and continues to swear the oath of allegiance. His infamous and dastardly *Seventh Report on Grievances*, which, as you know, helped unseat your own Sir John Colborne, was legally enough drawn up and, though sent by an unorthodox and clandestine route to Lord Glenelg in London, was nonetheless a powerful indication that, outside of his blather and rant, Mackenzie is still willing to work within the very system that has nurtured and tolerated his kind of dissent – often to its own detriment."

"And neither Joshua Smallman nor his daughter have been involved with Orangemen, Yankee extremists, or secret societies. Surely that is the point of all this speculation," Barnaby added.

"Lookin' back over the past months," Durfee said, "the only thing I can truly say is that my boyhood chum attended a number of meetin's and public rallies connected with the *Grievances Report*. An' since everybody 'round here knew he was a loyalist and a Tory supporter at the polls, they realized he only went along to escort Beth. After all, she was a widow, she couldn't very well run off to a public gatherin' by herself. Who else was there to go with her? Elijah? The crippled lad?"

"Surely Joshua's duty was to persuade her not to debase her character by attending the kind of meetings God intended for men," Child said.

"He could've tied her to a chair, I suppose," Barnaby said.

"With a second rope for her tongue," Durfee added, and laughed.

"You're all forgetting," Hatch said, "that Beth was carrying on the efforts that Jesse'd made in regard to the *Grievances* before he got so depressed and . . . did what he did."

"It is conceivable, then," Barnaby said carefully, without looking at Durfee, "that in an attempt to understand his son and perhaps even to comprehend the reasons for his taking his own life, Joshua did begin to become enamoured of the Reform position."

"Even so," Child said, "and I'm not granting your premise for a moment, that is no cause for the man to be murdered. Turning your coat in political matters may lose you a friend or some custom, but not your life."

"I have to agree, Your Honour." Barnaby smiled.

Only Durfee did not laugh. The brandy-whetted scarlet of his cheeks had suddenly paled.

"Are you all right, James?" Barnaby said.

"I've just had a frightenin' thought," Durfee said. "Suppose some people *did* think that Joshua's goin' to all them meetin's an' rallies was in earnest, whether it was or not. An' suppose someone or other at the rallies got the notion into his head that Joshua was pretendin' to be a convert – because of Jesse's grievances an' so on – but was actually an informer."

Marc held his breath, and his peace.

"Preposterous," Child said, circulating the cigar box and serving with his own hand a generous round of brandy. He even gave the slumbering fire an aristocratic poke with one of the irons.

Hatch became animated. "Not so, Squire. It makes a kind of sense, especially if you were a member of one of the fanatical fringe groups in the Reform party – a Clear Grit or whatever. Think of it from that point of view: a retired dry goods merchant comes into the district, a known Tory and occasional associate of the Lieutenant-Governor. Suddenly he starts showing up at Reform political do's everywhere with his daughter-in-law, a known sympathizer. Jesse campaigned over in Lennox for Perry, remember, and wrote up a petition that went to Mackenzie and the grievances committee in the Assembly."

"Aye, that's quite plausible," Barnaby conceded, and even Squire Child nodded meditatively.

Marc could hardly believe his good fortune. Here was the one motive for murder he himself believed to be the most compelling and for which he had inside knowledge he could not reveal. And now he would not have to. He tried to appear only casually interested.

"I see your point," he said, fingering his brandy glass.

"Nevertheless," Barnaby said, and he paused at the deflationary effect of that word. "Nevertheless, we are still faced with the same sort of question as before. What information would an informer – Joshua in this case – be able to gather, from ordinary political meetings and speeches, that would be seditious enough to pose a threat to some treasonous cause or specific persons espousing it?"

"Exactly," Child said. He turned to Marc like a wigged justice about to lecture the novice petitioner before his bench. "All you need to do is scan one issue of the *Colonial Advocate* or the *Cobourg Star* to realize that no rally, camp meeting, hustings debate, or underground pamphleteering goes unreported for any longer than it takes to set the type. One side inflates the rhetoric with hyperbole and bombast, the other edits and distorts at will – but no one's opinion, view, prejudice, or bigotry remains private for more than a day in this fishbowl of a province."

"True," Barnaby said. "There's a lot of bush out there, but not a single tree that would hide you for an hour."

"What we're saying," Hatch added, "is that the information would have to be truly seditious – like facts about proposed actions – not the empty-headed threats we see in the press every week."

For a minute or so the weight of this conclusion silenced the group, and fresh cigars were clipped and lit.

Barnaby spoke first. "I think we're agreed that truly treasonous information would not likely bubble up at the meetings Joshua and Beth attended last summer and fall. But what if those meetings were not the source?"

"What else could be?" Durfee said.

"You said yourself that Jesse Smallman was treading dangerous waters near the end."

"I only meant he was flailin' about – angry, in despair – at what was happenin' to him because of the Clergy Reserves. An' how he kept repeatin' that there didn't seem to be any political party capable of gettin' anythin' done."

"Is it possible, conceivable even," Barnaby continued, "that Jesse joined or thought of joining one of the annexationist groups, one of the secret societies, and that he might have been privy to treasonable information?"

"Now we're *really* grasping at straws," Hatch said.

"The man's also been dead for twelve months," Child said.

Barnaby, who was beginning to enjoy himself wholeheartedly, persisted. "What if Joshua discovered this information?

Among his son's effects, for example? And was thought to be an agent as well?"

"You've got a surfeit of 'what if's in that hypothesis," Child said.

"There's only one way to find out," Durfee said. "Only one person is left who can shed any light on Joshua or Jesse."

"You're not suggesting Beth might be involved in anything unsavoury?" Hatch said sharply.

"I think he's merely implying that some of the answers to our questions lie in the Smallman household," Barnaby said. "For the sake of the reputations of two men no longer able to defend themselves, I think it behooves us to engage in some hard questioning, indelicate as that might prove."

They all turned to stare, with expectation and much relief, at Ensign Edwards.

The arrival of Coggins with a tray of cheeses and sweetmeats and decanters of wine stinted the flow of serious conversation for some minutes. However, as soon as the sighs of satisfaction had abated, Philander Child picked up a thread of the previous dialogue.

"While I concur that we must press Mrs. Smallman as forcefully as her delicate circumstances permit in order to eliminate any possibility that Joshua Smallman might have been an informer or that Jesse was anything other than a committed Reformer, I would advise young Marc here to aim his investigation in more obvious directions."

"To those in the county already known to be fanatics," Marc said.

The Squire smiled patiently. "My years on the bench compel me to consider facts before hypotheses. Someone has to ascertain, among the living, whether there was any actual contact or real acquaintance between Joshua and known extremists. We need facts, dates, notarized statements, sworn informations or affidavits. No one gets himself murdered – and even that assumption is still conjecture, remember – without coming into contact, in some discernible way, with his assassin."

"So, I need to find out whether any such extremists knew Smallman or were seen with him over the past twelve months."

"And I can suggest two or three likely candidates," Child said.

Marc smiled. "Azel Stebbins, Israel Wicks, and Orville Hislop," he said, recalling these names from Sir John's notes.

"Sir John has been well briefed," Child said.

"When will you begin, then?" Durfee said.

Marc smiled. "I already have."

James Durfee and Charles Barnaby left together shortly after ten o'clock, because the doctor was tired after nine hours in his Cobourg surgery and Durfee wished to help Emma clear up after the chaos of the afternoon stage stop and the brisk evening trade of local elbow-benders.

As the remaining three were finishing their nightcaps, Hatch happened to mention to Child that Marc had manhandled a couple of Yankee peddlers on his way to Crawford's Corners.

"You *are* a soldier, young man." Child laughed appreciatively. "And a damn good one."

"Marc has reason to think they were involved in smuggling rum," Hatch said.

"What puzzles me," Marc said, "is why anybody, peddler or freebooter, would bring tariffed spirits into a province where whisky itself is duty-free and there seem to be more local distilleries than gristmills. Grog's a penny a cup at every wayside shebeen."

"A fair question," Child said, nodding towards Hatch. "But these smugglers are 'importing' high-quality spirits and wines:

rum from the West Indies, bourbon from the Carolinas, Bordeaux and Champagne from France, port from Iberia – and all of it, you can be sure, pirated or hijacked at some point along the way. They peddle it only around the garrison towns – Kingston, Toronto, London, Sandwich, Newark – to establishments that cater to a higher class of citizenry and that, in addition to cut-price vintage spirits, offer the further comfort of a warm bed and willing flesh." The Squire, long a widower, shook his head sorrowfully, as a man who has seen much folly and never quite accustomed himself to it.

"But that means tuns, barrels, packing cases," Marc said.

"Oh, the peddlers don't do the actual smuggling," Hatch said. "They're just petty advance men, drummers, messengers, and the like. Peddling door to door is a perfect cover for the work. The county is crawling with them, summer and winter."

"Erastus and I apprehended one of the blackguards a while back," Child said. "What was his name now?"

"Isaac Duffy," Hatch said, and his face lit up with pleasure at the memory. "Caught him trying to sell a bottle of His Majesty's finest Hunting Sherry to Emma Durfee, an item he'd most likely pilfered from some smuggler's drop he knew about."

"He's in irons down in Kingston," Child said, "but before we shipped him off, he gave us a lead to two scoundrels in the area we'd long suspected of actually hauling the stuff across the lake on the ice."

"Jefferson and Nathaniel Boyle," Hatch said. "Brothers who operated two so-called farms out past Mad Annie's swamp."

"Hatch and I hopped on our horses and rode right out there like a pair of avenging angels." Child laughed, and Marc did too, at the image of Magistrate Child's two hundred and fifty pounds of pampered flesh astride and agallop.

"Without a sheriff or constables?" Marc said above Hatch's chortling.

"I'd been after them Yankee cattle thieves for years," Child said with sudden vehemence. "I had a pistol tucked in each side of my waistcoat, and Hatch here had his fowling piece. My God, I can still remember every moment of that ride."

"By the time we got there," Hatch said, "they'd already skedaddled, as they say in the Republic."

"Those sewer rats can smell authority a mile away." The Squire sighed. "I hate smugglers of every stripe. They undermine the fragile economy here, flout the King's law, and offer incentive to others to do the same. And when they're Yankees to boot, I detest them as much as I do a traitor or a turncoat."

"All we found were two abandoned wives, just skin and bone, and a dozen half-starved youngsters," Hatch said sadly.

"Well, they haven't been seen since," Child said with some satisfaction.

"And when I took Winnifred out there with some food and clothes at Christmas," Hatch said, "the women and children had packed up and gone. The whole lot of 'em."

Marc had witnessed the effects of grinding poverty on the streets of London and never become inured to it, or to the callow disregard shown towards its victims by the prosperous and the morally blinkered. The thought of Winnifred's charity warmed him in ways the brandy, cigars, and stimulating company had failed to.

Philander Child wished Marc well in his efforts on behalf of the Lieutenant-Governor, complimented him on his good manners, and offered his assistance if it should be required. Walking back to the mill, appreciative of Hatch's companionable silence, Marc went over the evening's conversation. He concluded that he had been told much that had been intended and some that had not.

Coming up to the house, Marc suddenly said, "Who is Mad Annie?"

Hatch snorted. "You really don't want to know that long, sad story." He placed a fatherly hand on Marc's shoulder and said with mock solemnity, "I'll give you the gory details in the morning."

Marc lay awake for a long while that night, mulling over what had been said, half said, not said. What was really keeping him from sleep was the dread of interrogating Beth Smallman about two men whom she loved and who had been taken from her in the most horrific manner imaginable. At the same time, he was not prepared to discount any suspect, especially an attractive and vulnerable one, in advance of the facts. But he was happy that the four gentlemen with whom he had just spent a most pleasant evening had themselves been together during the critical hours of New Year's Eve. He was just about to drift off upon this comforting thought when he heard a door open and a familiar footstep in the hall outside his room.

He waited several seconds before easing himself out of bed, slipping the door ajar, and peering down the dark hallway. This time he caught a glimpse of white nightdress and a fleeting image of the female form undulating within it before the door to the back section of the house shut it out of sight. Then came the same giggle he had heard the previous night, the only difference being that the figure he'd just seen animating the nightdress was a head taller and a good deal more Junoesque than Mary Huggan's. It was undoubtedly the handsome Miss Hatch.

CHAPTER SIX

"Well, lad, what did you learn of value last night?" Hatch said to Marc, stabbing a sausage.

The question startled Marc, not because it was impertinent or sudden but because he had been absorbed in close observation of Thomas Goodall and his mistress, Winnifred Hatch. That they were lovers, and by all the evidence frequently and consensually so, could not have been inferred from the cool and formal intercourse between them over the Thursday morning breakfast table. Winnifred moved briskly about, neither smiling nor unsmiling, until the three men had been served, then sat down next to Marc across from her father and began her own meal. Mary Huggan soon joined her, and the two women exchanged pleasantries. Goodall, as was his custom, kept his eyes locked on his food, which he consumed rapidly but mechanically, as if eating were a duty. Like the miller's, his hands were large, roughened by cold and searing sun, and shaped to the plough and axe-handle.

Was it possible that the proud Miss Hatch was ashamed to admit her attachment to such a plain and taciturn man? Or had it more to do with a sense of obligation to her father? Marc had begun to realize that he had much to learn about the ways of these country folk, and that such knowledge might be necessary to unravelling the mystery of Joshua Smallman's death.

"Did we give you anything useful?" Hatch said to Marc, and he nodded towards the two women as if to say, "Keep it general."

"Yes," Marc managed to say. "Yes, you did. You gave me something definite to ask the gentlemen whose farms I plan to visit today."

"That's good, then." Hatch reached across the table and, with Mary Huggan's consent, tipped her uneaten egg and sausage onto his own plate.

"Thank you, Mary," Hatch said, and the girl blushed to the roots of her pale hair. Winnifred gave her a sharp look, and she blushed anew.

"We'll have to get that blush of yours repaired one of these days," Hatch said impishly.

"Leave the lass alone," Winnifred said, and before her father could recover from his surprise, she turned to Marc and said, "You're likely to find most of the surplus grain among the farms on the Pringle Sideroad north of the second concession."

Marc suddenly found her face, with its strong bones and dark, perceptive eyes, no more than a foot from his own, and he could hear the whisper of her breathing beneath the taut bib of her apron. Across the table, Thomas uttered a satisfying belch and pushed his chair back.

"Oh, why is that?" Marc said.

"They're good Tories, of course," Winnifred said, and Hatch let out an approving chuckle. "The Reformers on the Farley Sideroad," she continued, "are too busy organizing petitions to get a decent crop in, or keep it from the thistles when they do."

"Winnifred keeps all the accounts here," Hatch beamed.

"She knows the worth of every farmer in the district to the nearest shilling."

"Don't exaggerate," Winnifred said, nudging Mary Huggan, who jumped up gratefully and began clearing away some of the plates. Goodall had already stumped out to his chores, unremarked by anyone.

"I'll take your advice to heart," Marc said gallantly.

"It would be more useful in the head, I believe."

Mary knocked over a cup; Hatch reached out, caught it, and handed it back to the girl, rousing a more furious blush.

"Go put some more water on," Winnifred said firmly to Mary. "I'll finish up here." She rose and began stacking the dishes. There wasn't an ounce of self-consciousness anywhere in her body. "I wish you good hunting, Ensign Edwards," she said with cool solicitude as she went back into the kitchen.

"Don't mind her none," Hatch said. "She's a bit set in her ways."

And her straightforward, no-nonsense ways were certainly not those of the young ladies Marc had encountered at the mess parties and the soirees of Government House, ladies whose "aristocratic" breeding and overwrought manners seemed superfluous among the indignities of mud-rutted streets, slatternly servants, uppity tradesmen, and stiff-fingered seamstresses.

"She's quick with figures, mind – like her mother," Hatch was happy to add. "And a handsome lass, eh?"

Summoning his own good manners, Marc said, "Most men would describe her so."

Marc was looking forward to the challenge of eliciting essential and perhaps incriminating information from Israel Wicks, Azel Stebbins, and Orville Hislop – the trio of suspected "aliens" passed on to him by Sir John. But he was not anticipating with any pleasure the imminent interview with Beth

Smallman. The death of a loved one – especially a parent – was devastating. And while he himself had been a mere five years old when both his parents had died of cholera, he could still recall the numbing sense of loss, the abrupt rupturing of the world he had believed permanent and incorruptible, and the long, bewildering absence that followed and would not be filled. More immediate perhaps was the love he felt for "Uncle" Jabez, who had adopted him and raised him up in ways that would have been inconceivable had his parents survived. Beth Smallman had seen her husband hang himself out of some deep despair, the roots of which Marc knew he must probe, and barely a twelvemonth later she had suffered the unexplained death of a father-in-law she had come to love as much or more than she had her husband. How and why that affection had grown, and its consequences, were facts he had to learn, if his investigation was to be rigorous and objective.

Taking a deep breath, Marc turned onto the Smallman property.

"You again, is it?"

"My visiting your mistress is of no concern of yours," Marc said when he had recovered from the shock of Elijah's sudden materialization – this time from behind the manure pile in the stable yard. He realized immediately the ineptness of such a reprimand here in the bush, but not before Elijah had guffawed with his own brand of upstart contempt.

"The missus an' me'll decide what concerns us," Elijah said. "We ain't impressed by no fancy uniform."

Marc ignored the remark and switched tactics. "When did you leave your cabin and walk up to Philander Child's place on the day your master died?" he demanded in his best drill-sergeant's voice.

Elijah's eyes narrowed, and his ungloved fingers squeezed

more tightly around the handle of his pitchfork. "An' who wants to know?"

"The Lieutenant-Governor," Marc said, bristling.

But Elijah had already turned away and was now ambling towards the barn. As he went in, he called back over his shoulder, "Don't tha' be long up there. I won't have ya upsettin' the missus."

So much for the Governor's authority.

"You're wonderin' why I'm not draped in widow's weeds," Beth Smallman said.

In truth, Marc was silently noting not the absence of mourning attire but the arresting presence of a plain white blouse, brown woollen skirt, and an unadorned apron that might have been stitched together out of discarded flour sacking. Once again her flaming russet hair was behaving as it pleased.

"Well, there's no one would see them, is there?" she said, once again seated across from him in the tender light of the south window. "Besides, grief goes much deeper than crêpe or black wreaths upon doors."

"I apologize, ma'am, for the necessity of this interview –"

"Please don't," she said. "I'm as eager to learn why Father died in the way he did as you an' the Governor are." Her face was grave but not solemn. She struck Marc as a woman who would do her weeping at night – more Scots than Irish. "Livin' with 'whys' that never get answered is as hard as grievin' itself."

That she was alluding to her husband's death as much as to her father-in-law's was not in doubt. But Marc was not ready to take up that cue. Not yet. "It is the why, the motive, that I need to discover," he said quietly. "And to do so, I must learn as much as possible about your father-in-law's thoughts and feelings and actions over the past few months."

"I understand," she said. Her voice was breathy and low: she would be an alto in the Congregationalist choir, he thought. "I'll help in any way I can."

"My task is made somewhat easier by the fact that until your husband passed away a year ago, your father-in-law lived and worked in Toronto. We need to focus then on those activities he took up here subsequent to his return."

"He was born here," she reminded him, "an' grew up on a farm near Cobourg. When his father died, he sold the farm an' moved to Toronto – it was still York then. He enjoyed the country very much, but his talents lay in business, in the life of the town."

"And your husband's?"

Beth paused, smiled shrewdly, and said, "They did not share similar interests."

Marc decided it was politic to sip at his tea and sample a biscuit before he spoke again. "Jesse was not enamoured of dry goods?"

"While his mother was alive, he pretended to be. When she died seven years ago, Jesse took the money she left him from her own father's estate, moved back here where they were just opening the township, an' bought this farm." She looked down at her tea but did not drink. "He felt he'd come home."

The scraping of a boot along floorboards announced the entrance of Aaron. Marc waited patiently while Beth fussed over the boy, tucked a biscuit into his twisted mouth, did up the top button of his mackintosh, and escorted him back outside, whispering instructions into his ear as if she were not repeating them for the hundredth time.

When the tea was replenished and she was seated again, she said, "You'll want to know how we met."

"Pardon me for saying so, but you don't look as though you've been a farm girl all your life."

"You're very observant for one so . . . young," she said. And so coddled and pampered and protected from the true horrors of the world, she implied with her single, taut glance. "But these are genuine calluses." She showed both her palms while the cup and saucer teetered on her knees. "You learn how when you have to, an' quickly." That she herself was younger than he appeared to be of no relevance.

"You met your husband here, then?"

"My father was the Congregationalist minister in Cobourg. We came up here when I was eight, after my mother died back in Pennsylvania."

"But your husband was Church of England," Marc said.

Once again he was raked by that appraising gaze. "A venial sin," she said. "Congregationalists are a tolerant lot. An' democratic to boot." She watched to see the effect of this last remark.

"Would you say that relations between Jesse and Joshua were strained?"

"Did Father come to the weddin', you mean?"

"Did he approve of the . . . way his son's life was going?"

"He came down for the weddin' at St. Peter's in Cobourg."

"And that was . . . ?"

"Almost four years ago. Jess and I came directly here."

"Did his father visit?"

Each new question seemed to disconcert her just a bit more, but the only outward sign of discomfort was the length of the pause before she could answer. When she did, Marc could see no indication that she was reluctant, withholding, or evasive.

"Only at Christmas. And once at Easter."

When the thorny issue of whose church to attend must have complicated matters.

"Perhaps if there had been children . . ." Her voice trailed off.

"But there weren't," Marc prompted, uncertain now of his ground.

Her smile was indulgent but nonetheless pained. "No miscarriages, no stillborns, no infant deaths," she whispered. "Nothing."

"But Joshua came immediately when he was needed," Marc said with feeling, "and he stayed."

"Yes."

"And gave up dry goods to become a farmer."

Her "yes" was just audible.

Marc was grateful for the sudden arrival of Mary Huggan through the kitchen door.

"Oh," she said to Beth, "I didn't know anybody was with you." Mary seemed to have arrived in a state of some turmoil, but when she saw the tears sitting on Beth's cheeks, she looked bewildered and began backing away. "I'm sorry, I've come at a bad time."

"It's all right, Mary. Ensign Edwards and I have some distressin' but necessary things to talk over."

"Oh," Mary said, then whirled and fled.

Beth called out, "Come over after you've served dinner!" She had drawn a cotton handkerchief from her apron pocket and dried her cheeks before Marc could find his own linen one and offer it. "I'm ready to go on now."

"If your father-in-law made an enemy, even one he didn't know he'd made, I need to find that person – or group."

"As in political party."

"Or faction. Erastus Hatch and others have given me a rough sketch of the various parties and factions contending in the county. He also mentioned that –"

"I dragged my Tory father-in-law off to Reform rallies in five different townships when I'd be servin' my monarch better by mindin' the house, lookin' for a husband who could give me babies, an' helpin' to raise enough corn to keep the bailiffs out of the barn."

"Something of that order," Marc managed to reply.

"I also read newspapers, and I helped Jess write two of his petitions to the Assembly."

"I've been led to believe that Joshua accompanied you to Reform rallies as a means merely of seeing you properly chaperoned."

"He was a gentleman."

"Was he not in danger of being . . . embarrassed or otherwise discomfited? After all, his Tory leanings, his former business in the capital, the friends he selected here upon his return – these would be well known."

"Everything is eventually well known in Northumberland County."

"Did he participate in any way when he accompanied you?"

Again the indulgent smile, with just a touch of scorn in it. "I see you haven't attended the hustings or any of our infamous political picnics."

"As a soldier I have other pressing duties."

"So I've been told." This time her smile was warm, accepting. "But if you had, you'd know that opponents of every stripe show up an' pipe up at every opportunity. The give an' take of public debate is a polite way of describin' the shoutin' matches an' general mayhem. Sometimes it takes fisticuffs or a donnybrook to settle on a winner."

"No place for an unescorted lady, then." For a brief moment he pictured her dependent upon his strong, soldier's arm.

"You want to know, I think, but are too gentlemanly to ask, if Father became embroiled in the debates? The answer is no. He was a friendly but reserved man." She paused. "He was that rare thing among men: a listener."

Marc got up and walked to the window. He drew out his pipe and, receiving silent permission from his hostess, began stuffing it with tobacco from the pouch on his belt. When he turned back, Beth was beside him, a lit tinder stick in her hand. She watched him closely – with the same kind of marvelling intensity he himself had once used when observing his Uncle Jabez shaving – as he got the plug going. With a start he realized she had done this many times.

"My feeling from what Sir John told me of Joshua, and what I've learned here thus far, is that there is more likelihood of his *listening* to what was being said, of taking it in –"

"Or bein' taken in by it?" she said quickly.

"That too."

"Well, I can say one thing for sure: he began more an' more to understand what it was like – *is* like – to try an' eke out a livin' from the land when so much of the province's affairs are run from Toronto by gentlemen who've never hoed a row of Indian corn an' who think every person with a rightful grievance is an insurrectionist."

"You said a moment ago that some folks thought you should stay put on the farm to help keep the bailiffs away. Did you mean that literally?"

"Almost. If it hadn't been for Mr. Child extendin' us a mortgage, Jess an' me might well've lost everything."

"Philander Child holds your mortgage?"

"He did. An' when the second drought brought us to our knees, he kindly offered to buy the farm from us, for a lot more than it was worth."

"He doesn't look like a farmer to me."

Beth smiled indulgently. "You can be interested in agricultural land without wantin' to hoe beans or muck out stalls."

"Point taken. But you were not tempted by his offer."

"*I* was. But not Jess. He was not about to admit failure to his father."

"But then –"

"Then he died. And it was *me* that vowed never to sell. Then Father arrived and paid off the mortgage."

"I see."

"Mr. Child also arranged for Elijah to help Jess an' me out that last year." She caught Marc's wince of disbelief. "Elijah's a miserable old coot till you get to know him, but he worked for his board an' what little we could pay him at harvest time. He's got no family."

"Is he a local?"

"No. Some crony of Mr. Child's in Toronto was lookin' for a safe home for him an' he ended up here."

"But the land around here appears to be extremely fertile," Marc said. "And you've already cleared most of your acreage by the look of it."

Beth took hold of his arm. "Let's go for a walk. It's time you learned somethin' about grievances."

As they made their way to the door, Marc caught sight of a brass bedstead behind partly drawn curtains. On either side of the bed, a pair of tall shelves listed under the weight of books. The title of one leapt out at him: Thomas Paine's *The Rights of Man.*

Following the direction of his gaze, Beth said, "My own father's bed – his legacy, along with his library. I left the religious tomes back in Cobourg, for the Reverend Haydon." When Marc continued to stare, she said, "You enjoy readin'?"

"Very much," he replied, uncertain of the question's intent. "I spent two years as a law clerk."

She smiled. "I guess that counts."

Outside, the sunshine and cold air made walking a pleasant exercise. As they passed the barn to veer northwest towards the farm's fields and pastures, they could hear Elijah mucking out the pigpens and singing vigorously. No recognizable word emerged from his song, though the hogs joined in as they were able.

"Does Elijah have a last name?" Marc said.

"I suppose so," Beth said. "But he's never said and I've never asked."

A few yards beyond the barn Beth began to point out to Marc the location of fields, all alike now under two feet of snow, and their pertinent features: this one already bursting with winter wheat though you couldn't yet see its green sprouts; that one to be seeded with maize in April; this one lying fallow; that one an alfalfa field waiting for spring rains. The snow-packed trail they were following appeared to Marc to be shadowing Crawford Creek but at a consistent distance of thirty yards or so.

"Wouldn't this path be more scenic if it were closer to the creek?" he asked when they stopped at a field where tree stumps and random branches jutted brutally through the snow – a familiar sight, even to a newcomer like Marc, in a country whose arable land was still nine-tenths forest.

"It would," Beth said, her gaze still upon the stump-scarred field in front of them, "if we owned the land next to it."

"Where we've been walking is your property line, then?"

Beth murmured assent. "This was the last of our fields to be cleared. We worked on it all one summer and fall. It was the last thing Jess an' me did together."

Marc offered his arm in a gentlemanly gesture. She did not lean upon it, but he could feel the pressure of her fingers and found it pleasantly disconcerting.

"From what you've just told me and from what I've seen of

your livestock, you appear to have a prospering operation here."

"It must look that way now," she said, staring ahead. "The land was cheap so long as we cleared our quota an' did our bit on the roads. The mortgage was mostly for the new barn, the cows an' pigs, an' some machinery that needed replacin'. We even had a team of oxen once."

"Surely two or three good crops would have seen you solvent," Marc said, as if he actually knew what he was talking about.

"True. But just as we needed them, as I said earlier, the drought struck."

"But you've got a creek over there twice the size of most rivers in England!"

"I'm not talkin' about the kind of drought you get in a desert or the kind that drove Joseph into Egypt. It only takes three or four weeks of little or no rain in June or July to weaken a crop. The thistles an' blight get in, an' the kernels shrivel up so you're lucky to get ten bushels to the acre."

"And that happened three summers ago?"

"And the summer before last, too. If you look back towards the barn from this high point where we're standin', you can see that the main section of growin' land is very low. In the spring, it's actually swampy, an' difficult to plough an' seed. We had two wet springs in a row."

She said this as if rain and drought were the whims of a Fate determined to tease and madden, the kind that brought plagues to the Pharaoh and mindless ordeals to Job.

"The squire next to us back home had swamp ground like that, and he drained it with tile," Marc said.

"But we don't own the land next to the creek," Beth said.

"But the creek is right there," Marc persisted. "There's nothing but bush on either side of it, no one is using it. It's the same creek that drives Hatch's mill and feeds half the wells of the township." He was trying to keep the note of impatience out of his voice, any sense that he was instructing the naive or the unreasonably discouraged. "Nobody'd give a tinker's dam if you drained your swamp into it or drew water out of it for irrigation. Hatch says a quarter of the farmers here are still squatters, and no one pays the slightest bit of attention."

"That's exactly how Jess used to talk," Beth said. She turned and trod through the snow towards Crawford Creek. Marc floundered behind her. When he caught up, she gestured towards the frozen ribbon of water and the hardwood forest fringing its banks.

"Under those trees is prime farmland, rich soil, good drainage, a sugar maple woodlot, shade to protect the cattle . . ."

"You couldn't afford to buy it? Not even the part of it that includes the creek on this side?" Marc's eyes followed what he could now see would be the unalterable survey line that made every farm a rectangle, or set of contiguous rectangles, regardless of topographical caprice or nuance of Nature. The bow in Crawford Creek took it away from the straight boundary line that marked the western limit of the Smallman farm, when the curve of the creek itself cried out to be the natural border between the adjacent properties, assuring each a precious share of the creek's water.

"We couldn't buy it," Beth said, "even if we had the money."

Before he asked why, Marc had to suppress the unsettling thought that Joshua Smallman had been a wealthy man by provincial standards, having leased his lucrative business on "fashionable" King Street and paid off his son's mortgage, and that his daughter-in-law, so recently restored to his affection, would surely inherit whatever remained.

"What you see over there," Beth said, "and all along this side of the creek, is a lot owned by the Crown. If an' when the government ever decides to sell it, the proceeds'll go to the clergy."

Light dawned. Inwardly Marc blushed at his own obtuseness, his failure to see how Beth Smallman had been leading him patiently towards this conclusion. The Clergy Reserves had headed every list of grievances headlined in Mackenzie's *Colonial Advocate*. This was a phrase flung like a goad against the worthies of the province and the Governor's appointed Legislative Council.

"Ahh . . . yes. Every seventh lot to be reserved for the use and maintenance of the Protestant clergy," Marc said, the legalese slipping easily off the tongue.

"Pro*test*ants but not dissenters," Beth said.

"I see. But surely the assignment of such lots is not random and self-defeating. Surely both parties, the Church of England and the farmers, stand to gain by the rational allotment and sale of such reserve lands."

"The surveyors laid out these lots ten years ago and applied the grid plan they'd been given by the Executive Council. It's the same for every township in the province. The disposition of lots is decided in advance. What's actually on them or not on them is irrelevant."

"That's preposterous!"

"Mr. Mackenzie himself used that very word."

"Even so, can no one buy that lot over there?"

"Clergy Reserve lots are bought and sold all the time. Archdeacon Strachan an' his cronies in the Council trade them – like marbles. But only when the value's been raised or it appears convenient or necessary to their interests. That one over there will be sold when all the property 'round it is cleared an' improved and a concession road cut out to the north of it. It'll be worth ten times what it is now – to someone. Our farm and it would make a natural an' very profitable pair."

"But couldn't you and your husband have run your tile down to the creek and set up some irrigation pipes in the

97

interim? You could've put a squatter's shack on that piece by the bank, for God's sake!"

"We could have. But what's to stop the leaders of the Anglican Church with influence in the governor's Executive Council from suddenly decidin' to sell that lot to one of their friends, an' that friend then comin' in an' rippin' up our tile – leavin' us high an' dry like we were in the first place? Not a thing."

"They don't have to sell at public auction?"

"Not if it doesn't please them. An' don't forget, Jess an' me were radical Reformers through an' through."

Recalling Joshua Smallman's friendship with Sir John Colborne, Marc said, "But perhaps your father-in-law could have petitioned the Executive Council on your behalf?"

"He didn't believe in that kind of shady dealing," she replied, with more pride than regret. "He was too honourable."

"But you're not suggesting that the government would let politics corrupt its legal responsibilities?"

The ingenuousness of the question surprised and amused Beth Smallman, but she suppressed a laugh.

"All this has been set out in the *Report on Grievances* that Mackenzie sent across to Lord Glenelg?" Marc continued.

"The *Seventh Report on Grievances*."

They walked slowly back towards the barn, Beth ahead, Marc behind. At the point where the path dipped south towards the mill property (that, as chance would have it, straddled the creek down its full length), Marc took Beth's hand and brought her mittened fingers to his lips, a gesture ingrained by long habit and prompted now by something more than courtesy.

"Thank you for being so candid and forthcoming," he said formally. "And good day to you."

She left her fingers where they lay for a second or two after Marc released them, and she looked steadily at him, as if he were one of her father's books that might possibly deserve reading.

"I intend to find out what happened to Joshua," he said.

"I believe you will."

He watched her until she had passed the barn and disappeared into the summer kitchen attached to the rear of the house. Then he turned to make his way to Hatch's house, but a banging noise brought him up short. He stopped to listen. Somewhere a door was flapping freely in the light breeze. He checked the barn, then swung his attention to Elijah's cabin near it. The old goat had left his door unlatched and, if the wind picked up even slightly, it would soon blow off its leather hinges. Reluctantly, for he did not wish the pleasant afterglow of the interview with Beth to be disturbed, Marc walked down towards the cabin.

He grasped the plank door by the knob, but before fastening it, he decided to have a look inside, in case the wretched fellow had fallen or taken ill. In the grainy light that illuminated the interior, Marc could just make out the unmade and unoccupied bed, an empty chair, and a makeshift desk cluttered with papers. Marc stepped back outside and peered around for any sign of Elijah. A movement up beyond the house caught his attention: someone was trundling across the road and into the woods on the far side, where the path led up to Squire Child's estate – Elijah What's-his-name scuttling, quick as a dog in heat, over to call upon his lady friend, Ruby Marsden.

Marc latched the door and turned to leave, then suddenly wrenched it open again and stepped boldly inside. He moved swiftly over to the desk and sat down on the rickety chair in front of it. The desk was a mass of jumbled newspapers, pamphlets, and broadsides, speckled with ash and shards from cracked pipe bowls. For a man reputed to be illiterate, Elijah had chosen some unusual recreational materials. One by one

Marc held these up to the dim light that fell through the window. On every item, passages had been underlined or crudely circled with charcoal. The subject of each marked passage was instantly clear: political statements, whether they were in the reports of the minutes of the House of Assembly, a manifesto in broadside or tract, or a hyperbolic claim in the capitalized line of a poster. And each of them bilious with the rhetoric of the left – the bombast of the radicals. Among this detritus lay a single leather-bound book, *The Holy Bible*.

Gently Marc opened it, and he peered at the fly-leaf. A name was scrawled there, faded but legible. The word "Elijah" was readily decipherable, but the letters of the last name were tangled and blurred. After some minutes, Marc deciphered them as: C - H - O - W - N.

Elijah Chown.

So, Elijah had secrets to keep. He was a furtive reader and a closet Reformer. Little wonder, then, that he had been so protective of the Smallmans. But why the secrecy? Beth herself did not know he could read – or else she had lied about it yesterday when she had implied that only she among the New Year's guests was literate, a conclusion he now rejected out of hand. And what else might he have to hide? Somehow, Marc thought, he was going to have to find a way of interrogating the prickly old misanthrope. He needed to know much more about what was really going through the mind of Joshua Smallman in the weeks before his death. And he needed to hear it, unfortunately, from someone less partisan than his daughter-in-law.

At any rate, the hired hand would bear watching.

CHAPTER SEVEN

J ust as Marc rounded the north silo and turned towards the miller's barn, he heard a high-pitched squawk that rose to a terrified shriek, then stopped, as if an organ-pipe had been throttled with a vengeful thumb. Then, before he could even hazard a guess as to the tortured source of the sound, the elongated and fully engaged figure of Winnifred Hatch emerged from between the barn and the chicken coop. In the vise of her left hand, the silenced but thrashing body of a bulb-eyed, dusty-feathered capon struggled futilely against the inevitable. In her right hand, she clutched a hatchet. The miller's daughter – garbed in sweater and skirt and an intimidating leather butcher's apron – marched to a stump near Marc, one that had been set firmly in the ground for her purpose. She plopped the lolling head of the doomed creature upon it and brought the hatchet blade down with the zeal of a Vandal. Blood burst everywhere. Marc leapt back, then stared down at the crimson spatter on his boots and the gaudy petit point etched suddenly in the snow. As Winnifred jerked the decapitated fowl up by its feet to let the blood drip out, she noticed the spectator for the first time.

"Around here we do our own killing," she said. Then she wheeled about and strode into the barn. At the base of the stump, the creature's dead eye was wide open.

Marc scrubbed his boots in the snow and carried on. At the door to the back shed, he noted the probable cause of Winnifred's scorn, if that's what it was. Standing just inside, obscured by shadow, Mary Huggan was twisting a cotton hanky in her fingers and doing her best to hold back her tears.

"It's all right now, Mary," he said in what he hoped was a soothing tone. "You can go on over there. Beth's expecting you."

Mary blushed and sped away. If she saw the blood-drenched path beside the coop, she didn't let on.

After a midday meal of cheese, cold ham, and bread, Marc and Erastus Hatch walked down to the barn, where Hatch asked Thomas Goodall to saddle their horses. They continued on to the mill and sat smoking in the tiny office the miller kept there, more as a sanctuary than a place of business.

"I could go out there on my own," Marc said.

"I'm sure you could, son. But this ain't England, you know. That tunic of yours is more likely to raise the bull's hackles than to instill fear, or even generate a modicum of respect." He was chuckling but nonetheless serious.

"I do know that," Marc said. A mere eight months in the colony had taught him to disregard the graces and rules of the society he had been raised in. In Great Britain there were dozens of offences for which a man who forgot his place in the unchangeable scheme of things might be hanged – and frequently was. Here in Upper Canada, you had to murder a man in front of ten unimpeachable witnesses before the scaffold was brought into play. And dressing down an insubordinate or an offending citizen was just as likely to get you a string of retaliatory oaths as a cap-tugging apology. Even women who professed to be ladies smoked pipes in public and could not be trusted not to utter a curse or two when provoked. It was only at Government House and at the few mixed gatherings of the officers' mess that his scarlet tunic and brass set tender hearts aflutter or elicited respect amongst the enlisted men and servants. That he had been the son of a gamekeeper and his wife was neither here nor there, especially if no one were ever to find out.

"I'll just ride on out ahead of you," Hatch said, "and let Wicks and Hislop know you're coming, and why. Then I'll leave you to them."

"That's extremely kind of you."

"Still, even if they accept you as an advance man for the quartermaster, I don't quite see how you're likely to bring the conversation around to a death almost everybody in the township believes to be an accident."

"I don't rightly know myself," Marc said. "But I think I've learned enough to improvise something. It shouldn't be hard to *start* a discussion of Joshua's accident: there's certain to have been lots of gossip and speculation about it. All I need is a cue to ask whether or not these people ever knew or met him. I might suggest that I knew him a bit back in Toronto. None of these men will know precisely when I came here or how long I've been in the garrison at Fort York."

"You could even mention you're going to make an offer for the two hogs Elijah is fattening up for the spring."

"Am I?" said Marc.

"I'm sure your quartermaster would approve," Hatch said, laughing.

Half an hour later the two men were riding up the Farley Sideroad towards a group of farms locally dubbed "Buffaloville." Hatch had just suggested that Marc pull his horse into the protection of some cedars while he went on up to the Stebbins place to prepare for Marc's arrival and secure his cover story, when onto the road in front of them swung a two-horse team and cutter. Moments later, the vehicle went whizzing past them at full trot. A curt wave from the fur-clad driver was all the greeting they got as he raced down the concession line.

"Azel Stebbins," Hatch said. "Prime suspect."

"Where would he be going in such a hurry at one in the afternoon?"

"By the looks of that harquebus sticking up behind the seat, I'd say he was going hunting. Some deer were spotted up that way yesterday."

"Is everyone around here armed?"

"Well, they all hunt."

"I take it we can write off Stebbins for the day?"

"Unless you'd like to spend the afternoon watching young Lydia Stebbins bat her big eyelashes at you."

As good as his word, Hatch did go on ahead to the farm of Israel Wicks to prepare the ground for an official visit from the regimental quartermaster's emissary. When Marc rode up the lane alongside a windbreak of pines, he spotted a tall, bearded fellow sporting an orange tuque waiting for him in front of a low but extensive square-log cabin, onto which a number of ells and sheds had been added over time. Behind it stood an impressive barnboard structure, several smaller coops and hutches, and a split-rail corral where a pair of matched Percherons idled in the cold sunshine.

Wicks held out a friendly hand when Marc dismounted, and led him into the house. "Erastus says you're from the garrison in Toronto, scoutin' for grain an' pork."

"That's right," Marc said. "I'm authorized only to line up

potential supplies, to save Major Jenkin time when he makes the rounds of the eastern counties next month."

"We'll have some coffee and a shot of somethin' stronger before we talk business," Wicks said, pulling off his coat and scarf. He hollered towards the partitioned area at the rear of the house, "Moe, come out here. We got company!"

Wicks appeared to be about forty-five years of age. He had a grizzled beard, grooved brow, and deep-set eyes that revealed the confidence and the anxiety that comes from prolonged experience of life's vicissitudes. He took Marc's greatcoat and draped it carefully over a chair beside the fire blazing in the hearth, above which a brace of Kentucky shooting guns were on display.

"Ah, Maureen."

Marc turned to be introduced to Mrs. Wicks, a spare, fretting little woman who reminded him of a nervous songbird that's forgotten to migrate and seems perpetually puzzled by the consequences. She stopped abruptly when she sighted him, as if bedazzled by the blast of scarlet before her.

"Say hello to Ensign Edwards, Moe."

"Ma'am," Marc said, but his bow was missed by the averted eyes of his hostess.

"We don't get much company out here – in the winter," Wicks said.

"I'll fetch us some coffee," his wife said. She scuttled back into the safety of her kitchen, and the clatter of kettles on an iron stove was soon heard.

"You've no children?" Marc said.

"Two lads," Wicks said, in a voice strong and rich enough to grace a podium or the hustings in the heat of a campaign. The vigorous health that is the gift of an outdoor life shone through his movements and ease of bearing. Marc suffered a pang of envy and felt suddenly ashamed of his deception. "They're both out doing road duty for a couple of days."

Maureen Wicks flitted in with a tray of coffee and biscuits and flitted back out again. Wicks tipped a generous dollop of whisky into the mugs, and the two men drank and ate.

"I've got about fifty bags of wheat in storage at Hatch's mill," Wicks said and, looking closely at Marc, added, "but then you already know that."

Marc finished chewing his biscuit before replying. "Erastus hasn't written down the amounts for me yet, but he's suggested I see men like yourself because he knows you may be interested in any offers."

This answer seemed to satisfy Wicks. "I'd be willin' to sell half of that, as grain or flour when the mill starts up again. Hatch can vouch for the quality."

"Any livestock?"

"Half a dozen hogs fat enough by April, if that's okay. Do you need to see them?"

"The state of your buildings and the neatness of your house tell me all I need to know about the fastidiousness of your farming," Marc said, hoping he was not overplaying the flattery card, "and, of course, what Hatch has already told me about you."

They chatted informally about potential prices, the prospects for a good spring, and the severity of the past two winters before Marc said casually, "Hatch tells me the winter's been hard on his neighbour."

"Mrs. Smallman," Wicks said, eyeing him closely.

"Something about her father-in-law getting killed in a freak accident."

"A tree fell on him. New Year's Eve."

"What kind of fool is out cutting trees on New Year's Eve?" Marc said, feigning incredulity.

Wicks eyed his guest carefully, then said, "Joshua Smallman was no fool."

"You knew the man?"

"Just to see him," Wicks said with calculated offhandedness. "I knew his son Jesse a while back. The father was a merchant from your town – an old Tory, I'm told, but a gentleman all the same."

"Not the dry goods man?"

"That's right. He come back here to run the farm after Jesse died."

Marc smiled. "And I take it that you are not a Tory?"

Wicks laughed, and the tension in him dissolved. "I see that my good friend Constable Hatch has been praisin' more than my ploughin' techniques. In this province, once an American, forever a Yankee." The laughter faded. "I'm more the fool for thinkin' that'll ever change."

"My quartermaster doesn't distinguish between Yankee wheat and English corn," Marc felt compelled to say.

"That is quite true," Wicks said, pouring them each another whisky. "And it's one of the many reasons I've chosen to stay here an' raise my family. Though I still have days when I wonder if I'm crazy to do so."

Marc shifted in his chair.

Again, Wicks's smile was as broad as it was enigmatic. "You haven't been in this country long, have you?"

"A year or so," Marc said.

"So far I bet you know mostly what you've been told by the self-serving grandees around you, includin' a lot of lies and exaggeration about the Yankee settlers doin' all the agitatin', or secretly yearnin' for the democracy they so foolishly abandoned."

"I've heard that kind of talk," Marc said. "You think I shouldn't believe it?"

"I'd be astonished if you didn't," Wicks said. "But you've been given a chance – bein' sent out here to the untamed, insurrectionist countryside – to see for yourself. Which is somethin' the Family Compact – with its rectors an' bankers an' lawyers – an' the toadyin' members of the Legislative Council in Toronto have never bothered to do."

Marc seized his opportunity. "I did see for myself only this morning the tragic effects of the Clergy Reserves policy – on the Smallman farm."

"You can multiply that by a thousand," Wicks said, seemingly without rancour. "But since you are interested an' may be young enough to learn somethin' new, let me tell you a bit about the so-called Yankee troublemakers in this province."

"I would be happy to listen," Marc said, barely able to contain his delight.

"I was a Yankee born an' raised up, like so many of us who came up here after 1815: free-spirited, happy-go-lucky, fearin' no man an' certainly no government, genuflectin' to nobody. My parents had carved out a farm in the Ohio Valley an' helped to push the frontier towards the Wabash. But when they died, what they left me was not peaceful fields an' prosperous towns. They left me Indian wars an' military service and all the horror an' lawlessness that comes with social chaos an' the seductive power of sudden riches."

Mrs. Wicks, detecting perhaps some sea change in the familiar rhythms of her husband's speech, poked her nose around the partition.

"I was forced to serve my three months with the Ohio Volunteers during the Indian wars. I was at the Battle of Frenchtown on the River Raisin. A slaughterhouse it was. I saw the great warrior Tecumseh up close before some tomahawk clubbed me unconscious. I was one of the lucky ones: I got dragged back with my unit when we retreated. Several hundred of our wounded were massacred later that night an' their bodies tossed into the bush to be eaten by bears an' coyotes. An' later on, when we got a chance to get our own back, we did: I watched women an' children hacked an' slashed like butchered swine. I myself held torches to houses, some of them with people still inside, refusin' to leave. I still wake up at night, screamin' with the agony of it."

"War is sometimes an unpleasant necessity," Marc said lamely.

Wicks did not hear. He stared into the fire for a while, then said, still looking down, "Most of us came up here for a little peace an' stability, a little law an' order, and a chance to prove we could be good farmers an' better citizens. When Governor Peregrine Maitland called us aliens an' sought to have us barred from holdin' office or a seat in the Assembly, we had no choice but to do the very thing most of us were tryin' to escape: get embroiled in politics. For a time even our property rights were threatened."

"So you joined forces with the radicals in the Reform party?"

"Who else was goin' to look out for our rights?"

"And so you met Jesse Smallman, who also had his grievance."

"An' dozens of others – local-born, Scotchmen, Irishmen, a few fair-minded loyalists. An' we got the alien question settled once an' for all."

"But I've been told that a new petition of grievances is in the Colonial Secretary's hands at this very moment."

Wicks had lit his pipe and was now puffing contemplatively at it. "I do read the papers, young man, even the radical *Advocate*. But my property is now secure. My two sons, who can't remember any other home but this, are out doin' public service on the King's Highway. My own concerns are no more than the weather an' the price of grain."

"I'm most happy to hear it," Marc said, rising. "Thank you sincerely for your hospitality and your frankness."

As Marc was buttoning his greatcoat at the door, Wicks said, "When you make your report to Colonel John Colborne, be sure and ask him how keen he'd be to repeat the carnage of Waterloo or Toulouse."

Riding away, Marc was still too flummoxed to notice Maureen Wicks's angst-ridden face in her kitchen window, like a winter moon with all the harvest-blood drained from it.

CHAPTER EIGHT

M arc continued north along the Farley Sideroad towards the last farm before the serious bush began, though to someone not familiar with the Upper Canadian landscape this frozen twelve-foot swathe bordered by cedar, pine, and leafless birch would seem more like a logging road in a wilderness than a neatly surveyed thoroughfare. At the moment, the isolation and silence suited Ensign Edwards, who was deep in thought.

He guided the horse through a gap in the evergreens and was astonished to see before him a very large area, perhaps a hundred acres, completely shorn of trees and seemingly of all vegetation. Not a bush or vine peeped above the rumpled counterpane of snow. At the far edges of the clearing Marc could see a ragged fence of uprooted stumps and charred limbs. Three buildings interrupted the horizon: a low, ungabled log house with oiled-paper windows; a ramshackle barn whose wings, ells, and jetties seemed to be patched together; and beyond that a sort of lean-to fashioned of cedar poles and layers of bark or wind-stiffened sailcloth. From the house a limp plume of smoke rose out of a crumbling chimney.

Marc rode up to what he deduced to be the front door, dismounted, and, failing to find a hitching post or ring of any kind, wrapped the horse's reins around one of the protruding log ends. The door itself drooped on stretched leather hinges and boasted a number of gouges and splinters where a boot or fist had met it in anger. Marc gave it a tentative rap, fearing he might knock it irreparably askew.

A booming voice that might have been female answered from the depths inside: "For Chrissake, don't just stand there pickin' at your scab, open the goddamn door an' come in!"

Marc did as he was bidden. Seated in the centre of the room in a horsehair chair of princely proportions was a woman of ample dimension and extraordinary presence. Marc recoiled visibly, as if unable to take in the image of her all at once.

"Cassie, get off your plump rump an' take the gentleman's hat! Buster, vacate that chair this instant or I'll take a strip off yer arse an' turn it inta a red bandanny!"

The fire in the hearth, fitful and smoky, flung a dim glow through the almost windowless room. Cassie came meekly out of one of its shadowy corners: a young woman clad only in a shift and moth-eaten sweater, whose beauty was marred – or perhaps made more exotic – by a glassy walleye and a mole at the base of her throat. Staring at Marc, abashed, from her one clear, blue eye, she stretched out a trembling arm for his coat and shako cap. She continued to stare at his uniform.

"You keep yer eyes on the floor, milady!" the girl's mother – as Marc assumed her to be – roared with an accompanying guffaw that shook the room with the vehemence of a fart. "Young Cassie's got a thing for soldiers. Come militia day, an' we gotta lock her in the pigpen!"

"Good day, madam. My name is –"

"I know what yer moniker is, young gentleman. I've been forewarned, ya might say, and I know why you're here. Take that chair by the fire. Buster, get yer greasy paws offa it! You get the loo-tenant's uniform dirty an' he'll take you outside an' shoot you silly with his Brown Bess."

Marc smiled reassuringly at young Buster, who seemed deaf to his mother's entreaties and more intent on looking for any sign of said gun. Marc sat on the edge of the chair.

"I'm Bella Hislop," the woman said, "as I'm sure you've figured out already. You met Cassie, my oldest an' prettiest – don't blush, girl, beauty's not a gift to be sneezed at, the good Lord only doles out so many talents – an' Buster there, with the gawkin' eyes an' big nose, my eldest of the bollocked variety. And up there the other six are skulkin' an' tryin' to keep outta my reach, *aren't ya, ya little buggers!*"

On this last note, Bella Hislop wrenched her thick torso a quarter-turn, which allowed her to gaze up into a huge loft that covered almost half the house at the north end. Several titters and much rustling ensued, and Marc could just make out in the gloom a row of dirty children's faces peering down with curiosity and trepidation.

"Mr. Hatch has been here, then?" Marc said.

"Indeed he has, the old crook. I damn near run him off the place."

"He has wronged you somehow?" Marc said, unable to hide his surprise or his irritation.

Bella Hislop rose in her chair, lifting her heavy flesh into a posture of indignation and contempt, like an overweight marionette whose slack strings are suddenly jerked upwards with a singular flourish. Her voluminous dress went dangerously taut, threatening to burst. Her jowls quivered stiffly and her eyes blazed.

"He merely swindled my husband outta twenty barrels of flour, that's all. And us with eight mouths to feed an' me still teat-feedin' the young'un. 'Full of chaff an' tares,' the bastard says to Orville, right in front of half the neighbourhood. That's all he's got to say for comin' up twenty barrels short on our millin', our whole summer's harvest. Well, we got our pride if we got nothin' else. My Orville just turns an' walks away, real dignified, like the gentleman he was brung up to be."

"I'm sure the miller is not a man to cheat his customers," Marc said.

Bella gave him a withering look, then abruptly relaxed, her flesh and bones sagging thankfully back to their accustomed position. She emitted a thunderous chuckle. "You are a *young* man. You know little of the ways of the world and its thousand iniquities. All millers are cheats an' mountebanks. If they were honest men, they would till the soil themselves instead of feedin' off the sweat of their fellows. An' what redress have we got anyways? You think my sweet Orville – as honest as Esau, as upright as Solomon – can trot along cap in hand to the constable to swear out a complaint?" She burst out laughing. "Is that bugger Hatch gonna arrest *himself*!"

"There is a sheriff for the county," Marc pointed out. "And a magistrate a stone's throw from the mill."

"Randy-the-dandy MacLachlan, you mean!" she roared, and the shock wave made the peering faces in the loft bob. "I wouldn't let my six-year-old Susan near him. And who do you think is a charter member of that faggots' club up at the Squire's?"

"I would be most pleased to forward any written complaint or petition on your behalf," Marc said, not for a second believing Bella's charge but nevertheless feeling some obligation to demonstrate the absolute objectivity and probity of British due process.

"What makes you think Orville an' me got any surplus to sell to the English army of occupation?" Bella said, and she pinned him with a stare.

"That's what I'm here to find out, ma'am. I'm merely an emissary."

"A papal legate, sort of," Bella grinned. "You payin' with cash?"

"Pound notes only."

"None of that funny money, now, that army scrip yer betters palmed off on us last time. An' no notes drawn on the Bank of Fuckin' Upper Canada."

Marc flinched, noted no reaction from the two eldest at the obscenity, and forged ahead. "We're looking for pork as well as grain," he said.

"Our pigs aren't doin' so good this winter. Some kinda fever gettin' inta them. The boar's doin' poorly too. Unfortunately, a boar is a necessity, ugly as it may be, eh? Like God an' shitty weather."

"Is your husband at home, madam?" Marc said.

"Jeezuz, I ain't been called 'madam' since the time I stumbled inta a hooer-house in Syracuse lookin' fer that arsehole that got me up the stump an' had to marry me or take a load of buckshot in the underparts!"

"I can return another time," Marc said, starting to get up.

"Siddown, for Chrissake, nobody's tryin' to scare ya off. Cassie, bring out the jar of hooch an' pour a mugful fer me an' Officer Edwards."

"Really, ma'am, I couldn't –"

"You call me 'ma'am' once more and I'll toss ya headfirst inta the fire. Now unhitch yer high horse an' relax. I got some questions I wanta ask *you*."

Cassie did as she was commanded, blushing fiercely as she served Marc and sensed his eyes upon her flimsy dress and what it inadequately concealed.

"Pretty one, ain't she?" Bella said, downing half her drink in one gulp. "Spittin' image of me, though you'd hardly think so now. 'Course I had two eyes to see with back then an' still ended up in this shit-hole."

"How may I help you?" Marc said.

"I wanta know why you're really here."

"But I've told you that . . . Mrs. Hislop."

"I hear Monsieur Papineau an' Wolfred Nelson're kickin' up shit in Quebec. Colborne an' his Tory ass-lickers think the same trouble's about to start up here, don't they?"

"I am not at liberty to comment," Marc said, swallowing his astonishment.

"Aren't ya, now. Well, that's one of the things wrong with this province, ain't it? The people in power don't feel the need to be at liberty to say anythin' by way of explanation to the wretches who've got no power of their own."

"The people here, I'm told, elected an Assembly in which the majority of seats are held by members of the Reform party."

"Well, you *are* up on yer politics, ain't ya?" She polished off her "whisky" and waited until he had at least sipped his. (Jamaican rum, he was only mildly surprised to discover.) "What *I* am at liberty to say to *you* an' yer limp-pricked major-domos back in Toronto is that my Orville worked as hard as any man to get Mr. Perry elected to the Assembly. He even escorted Mr. Mackenzie on his tour through this district in thirty-four – him and a dozen others, like Wicks an' Stebbins an' poor young Jesse Smallman that hung himself for grief over the state of affairs. That don't make my Orville a revolution-ary. His grandpapa, now there was a true revolutionary. Fought side by side with George Washington at Valley Forge an' got his left leg blown to kingdom come. Folks up here don't know chapter one about real revolution."

"I assure you, madam –"

"We got more assurances from your bigwigs than we could use to paper a privy." Her mammoth breasts heaved above the stretched waistline of her dress, but it was the flare of her eyes that held Marc spellbound. "If it was up to me, I'd've organized a posse of Minutemen, marched on Toronto, an' done what my countrymen did to it in the War of 1812: jam a stick of dynamite under it an' blow it inta Lucifer's parlour." She sighed extravagantly, like a basso profundo at the end of an aria.

"That's treasonable talk, madam."

"Lucky fer you I didn't, eh? You'd have no toy soldiers to play with. But I'm only a woman, and Orville ain't what he useta be." She chuckled softly. "Poor Orville wasn't *ever* what he useta be."

"Your husband is ill?"

Bella guffawed, sending a spray of spittle past Marc's knees. "Not as ill as he oughta be! He can still get it up, if that's what you're inferrin'."

"Madam, there are children present."

"Don't I know it. I got eight livin', all of 'em in this stinkin' room. But I've had twelve all told. It'd've been a goddamn good trick if I could've organized a revolution between the ploughin' an' the begettin', wouldn't it?"

Marc got up and pulled his coat on quickly before Cassie could arrive to assist him. Buster meantime had sidled up to him and was stroking the brushed wool as if it were ermine or beaver, or a pet that would purr in gratitude.

"I hear tell the new governor ain't a military man," Bella said, still wedged so firmly in the big chair that if she were, on a whim, to have stood up it would have come with her like a monstrous bustle. "That should be an improvement right there."

"Mr. Hislop is not here?" Marc tried again.

"*Mister* Hislop is out in the barn somewheres or else skunk-drunk in a snowdrift. *Mister* Hislop don't spend much time in his house these days, or nights."

Cassie looked ready to interrupt her mother; her lower lip trembled and tears sprang into her eyes.

"Don't you shush me, girl," Bella hissed at Cassie. "I'm all you got in this world, an' don't forget it." She turned back to Marc, who now stood rooted to the door jamb. "I've had all the babies I'm ever goin' to. I've made that perfectly plain to his nibs." She reached under the horsehair cushion and produced a menacing pair of tin-snips. She snapped the pincers together with an ominous click. "If he so much as breathes on my bed with his hoe-handle at half-mast, it's snip, snip – goodbye an' good riddance. An' he'll get some of the same if I see him within spittin' distance of my Cassie."

Just before he shut the door behind him, Marc slipped a shilling into his young admirer's grimy palm.

As he walked to the corner of the house where his horse was tethered, Marc noticed a male figure scuttling in his direction. It seemed to have emerged from between the barn and the lean-to beyond it. The figure stopped, appeared to take its bearings, then hailed him. Marc dropped the reins and strode out, not without curiosity, to meet, he presumed, the treacherously sweet Orville Hislop.

"Who the hell're you!" Hislop shouted querulously. He started forward.

Marc continued on towards him. Hislop stalled, uncertain of his ground. His glazed eye had caught the tufted shako and flash of scarlet at the open throat of the military greatcoat. Hislop himself was clad only in overalls, boots, and a bulky sweater, which struggled to envelop a low-slung belly that seemed at odds with his otherwise muscular and work-hardened body. He wore no cap, and the brindled mop of his hair was littered with straw, and worse.

Marc shot out his hand. "I am Ensign Edwards," he said, "on assignment from the quartermaster at York. We're looking to buy surplus grain or pork for the army, as soon as possible."

"Are ya, now? You don't look like no quartermaster to me," Hislop growled. "An' what've ya been foragin' at in my house, eh?"

"Your good wife directed me out here to you," Marc lied, with an ease he was growing accustomed to.

"Good wife, my arse," Hislop said, and Marc could see now that he had been drinking – a lot – and that he had become suddenly aware that this uniformed stranger had noticed it. He grinned broadly, exposing three yellowed stumps of teeth, and winked. "You'll know all about it when you're married."

"I understand from Mrs. Hislop that you've had a bad year and that I'm not likely to find what I'm looking for."

"She told ya that, did she, now? Weren't that just splendid of her! Well, Mr. Ensign Edwards, you just come along with me and I'll show you half a dozen of the finest hogs in the county."

Marc followed Hislop into a rickety, shed-like appendage to the barn, trying to keep upwind of him. Inside, the stench was overpowering: the result of a pigsty unmucked for weeks, mixed with a similar stink from the adjacent cattle stalls.

"Takes a little gettin' used to." Hislop chuckled, peering sideways at Marc as the latter thrust a handkerchief over his mouth and nostrils. "Just plug yer nose an' take a gander at them barrows. They'll be as fat as my wife's tits by Easter." Marc could just discern the scrawny outlines of several young, castrated hogs, so begrimed it was only their occasional twitch or shudder that distinguished them from the mud and excrement they inhabited.

"Good thing we don't eat the outside of 'em," Hislop said encouragingly.

"Yes," Marc said, and he stumbled back outside. A few yards away was the peculiar lean-to affair. "That where you keep your sick boar?" he said between gasps.

Hislop squinted, coughed, gargled a mouthful of phlegm, and said, "That's right. I been tendin' to the poor bugger all afternoon."

"I was raised on a farm, believe it or not," Marc said. "My uncle worked wonders with sick animals. I'd be glad to have a look at him for you."

Hislop's eyes widened as far as his alcoholic haze would permit. "That's mighty considerate of you, sir, but it's just a touch of colic." He had Marc by the elbow and was ushering him towards his horse. "You be sure to let me know about them barrows of mine. I'll take any price that's fair, especially if you're payin' cash this round. We don't see much minted money in these parts. I can give ya the names of some other fellas in the township –"

"Quartermaster Jenkin will be in touch with you next month, provided those hogs are healthy . . . and clean as a babe in its bath," Marc said, mounting his horse. Then, without a nod or farewell, he rode straight out to the sideroad.

At first he headed south towards the highway, but when he came to a path that wandered west through the bush below the Hislop place, he urged his horse onto it. He followed it slowly in a wide arc until he was at the rear of the farm, where he had a sheltered view of the lean-to and the barn behind it. He was just in time.

Glancing around every few seconds, Hislop was skulking his way towards the lean-to. He staggered around to the near side of it, where a rickety door or hatch had been propped up to block the low entranceway. He stood still, as if listening intently. From inside the lean-to came a mewling sound, most un-pig-like in its keening persistence. Seemingly satisfied, Hislop jerked the hatch away and flung it aside.

"Stop yer whinin'! Ya want Bella out here with the snips?"

The keening increased, broken finally by a series of hiccoughing sobs.

"Get yer skinny arse outta there, the fun's over."

A moment later a woman's head pushed its way out of the murky interior: first a tangle of red curls, then a pale face.

"Outta there, ya little hooer," Hislop barked. He reached down to grasp the girl – for she was only that – by one thin wrist and heaved her up and out into the nearest drift. She landed on both buttocks, her equally thin legs splayed and one oversized boot ripped off. She was clothed only in a flannel nightgown and a man's sweater that she had not succeeded in getting over her head in time.

"I want my shillin'," she said with a perfunctory whine.

"You almost cost me twenty dollars – if I'd've missed that soldier, out here with the likes of you."

"I'll holler my head off –"

But she didn't. Hislop kicked her in the stomach, knocking the wind and any resistance out of her. She let out a gasp, curled up into a ball of bent limbs, and started to whimper.

Marc was just about to spur his horse forward when the girl leapt up and turned to flee. Hislop whirled around and snatched at her nightgown, and as she wrenched herself away from him, the entire gown with the sweater came off in his hand. Hislop's chin dropped in amazement. The girl saw her chance and sprinted towards the sideroad, stark naked but for one blackened boot that thumped into the snow like a club foot.

Marc realized immediately that she would come out onto the sideroad only a few yards from where the path he had taken met it, so he headed at full gallop back through the bush. As he charged out onto the road, the girl was just coming through the trees. Unexpectedly she turned north and, still bounding like a spooked doe, oblivious to her nakedness or the freezing air around her, she sped towards the end of the road. Marc caught up with her just as she veered back into the bush. Leaning down, holding the reins slack in one hand and guiding the horse with his knees, Marc grasped the girl under her arms at the apex of one of her leaps and swept her up in front of him onto the horse's withers. She let out a surprisingly loud shriek and tried to strike him.

"I'm not Hislop!" he cried. "I've come to help you." The horse kept on going along a faint trail through the bush. The girl's struggles eased – in relief or exhaustion. Marc brought the horse to a halt and dismounted.

"I'm going to take you down from here and wrap you up before you freeze to death," he said. "Please don't scream. There's no need. I'm not going to hurt you." She said nothing. Her body went limp in his arms.

He drew her gently down and, holding her under the arms – his gloved hand crushing one of her small, stiff-nippled breasts – he tugged a blanket out of his saddle-roll and pulled it about her, twice. Tiny shudders racked her wasted body, no more than a hundred pounds in all. Her lips had turned a ghastly purple, her teeth chattered, and her eyelids blinked frantically. She's dying, Marc thought. He'd seen death like this up close, not on any battlefield, but in the alleys of central London where, every morning as he walked from his rooms to the offices of Jardin and Musgrove, he passed the casualties of lust and other hungers: prostitutes with the rags of their trade falling off their ruined flesh, their emaciated faces peering up at anyone foolish enough to bend down to them and venting a final curse or death's-head plea as their eyelids fluttered and closed.

He opened his greatcoat and crushed her body in against his own warmth, cocooning her, willing her to survive. Foolishly he kissed the top of her head, pushing his nose into the thick, reddish curls, as if the least gesture of affection might astonish and resuscitate. Gradually the shuddering diminished, her cheeks went suddenly rosy, her eyes swelled with tears, and a pink sliver of tongue slipped out to lick her upper lip. Then she snuggled farther into the hug that held her.

The girl sighed, closed her eyes, opened them again, and said in a low, sweet, Sunday-school voice: "You gonna poke me?"

Her name was Agnes Pringle, and they were on a woodsy trail that, as long as you knew where you were headed, would lead them to her home. With the blanket and greatcoat still wrapped around her and Marc's extra mitts on her feet, she insisted she was well enough to ride up behind him, holding tight with both arms around his chest. The horse moved at a sedate pace.

"You don't mean to say your mother's Annie Pringle?" Marc said.

"That's right, Mad Annie," Agnes said cheerfully.

Erastus Hatch, as promised, had explained to Marc who Mad Annie was, and had sternly warned him to steer clear of her squattery out on the marshland north of the surveyed concessions. The only route into it lay in a maze of trails, the miller had said (not without some admiration), most of which were booby-trapped and life-threatening to the unescorted. What lay at the heart of this mischievously mined moat was the subject of much public speculation and sustained moral outrage. "Just Mad Annie, a still, and her brood of ne'er-do-wells," Hatch had suggested, "but you could get maimed trying to prove it!"

"You can just let me off at the end of this here path," Agnes said. "I know my way up to the house."

"I could make a lot of trouble for Hislop," Marc said.

"An' he'll only make more for us."

"But he assaulted you."

Agnes giggled. "He did a lot more'n that to me."

"He owes you a dress," Marc said.

"We take care of our own," Agnes said.

Hatch had warned him also about the infamous Pringle boys, Mad Annie's obstreperous male offspring, and Marc decided not to be nonchalant about this errand of mercy. A military uniform out here could easily be misconstrued.

"Nobody'll hurt ya," Agnes said, sliding off the horse. She removed the greatcoat with a slow, purring gesture, rubbed it sensuously against her cheek, then held it up to him. She watched him put it on, then said, "What about yer mitts an' this here blanket?" She started to draw the edges of the cloth away from her chest in a sad parody of seduction.

"You'll need them if you aren't to freeze," Marc said. "You sure you can make it home?" He was gazing dubiously through a screen of cedars at an uneven open area that was likely a swamp come spring, dotted here and there with scrub bushes, the remnants of cattails, and stunted evergreens. Several hundred yards farther, on the distant verge of the clearing, he spotted several shacks and tumbledown outbuildings. No welcoming smoke rose from any one of them.

Agnes was in the midst of nodding "yes" to Marc's inquiry when her eyes widened and her pale cheeks went paler. "Jesus," she hissed. Then she wailed, "*It's Ma!*"

From the cover of a nearby cedar stepped the woman known throughout the district as Mad Annie. Marc's initial instinct was to laugh, for she was at first glance not a prepossessing sight. From Hatch's descriptions and cautions, given in detail on their ride to Buffaloville, Marc had expected her to be a female of formidable bulk. But before him now, with her feet planted apart as if she were on snowshoes, stood a tiny woman clothed in a loose sweater, a lumberjack's tuque, woollen trousers fastened at the waist and ankle with binder-twine, and a pair of mismatched boots. Her face was misshapen, like a badly aged apple doll. But it was her eyes that caught Marc's attention. They were large and round – intelligent, belligerent, and curiously vulnerable. At this moment, they blazed with suspicion and imminent aggression. Marc could see nothing lunatic in them.

"Put the girl down," she commanded.

"She is down," Marc said firmly. "I've brought her home – to her mother, I presume."

"Who I am ain't your business, mister," she said, assessing the uniformed rider and his horse with a single cold, bright glance. Then she turned to the girl, as if Marc were now of peripheral interest at best. Agnes wrapped the grey blanket twice around her and shuffled across to her mother.

"What'd the bastard do with yer dress?" Mad Annie said.

Agnes ducked away from a blow that did not come. "Tore it offa me."

Mad Annie smiled with her lips only (she appeared to be toothless). "They do get excited at the sight of tits and a fur-piece, don't they?" When Agnes peeked up to acknowledge her mother's remark, Mad Annie cuffed her smartly on the back of the head.

Marc started forward in the saddle. He was still trying to square the image of this crone with Hatch's colourful account of a matriarch who had "whelped" seventeen times, including two sets of twins, only the first three of her litter being trace-able to Mr. Pringle, who had long since vamoosed or died happily by his own hand. Mad Annie caught Marc's movement out of the corner of one eye and wheeled about.

"You stay right where you are, mister. You're trespassin' on Pringle property."

"I suggest you leave the girl be," Marc said. "She's been kicked and abused enough for one day."

"That so?" Without looking, she reached out and grabbed the blanket covering Agnes's shoulder and hauled the girl before her. Agnes collapsed submissively at her feet. As she did so, the fabric parted, exposing her breasts, like two puffed bruises. "He pay you?" Mad Annie barked, glaring back up at Marc.

"It was Hislop, it was Hislop," Agnes whimpered. "He did me every way all afternoon in that . . . that *pigsty*, an' then he rips my dress an' throws me out."

Mad Annie ignored her daughter. "You poke her, you pay," she said to Marc.

"Madam, I find you a repulsive and unnatural human being. I recommend you take your daughter, who has suffered an outrage and nearly lost her life, and care for her with any kindness you can muster as her mother and protector. Otherwise I shall have the law on you."

Agnes was shaking her head at him.

"And I recommend you turn that ball-less bag-o'-bones around an' hightail it offa my land before I do somethin' beneficial, like blow yer pecker off." From under her sweater, or through one of its several vents, she had drawn a pistol, and she was aiming it at the Ensign.

Marc had never before stared into the business end of a deadly weapon aimed at him. His gut went queasy, but the disciplined training he had endured for over a year at Sandhurst held him in good stead. He blinked, but did not flinch.

Agnes took advantage of the momentary standoff by scampering up and away, clutching the army blanket to her throat.

With steely calm, Marc turned his horse and trotted deliberately back down the trail, his broad shoulders providing the perfect target for a bullet. At the first bend he stopped and turned to look back. Mad Annie had caught up to Agnes but was not berating the girl. Instead, the two women had joined hands and were making a rapid, zigzagging dash across the frozen marsh towards home.

Avoiding their own booby-traps, Marc thought. Only now did it occur to him that the pistol appeared to have been neither primed nor loaded. He rode slowly away, pondering what further assault might yet be made upon the dignity of the Crown's commissioned investigator.

CHAPTER NINE

"I know, I know," Hatch said, "back home the likes of Mad Annie and Bella Hislop would be thrown into Bedlam or packed off to Van Dieman's Land on the first boat."

"Hanged at Newgate more likely," Marc said, but in truth he was more disappointed than outraged. Any anger remaining was now directed at himself and his all-too-apparent inadequacies.

"The way many folks around here look at it, they really aren't doing much harm to anybody but themselves. Annie's gaggle do manufacture bad hooch from time to time, and once in a while the Sheriff catches one of her boys stealing a chicken and they spend a month or two in jail. And those Yankee farmers are just an independent lot by birth and upbringing. You never really stood much of a chance of getting anything useful out of them. Still, I think you did the right thing by carrying on to see Farley and McMaster. Those farmers have been here since before the war and are as tame as brood hens, but they're neighbours of the less trustworthy Americans out there and they'll soon report that you seemed to be what you claim to be. It'll keep Hislop and Wicks wondering and set you up for the Stebbins place tomorrow. You'll find them quite a different kettle of fish."

Marc and Hatch were seated before a lively fire mulling over the day's events and taking inventory of where they thought they were in their investigation. Erastus was being as encouraging as his good nature and the facts would allow. They were alone in the house.

After a fine roast-chicken supper, parts of which proceeding seemed to be coldly amusing to Winnifred Hatch, Thomas Goodall had hitched the Percheron team to the family cutter and joined Winnifred and Mary Huggan in the forty-minute drive to Cobourg, where a charity meeting of the Ladies' Aid had attracted the two women and an evening at the pub their driver. According to Mary, Beth Smallman had been invited to join them but had politely declined. Winnifred had dressed for the occasion in a carmine-coloured dress with ruched sleeves and jutting shoulders, of a material that crinkled and shook like shale ice.

"It's hard to imagine any of these expatriate American farmers forming a strong-enough personal hatred towards Joshua they'd want to see him dead," Marc said. "They all knew who he was, and showed no hesitation in admitting it. Their anger is focused on the government and the leaders of the Family Compact. You'd have to believe that they chose Joshua merely as a scapegoat for the Legislative Councillors or the Toronto bankers. If so, then why choose a man who himself had begun appearing at Reform rallies and listening respectfully to what was being said?"

"I agree, though I also think we're looking for *one* man with some kind of personal grudge. Stebbins is a known hothead and a very secretive chap. He seems to do an awful lot of hunting for a fellow whose smokehouse is usually empty."

Marc took note of the point, then said, "Most of these people will have known Jesse Smallman better than his father. Jesse was an associate during the period when the alien question threatened the political and property rights of the immigrant Americans, and tempers were naturally frayed. But the question has been more or less settled for a year. Any direct threat to the livelihood of Wicks, Hislop, or Farley is over. They do appear to me to be consumed by the demands of their farms. And, of course, Jesse himself died twelve months ago. It's an unequivocal connection between Joshua and some mad soul out there that I have to establish and interpret."

Hatch puffed on his pipe. "We also have to consider the possibility that we may well have a different sort of mystery on our hands – one that doesn't involve a deliberate murder."

It was something they had both been thinking, but, spoken aloud, it seemed somehow more daunting.

Once again Marc arrived late for breakfast. If Winnifred had slipped past his door last night on her way to another assignation with the hired hand, no hint of it showed in her face or demeanour as she went about helping young Mary serve up helpings of porridge and molasses, followed by pork sausages and boiled eggs, with thick slices of just-made bread and peach preserve. Thomas's chin drooped slightly more than usual below his downcast eyes (too much ale, or some more physical activity? Marc wondered), and Mary Huggan's cheeks glowed from something more than fanning the morning fire.

After breakfast, while Erastus and Thomas went off to the mill to check on some suspected damage to the mill wheel from shifting ice, Marc walked down to Crawford Creek. He could imagine the unerringly straight surveyor's line that permitted one curve of the meandering creek to be included in Hatch's property and another curve, in the opposite direction, to be excluded from the Smallman lands, depriving them of drainage and irrigation. Feeling vaguely impious, he tramped off the worn path and along the bank of the stream, impressing his regimental bootprints defiantly upon the clergy's preserve.

His efforts to revisit the facts of the case this morning, however, were waylaid by the sudden and disturbing image that popped into his head of Winnifred Hatch and Thomas Goodall entangled and thrashing on that simple ploughman's bed in the January dark. And that lascivious picture turned his thoughts to his own romantic past.

Outside of his early fumbled attempts with one of his uncle's maids, his only sustained and satisfying sexual relationship had been with Marianne Dodds, a ward of their illustrious neighbour, Sir Joseph Trelawney. Theirs had been a passionate affair, chaste at first, but after a tacit understanding of sorts had been reached, it had quickly become a complete meshing of body and youthful spirits. When Marc was sent up to London to apprentice law, letters of confession and promise and eternal steadfastness cluttered the mailbag of the daily coach between London and Kent. Then hers stopped. By the time Marc could get leave to return home, Marianne had been forcibly removed to a distant shire and his love letters had been burned in the great man's grate. No explanation was ever offered for either barbarity. Several months later, back in London, he learned that Miss Dodds had been married off to a vicar with five hundred pounds and a twenty-year-old son. Uncle Jabez, unfailingly kind and meaning to be helpful no doubt, had whispered some unconsoling wisdom in his adopted son's ear: "In this country, class is class and blood is still blood. I can give you everything you need and deserve, except that."

Marc's reverie was interrupted by the sight of a small figure making its way towards him along the trodden path behind Smallman's barn. He waved. Beth waved back.

In his suffering and bewilderment at Marianne's loss, Marc had plunged back into his work, happy now that lawyering was so hateful to him. And for the first time he had given in to the teasing of his fellow clerks, as young as he but infinitely more worldly, and followed them to the theatre and the fleshpots of London. Only once. The one good aspect of that night, ironically, had been his delight with the play itself, and his subsequent participation in amateur theatricals. His friends later accused him of moral priggery, but his abhorrence of the brothel and the offstage licentiousness of accommodating actresses was a physical revulsion, inexplicable but as uncontrollable as a reflex. There had been no woman in his life since.

Marc started across the untrodden snowscape of the Clergy Reserve towards Beth, who had halted at the edge of her property to wait for him.

It wasn't that there had been no opportunities for romance at balls in the neighbourhood, or later at the Royal Military School. At the suggestion of his "Uncle" Frederick, Marc had willingly been sent to the school to "mend his heart and seek the only commendable career for a young man of spirit." Even in Toronto, since his arrival last May, there had been possibilities. So far, Marc had danced, flirted, dallied, and generally enjoyed the company of women, but that was all. He had refused to join the subalterns on their periodic expeditions to the stews and gambling dens of Toronto that catered exclusively to the needs of officers robbed of combat by the prolonged post-Napoleonic peace. Despite his apparent prudery, Marc retained the respect of his mates, even their affection.

"Good morning, Ensign Edwards," Beth said as he puffed

up the path towards her. "I see you decided to take the military route."

"Did Joshua have any sort of contact, friendly or otherwise, with any of the extremists out there in Buffaloville?"

They had walked, without predetermination, into the woods on the Crown land above the Smallman farm, savouring the air, enjoying the challenge of ploughing their way through the pure drifts.

"None that I know of," Beth said. "Apart from his evenings with that Georgian crew and our trips into town for supplies, an' the half dozen rallies we went to over the summer an' fall, Father went nowhere. It took every one of us to keep the farm afloat, even with the mortgage lifted. The drought was severe. Everybody suffered to some degree."

"You can remember no altercations at any of the rallies?"

"None. Besides, Azel Stebbins was about the only one of those people to come to the meetin's. After the business with the Alien Act was over and they got back their rights, most of them lost interest. They had farms to run. Like us."

"But *you* kept attending," Marc said gently.

"I had my own reasons."

"I suppose Jesse knew more of these people than his father did," Marc said, then he took her mittened hand briefly to guide her over a windfall.

"Yes. They worked together off and on through the election year of thirty-four. An' Jesse did some carpentry for a couple of them – corncribs, I think. He was a wonder with his hands."

"And your efforts helped to get radicals like Dutton and Perry elected in this end of the province, to establish a Reform majority in the Assembly, and even get the alien question settled in your favour . . ."

"But?"

"But even with your majority and Mr. Mackenzie's underhanded manoeuvring to get the *Seventh Report on Grievances* across the Atlantic, even then you were no closer to winning your claim against the injustices of the Clergy Reserve allotments."

Beth stopped so she could read his expression. "So you think our claims may be just, do you?"

"All one needs to do is take a morning constitutional to see that."

"You should've brought Sir John along."

"It's easy now for me to understand how angry and frustrated your husband must have been last year. To have achieved a majority in the House and have so little to show for the effort, and risk."

"And a governor standing on the dock at Toronto ushering in penniless outcasts from the Auld Sod, sure to be grateful voters in the next election."

"From Jesse's perspective, it must have seemed like 'now or never.' In two years' time the entire government might have been Tory."

"With ample means of avenging themselves on traitors an' mischief-makers."

A new thought occurred to Marc, and he said, "His father must have learned these things, just as I am beginning to, soon after he arrived here. And Tory though he was, he must surely have built up some feelings of resentment over what happened to his son."

"He was very fond of Jess," Beth said, looking straight ahead.

With mixed emotions, Marc pressed on. "Might he not have drawn the conclusion – as he attended the Reform rallies – that it was all that radical and inflammatory talk that had pushed Jesse to the edge? And could such resentment have resulted in some harboured enmity on Joshua's part towards one or more of these radicals, which, unknown to you, led him to accuse or challenge or even threaten that person or persons?"

Beth seemed to be giving the notion due consideration. After a while, she said, "I reckon it more likely he came to understand exactly why his son did what he did."

"I don't follow," Marc said.

Beth took his arm. "Then it's time I explained."

They stood side by side in the barn. The sun bored through the unchinked log walls and spilled at their feet. From the hayloft at one end of the single, spacious room a square crossbeam ran to the far side. In the shadows, a pair of pigeons cooed amiably. Behind them and under the loft, cows chewed at the clover hay thrown to them earlier by Elijah, their literate caretaker.

"I found him hanging there. Just after noon. I wondered why he hadn't come in for his meal. Thank God I didn't send Aaron after him. Jess knew Aaron and I were spendin' the mornin' with Mary Huggan's family. So nothin' would disturb him."

"I don't need to know –" Marc said, wondering whether his touching her would be welcomed or resented.

"I think you do. That milkin' stool was tipped over. He'd used it to stand on, then kicked it halfway across the barn. He'd even made a kind of rope-manacle for his hands an' somehow tied them behind his back."

"Behind his back?"

"He wanted nothin' to tempt him from his purpose."

They stood staring up at the scar on the beam where the noose had rubbed it – one of them imagining, the other reliving.

"You see, I misled you a little last time when I said Jesse wasn't tempted by the radical solutions bein' whispered throughout the district. In truth, he'd become desperate an' depressed."

Marc spoke only because the silence continued longer than he could bear. "Do you know if he actually had contact with any seditionists?"

"He may have. If he did, he didn't tell me. There seemed to be a lot of things he couldn't tell me . . . near the end."

"I'm thinking that he may have learned something that his father might have subsequently come across, something incriminating –"

"But that's what I'm tryin' to show you," she said. "Jess was unlike his father in many ways, but there was one thing they had in common. They believed in the law an' the rights it gives us an' the duties it demands in return. In any other time an' place, my Jesse would've been as conservative as his father. I believe he stared sedition in the face, he may even have let it whisper treason in his ear, an' when he realized the rule of law was about to fail him, he had only two choices left."

"To break it –"

"– or take himself out of its reach," she said, weeping.

Marc held her, and she shuddered against him, letting her hurt and anger pour out.

"There was nothing you could have done," he said as she wiped her cheek with his handkerchief, then blew her nose in it.

"I know that," she said. "But I can't make myself believe it."

As they were about to leave the barn and the scene of its past horror, Marc paused to stroke the nose of a dappled draught horse in a stall near the door.

"She used to pull our cutter," Beth said, "but we had to sell it last week. Bessie here goes off to a man from our church next Monday."

"But your father-in-law will have left you some money and valuables?" Marc said with some surprise.

"He intended to – that I know – but he left no will," Beth said matter-of-factly. "When Father came back here to live, he engaged Mr. Child as his solicitor. And Father mentioned to him that he had a brother who went down to the States before the war, so there could be nephews an' nieces he never heard from. It might be months an' months before I know –"

"While your solicitor pursues them as part of the probate," Marc said with a rueful sigh.

"But Father did pay off our mortgage," Beth said firmly, "an' sweated behind a plough an' harrow." She turned abruptly as if to leave.

At the back of Bessie's stall Marc noticed that the horse had knocked over a bale of straw and exposed the barrel it had been concealing. A barrel with a spigot.

Beth came up beside him and followed his gaze. "Oh, dear," she said, but it wasn't in alarm.

"Whisky?" Marc asked.

"Rum, from Jamaica. Elijah thinks it's his secret cache." She smiled. "An' we've never had the heart to let on."

"Was it here when he came?"

The note of levity in Beth's voice evaporated. He felt her grow tense, and wary, as she had been in their first encounter. "Why can't you let him be?" she said. "Jesse wasn't a rum-runner. Or a bootlegger. Such men don't take their own life on a matter of principle."

"You're right," he said. "Please accept my apologies."

She leaned against him and, despite the layers of winter clothing, her womanliness and its effects were unmistakable. "Do you always talk like you're in some duchess's drawing room?"

"Always, ma'am."

"I've never been a ma'am, or even the missus," she said. "Just Beth."

"I'd be honoured if you'd call me Marc, then."

Beth tilted her face towards Marc's, who gathered her close. But the door behind them was jerked open without ceremony or concern for what it was interrupting. It was Aaron, wide-eyed.

"Co-come, qui-i-i-ck! You're wa-wa-wanted!"

"Who wants me?" Marc said sharply.

"Mister Ha-Ha-Hatch. He's seen the pe-pe-peddlers!"

Supernumerary Constable Hatch was waiting in front of Beth's house with his own horse and Marc's. He was flushed with excitement.

"Come on, lad. Durfee spotted the peddlers' donkey clumping onto the ice at the foot of his property."

"Which way were they headed?"

"There was only one of 'em, and he went east, real hasty, up the shoreline."

"Be careful!" Beth called after them.

They swung onto the Miller Sideroad and galloped down towards the highway.

"If he's headed east on the ice," Marc shouted, "we could surprise him and cut him off at Bass Cove."

"By golly, you're right," Hatch replied. "That donkey can't run too fast on the ice, and we'll save the horses by taking the road."

So they wheeled east onto the Kingston Road, galloping apace, and retraced the route they had taken an hour after Marc's arrival in Crawford's Corners on Tuesday. Twenty minutes' hard riding found them on the deer trail that wound its way up to the scene of the murder and the cave beyond. With no new snow to fill in their previous footprints, they were able to urge their mounts past the deadfall trap before abandoning them and surging ahead without the aid of their snowshoes.

"Christ, lad, he's in the cave!"

Marc looked up to see the snout and ears of the donkey poking above the rim of the ridge where the cave would be. The peddler, who appeared to be Ferris O'Hurley, was floundering towards it, spooked by their approach. An unexpectedly deep drift slowed Hatch and Marc down just long enough for the jackass and its master to scamper down the far slope and hit the ice of the cove. They were in full flight west.

"Don't worry," Hatch puffed when they had struggled to the top of the ridge. "I've got James watching the sideroad north. If the bugger tries to get back into the Corners he may end up with a buttful of Durfee birdshot."

"My hunch is he's heading back towards Toronto and Lewiston."

"Then why come east to the cove?"

"The cave, you mean."

They went to have a look.

O'Hurley had indeed been coming to the cave, for the evident purpose of collecting or destroying materials left there earlier. Ashes from a fire more recent than Tuesday were clearly visible, and papers had been torn and burned in it. Several bottles that had once held contraband spirits or wine had been smashed and scattered, their labels singed.

"They must've been here yesterday," Hatch said ruefully. "Somebody who should know better has told them we've become interested in this place, so the skinny one beetled out here to obliterate whatever they'd left in the vicinity – before picking up his partner in the bush farther down and lighting out for the States."

Marc sighed.

"What's wrong?" Hatch said cheerfully. "We've put the fear of Jehovah into them. They won't be back here for a while."

"Don't you see?" Marc said, sifting idly through the debris. "These fellows are likely advance men for smugglers. They've been using this cave as a hideout, a drop point, and a storage bin for a long time."

"And?"

"And that means that the snowshoe print and broken pipe stem we found on Tuesday could have been left here by one of these peddlers or by any one of a dozen possible confederates."

"And therefore not likely left by the killer of Joshua Smallman?"

"Right."

"But that pipe stem hadn't been here long," Hatch said. "That break on the stem looked fresh, and the thing wasn't completely covered with snow. Even though the ledge here is sheltered, a fair amount of snow would have drifted over it."

Marc nodded. But he was thinking of his conversation with Beth. "What connection, I wonder, could a man like Joshua Smallman have had with vagabonds like O'Hurley and Connors?"

"Maybe that money you found had nothing to do with rum or French wine."

"Perhaps," Marc said, "but have a look at this." In his hand was a strip of paper about twelve inches long whose right half was completely scorched. "See these names down the left side here?"

"Yes," Hatch said. "They're names of various types of whisky and such. Squire Child and I have come across these tally sheets before. Even the writing looks familiar."

"And below each," Marc said with a little more enthusiasm, "is the name of some bay or point along this shoreline, I'd wager."

"And you'd win," Hatch said. "The figures here are dates and times for the drop-offs. All that's missing are the smugglers' names – they've been burned to a crisp."

"Well, we know who Connors and O'Hurley are."

"True," Hatch said. "And you can be sure the alarm will be raised from Kingston to Buffalo. I'll pass this paper on to Sheriff MacLachlan anyway. I may even get promoted," he chuckled.

Marc was still rummaging about the debris, but he found nothing more of any value.

Riding slowly homeward, the two men kept their own counsel for some time. Then Hatch said, "We've got to face the fact that any connection between those sewer rats and Joshua's death is highly improbable. And that means that the cave itself may not have been his destination that night. Maybe the blizzard did confuse him, and he died in a senseless accident."

But Marc said, "I have good reason to believe that *Jesse* Smallman may have been desperate enough to try to raise money to save his farm by acting as an agent for those freebooters."

Hatch paused before responding. "Have you mentioned this to Beth?"

"Obliquely. But it's a topic she will not talk further to me about. That much I do know."

"Hard to blame her."

"Don't you see, though, it's possible that Jesse had garnered vital information about the rum-running trade and that, somehow – in going through Jesse's effects, for example – Joshua discovered this information. Being an upright man, he might have confronted someone more dangerous than he realized. Or he might have doubted its implications and set out to clear his son's name. In the least, I can't believe he would not attempt to find out more about why his son hanged himself."

"Well now, that makes rough sense, lad. But we're still left with the question of who."

"One thing I did learn yesterday was that most of the farmers out in Buffaloville have been hit hard in the last couple of years.

They're desperate for cash, offering me underfed pigs and mildewed grain. They're prime suspects for participants in a lucrative smuggling operation. And with Mad Annie's menagerie half a mile away and deep in a part of the bush nobody visits, I'd say the answer to your question lies out there."

"If there *is* a connection of some kind – and we don't know what, remember – then this cave is definitely where Joshua was heading the night he was killed."

"Exactly."

"And if the threatened person suspected that Joshua was more likely to be an informer than a convert, Joshua's possession of any incriminating evidence would be all the more dangerous. The likelihood of it being conveyed directly to the Lieutenant-Governor and, more important, being believed there without question, would be very high."

"Perhaps bribery was attempted," Marc elaborated, "and when that didn't work, murder was the only option remaining. Joshua Smallman knew too much and had to be stopped."

They rode on in silence. Since Hatch had raised the issue again, Marc felt the time had come to tell someone the truth about Joshua Smallman's role as Sir John's official and trusted informant.

"Well, I'll be damned," was Hatch's initial comment. Then he said, "You know what this means, though? If you're going to learn anything at all from Beth about Joshua's motives and behaviour last fall, you'll have to break the news to her as well, and admit that he managed to deceive everyone – except perhaps his murderer. And remember, when she *is* told the truth, she may be able to interpret past events and words in a far different light."

"I can't tell her," Marc said. "It's too soon."

Hatch was puzzled but held his peace.

As they sighted James Durfee, seated – peddlerless – on a

snowbank in front of his inn, Hatch said, "Well, at least when you go out to beard the Stebbins couple this afternoon, you'll be scouting evidence of the rum trade: that's a sight more solid than a lot of free-floating political nonsense about secret societies and Hunters' Lodges."

Durfee was waving his musket at them like a bosun's semaphore.

"You're right," Marc said, "but I haven't given up on the political angle. It's in the mix somewhere. And for Beth's sake, I intend to find it."

"Ahh," Hatch said, but he left it at that.

CHAPTER TEN

As it turned out, Marc did not get the opportunity to test either of his hypotheses regarding the motive for Joshua's murder (political treachery or a falling out amongst thieves) on expatriate Azel Stebbins until late in the afternoon of that Friday.

First, he and Erastus stopped to talk to James Durfee outside the inn, where they were informed by the scarlet-cheeked post-master that he had just discharged his weapon in defence of the realm. "Missed the bugger by a mile, but that mule of his sure got the message!" After a stiff whisky at his own bar (which did little to steady his heartrate), Durfee assured Constable Hatch that when the noon mail coach arrived, he would forward the news of O'Hurley's flight westward on the ice, and further assured him that if the blackguard were to put so much as his snout ashore he would be taken without mercy. The official alarm would be rung all the way from here to Hamilton and Newark.

After commending Durfee's valour and dispatch, Hatch took his leave, and he and Marc headed for their midday meal at the mill.

"I must remember to tell the Sheriff tomorrow about the

peddlers' loot Durfee is keeping for me," Marc said as they dismounted and let Thomas see to the horses.

"And you're gonna show him Sir John's warrant and his instructions to you?" Hatch said tactfully.

Marc smiled. "I did agree to do so, but I was hoping then to have a lot more to tell him than I do now. On the other hand, he may be able to interpret some of my observations in ways you and I have not thought of."

"I wouldn't be overly hopeful on that score, lad. Hamish MacLachlan's a fine fellow and a loyal servant, but he got the job because he's a cousin of the Attorney General."

After lunch, just as Marc was about to set out for the Stebbins place, a boy sent over from the inn brought a message for the Ensign to come there immediately. Marc pulled the boy up in front of him on the saddle and galloped him gleefully down the Miller Sideroad.

Durfee had summoned Marc because, among the post-luncheon crowd at the inn, there were several notorious supporters of the Reform party, men who were not resident aliens and lived nowhere near the Americans in Buffaloville. "I'll just get 'em talkin' an' you can sit up here nursin' a toddy with both ears open."

In the two hours that followed, Marc learned much about elections, the evils of the Family Compact, the toils of farming, and much else irrelevant and otherwise – but none of it incriminating or pointing in that direction. Everyone had known Jesse Smallman and was saddened by his senseless death. Little feeling of any kind attended the occasional mention of Joshua's name (adroitly dropped by Durfee at intervals). Only the bizarre manner of his death seemed of any lasting moment. The most telling consequence of the entire afternoon was that Ensign Edwards was seen weaving his way towards the double-image of Colonel Margison's horse.

A brisk north wind and a steady canter up the Pringle Sideroad, across the second concession, and up the Farley Sideroad into Buffaloville soon sobered Marc for the challenge ahead. Or so he told himself. The Stebbins farm lay just above the concession line and across the sideroad from the McMaster place he had visited the previous afternoon, following the drama of Agnes Pringle's rescue and return. From Hatch's briefing Marc had learned that Azel Stebbins was by far the youngest of the suspected extremists and the most recently arrived (from New York State). At thirty, and with less than ten years in the province, young Stebbins had established a reputation for himself as a hotheaded republican and an ardent supporter of Willy Mackenzie's oft-stated view that only by annexing itself to the United States could Upper Canada ever be free and prosperous. His wife was reputed to be much younger than he, a child bride brought back like a trophy on his saddle from Buffalo, where he used to go on a monthly bender to the stews and dives of that pseudo-egalitarian Gomorrah.

When Marc arrived, Azel Stebbins was walking towards his barn with a bit and bridle in one hand. When he saw the Ensign riding up and dismounting, he stopped, took him in with a searching stare, then grinned and shot his hand out to the visitor.

"Hello, there," he boomed from a barrel chest. "I'm Azel Stebbins."

"Good day to you, sir. I am –"

"Ensign Marc Edwards, come to have a gander at the tons of wheat I got lyin' surplus all over the farm." His laugh invited Marc to join in on the joke.

As Marc smiled he did a quick appraisal of the man he hoped would prove to be his prime suspect. Stebbins looked like a quintessential Yankee: tall and ruggedly handsome with blue eyes and hair the colour of bleached hay, big-boned and muscular (features even his coat and leggings couldn't hide), and sporting a hair-trigger grin offset by a calculating tilt of brow and chin, from which drooped a blondish goatee.

"The quartermaster at York has been authorized to purchase extra supplies in the coming months, grains and pork in particular," Marc said, glancing towards the barn and the coop, smokehouse, and corncrib behind it.

"A mite worried about the ruckus in Quebec, I'm told," Stebbins said as he took the horse's reins.

"That was a factor, I believe."

"And you're the drummer?" Stebbins said.

"Advance agent."

"Seen plenty of drummers where I come from, though not always glad to."

The quick grin telegraphed the joke, and Marc dredged up a weak smile.

"Anyway, I'd like to see whatever you might have to offer. The price will be good, and paid in pound notes."

"Well, I'm relieved to hear that, I reckon – though my Yankee blood hankers after currency you can sink your teeth into."

"Are you new to the province, then?"

Stebbins halted near the big double-door to the barn. No grin mitigated his next comment. "I figure you know to the day an' the hour precisely when I first set foot on His Majesty's soil, and a good deal of what I've been doin' an' sayin' since. You an' me'll get along just fine so long as there's no malarkey between us. You look like a sensible young fella to me."

"Erastus Hatch has given me a few details of your stay in the district, but for my part I assure you I am here to reconnoitre grain and pork. There's no politics to a soldier's hunger."

"When you've been here a while you'll learn that everythin's politics in this country. As it is in the United States. The difference is, back home everybody's given a chance to join in the game – and win."

The obvious rejoinder – "Then why didn't you stay there?" – was on the tip of Marc's tongue before he reined it in, took a deep breath, and said, "Be that as it may, Mr. Stebbins, I have a simple duty to perform –"

"Now, now, don't get yer garters in a snarl," Stebbins said, hitching Marc's horse to a post, dropping his gear, and starting to haul the doors apart with both hands. "An' for Chrissake, quit hailin' me as *Mister*. The name's Azel, though I been called worse from time to time."

"Then you've something to show me?"

"You think we're headin' inta my barn to take a leak?"

The interior of the barn was spacious, well laid out, and scrupulously maintained. Two rows of stalls housed Ayreshire milk cows, a team of Clydes, a roan mare, and a huge bull manacled to a concrete stanchion by a ring in its nose. Fresh straw was evident everywhere. The energy Stebbins was putting into his political activities and unexplained "hunting" forays evidently had not affected his proficiency as a farmer.

"We had a drought last July that hit the wheat hard," Stebbins said, "but I put in a fair amount of Indian corn for pig feed, and it's paid off. The hogs're in the back. Hold yer nose!"

When they'd finished admiring the hogs – robust Yorkies waxing nicely towards slaughtering time – and tallying a potential purchase by the quartermaster's self-appointed legate, Marc said casually, "You've done exceedingly well here in a short time."

"I have done, haven't I? And I've managed a wife an' two babes inta the bargain."

"I heard about the fuss over alien rights when I arrived last spring," Marc said in his most empathetic tone. When Stebbins ignored the bait, Marc added, "You must have been concerned you might lose all this."

"You're damn right I was! I built everythin' you see here, an' the house, too, with the aid of my neighbours and other Christians who cared not a fig about my place of origin or the way I voted. I put in my own crops with only my woman and a lad or two from the township. Our harvestin' is done together, farm by farm. We got no landlords or fancy squires in this part of God's world."

"And Mr. Dutton was your man for the Assembly?"

"I reckon he didn't need much help takin' this seat."

"Hatch was telling me a neighbour of his suffered terribly from the drought."

Stebbins paused at the bull's stall, seemed to make some sort of decision, and said, "Smallman. Aye, sufferin's an inadequate word to cover what happened to that poor bastard."

"Jesse was a friend?"

Again a brief hesitation, then, "Not really. More like a comrade-in-arms, but when you've fought alongside somebody for the same cause you can make friends pretty fast. Jesse thought we couldn't get a fair shake for our grievances under the present set-up in Toronto, but he couldn't bring himself to cross the line."

"Whereas others did?"

Stebbins grinned cryptically. "Now them are matters I wouldn't know nothin' about, would I?"

"I wasn't implying you did," Marc said lamely. "But we heard rumours of seditious talk down this way and meetings of some secret society."

"The only so-called secret society infestin' this county is the Loyal Orange Lodge, led by that lunatic Gowan."

"At any rate, the alien question's been resolved, hasn't it? Your land is safe and you can hold any office you can get yourself elected or appointed to."

Stebbins said, "You'll also be happy to know I've just applied for my naturalization papers. I been here longer than the seven years they're requirin' for citizenship."

Marc was glad they had turned to leave the barn because it gave him a moment to recover from the shock of hearing this news and the deliberate manner in which it was revealed.

"Yessirree, in a month or so, Azel Stebbins, his wife, an' his bairns're gonna be *bona fidee* subjects of King Willy the Fourth."

Marc was not ready to give up, however, and when Stebbins insisted they seal their verbal contract with a drink, Marc was quick to accept.

"I never trust a man who turns down a free drink," Stebbins said, and winked. He led Marc past the horse stall to a manger below the hayloft, reached down, and drew a clay jug into the weak light of the waning day. He tipped it up, took a self-congratulatory swig, wiped his mouth on his sleeve, and passed the jug to Marc. "That'll tan yer insides."

Marc made a valiant show of duplicating his host's gestures, appending only an explosive wheeze to the set. Stebbins's grin wobbled through Marc's tears. "My God, that's raw stuff," he managed to say.

"Mad Annie's boys ain't too particular, I reckon."

"You wouldn't have something a little less – intimidating?" Marc said.

"Annie's potion's about all folks around here can afford."

"That's probably why I haven't had a decent drink since I left the Fort on Monday."

"Well now, I surely wouldn't want a man who's lookin' to buy my crops to go back to his commandant an' bad-mouth the local hospitality. Nosirree." Stebbins winked lasciviously, offered a quicksilver grin, and began to brush away at the hay in the manger. "Ahh," he said, and he drew forth a dusty bottle whose smudged label bore no word of English or American. "Bordeaux, older'n my granny's cat. In Buffalo they call this stuff 'French leg-spreader.'"

Marc flinched when he saw Stebbins attack the cork with his jackknife. "There," he said, "all ready for the back of the throat. Be my guest."

Marc had no choice but to hoist the vintage red and let it slide its way, bits of cork still abob, over his tongue and down his astonished throat.

Stebbins then did the same, but continued gulping until the dregs arrived, prompting him to spit furiously. "Jesus, but that's good stuff. A man could do worse'n get pissed on that."

"I haven't tasted anything that good, even in the officers' mess," Marc said, dabbing his lips with a handkerchief, a move that set Stebbins grinning again.

"It ain't available to members of the Family Compact."

"Could an ordinary soldier lay his hands on any of it?"

"You can get almost anythin' fer a price," Stebbins said.

"What else have I got to waste my money on?"

"Well now, if I *did* know where to find such ambrosia, I'd be sure an' tell an ordinary officer like yerself."

"You didn't *buy* this, then?" Marc forced himself to look suitably crestfallen.

"'Twas a gift, from a friend of a friend. For services rendered."

"Ahh . . . that's unfortunate."

"An' we don't tell tales on our friends, do we?" With this caveat Stebbins turned and ambled placidly out of the barn. Perhaps he did not realize how much he had just given away to his interrogator: the confirmation of a direct link to smugglers and a more oblique one to Jesse Smallman and his father.

Buoyed by this thought, Marc was caught off guard when he reached for his horse's reins and Stebbins said heartily,

"Where'n hell do ya think you're goin'? Don't ya wanta stay fer supper an' meet the missus?"

Marc was most pleased to say yes.

Marc put his horse in an empty stall beside Stebbins's mare, removed its saddle, gave it a perfunctory rubdown, and threw a blanket over it. "Sorry, old chum, but that's the best I can do." He chipped the ice off the water bucket in the stall, noted the hay in the corner, and went off to meet the notorious child bride from Buffalo.

Lydia Stebbins was attired in a woollen housedress that hung loosely on her, laceless boots, and a maid's bonnet askew on her brow. She stood before several steaming kettles and pots over a balky fire – ladling what appeared to be stew, intermittently stabbing at the fire logs with a twisted poker, and wiping the sooty sweat from her face like the beleaguered heroine in a melodrama. None of this blurred or diminished her beauty. A two-year-old clung shyly to her dress and stared up at Marc.

"Good gracious, Azel, you didn't tell me we was expectin' company," she cried, and she swept the back of a hand across her forehead.

"You got enough stew there fer a herd of longhorns," Stebbins said, shucking his clothes in sundry directions. "Put on a couple of extry dumplin's an' set a plate fer Ensign Edwards. Then hie yer pretty little rump over here an' shake his hand, like a proper lady."

A proper lady she might have made in other circumstances. Her hair was as black and shiny as ebony and fell in generous, wayward curls over her neck and shoulders and partway down her back. Her face was perfectly heart-shaped, her skin the milk-white hue of the Irish along the windy coasts of Kerry or Donegal. Her eyes were deep pools many a homesick sailor would happily have drowned in. The figure complementing them could only be guessed at, but as she gave her husband a warning glance and moved across the room towards Marc, a dancer's grace and innate control intimated a slim waist and lissome limbs.

"Pleased ta meet ya." When she smiled, her teeth were even, flawless. "You just call me Lydia like everybody else 'round here."

"And I'm Marc," he said, taking her hand and drawing it up towards his lips.

"Jesus!" she yelped. "He's gonna kiss it!"

"That's what they do to ladies over in England," Stebbins said scornfully.

Marc pressed his lips to the back of her hand. Lydia giggled but did not pull away. "You all done?"

"That's all there is to it, girl." Her husband laughed. He was over at the fire now and sniffing at the stew.

"Christ, I been kissed better by a pet calf," she said, her eyes dancing.

As Marc removed his coat and hat and searched for a chair or stool to drape them on, Stebbins came up behind his wife, flung both arms around her waist, and grabbed her breasts. "The littl'un's still pullin' on these," he said to Marc, with forced humour. "That's why they stick out so."

Lydia scowled and brought an elbow sharply into his ribs. "I told ya not to do that!" she snapped. "I ain't no cow!"

Stebbins cried out once, glowered at her, and for a second Marc thought he would strike her.

"Now, now, my pet, you know I was only teasin'," he soothed, and he let his head loll penitently on one of her shoulders. She reached back and stroked his thick hair, inadvertently illustrating her husband's crude point.

Marc looked away.

"C'mon now, luv," Lydia said, "we're embarrassin' Officer Edwards from England."

The stew was surprisingly tasty and the dumplings even better. Mr. and Mrs. Stebbins were now on their best behaviour, though Marc expected that the elaborate politeness of their "Mrs. Stebbins, would you kindly pass the bread?" and "Certainly, Mr. Stebbins, but not before our guest's been served" was a parody for his amusement or discomfiture – he was not certain which. In light of their performance, and the indignities of yesterday's encounters, Marc began to doubt the possibility of creating in Upper Canada an alternative society to the rabid and reckless democracy south of it – a New World country where decorum, reverence for the law, and respect for one's betters would be the accepted norms. It certainly seemed to be a moot question at best.

While Lydia washed the plates and spoons in a kettle at the fire, Stebbins and Marc sat at the deal table and drank several mugs of coffee tempered with dollops of Jamaican rum. With each swig the layers of civility fell away from Stebbins.

"Lookit that." He grinned mischievously towards his wife, stooped over her task. "You'd never believe she used to have the neatest little arse in Buffalo."

Marc could have disputed the claim but withheld comment.

"Her daddy owned the Buffalo House hotel on Seneca Street."

"He still does," Lydia shouted without turning around, "an' don't you ever forget it. My daddy was a colonel in the War of 1812. He killed an' scalped half a dozen Injuns bigger'n you."

"An' some evenin's he'd let his little darlin' get up on the stage there an' dance an' sing her pretty little heart out." Stebbins drank. "But she's runnin' to fat, for sure. One more kid'n she'll blow up like a pig's bladder. She couldn't sing fer her supper now, an' that's a fact."

As if on cue, Lydia began humming a tune, to which she added some audible but unintelligible words: her voice was melodic and sweet-soft as a canary's. Marc would have bought her supper or any other meal she fancied.

"You're just showin' off for the Colonel here," Stebbins hollered at her backside. He swung an inflamed eye around to Marc. "Now that there sounds like an old hooer of a crow squawkin' an' squeakin' from a barn roof, don't it?"

Marc reached for the rum jug.

"Don't wanta answer me, eh?"

Lydia ceased singing and swivelled around to face them. Her cheeks were scarlet from the heat; tiny pendants of sweat beaded her forehead and trickled down into the hollow of her throat. "Stop badgerin' the man," she said. "You don't know when to stop, do you?"

He glared at her and clenched both fists.

"You never did an' you never will." She grabbed the jug from under his reach and, with cool unconcern, walked it over to a cupboard.

Suddenly Stebbins leaned back and let out a huge, purging laugh. "She knows me better'n I know myself, that sweet, tiny-arsed waif of a woman. I gotta stay sober tonight," he said to Marc. Then he lowered his voice to a whisper, and added, "Gotta big meetin' to attend."

His laugh apparently disturbed the baby, who had slept through supper and its sideshow in a cradle beside the fire. The two-year-old had fallen asleep halfway through her meal and been tucked into bed in the loft above. Lydia went to the crying infant, clucked over it for a few seconds, then began to rock the cradle with one delicate, booted foot.

"Time for me to vamoose," Stebbins said, and he seemed to shush himself by holding two fingers to his lips.

Marc rose and said quietly, "I'll ride as far as the highway with you."

Stebbins hesitated. "Okay by me. You've been damn good company so far."

Marc bowed to Lydia (he thought he detected an amused exchange of glances between man and wife), and then the two men tiptoed out.

"No so hard, ya little nipper," he heard Lydia say as the door closed behind them.

Side by side they saddled their horses in the glow of a single lantern. The sky was clear, but the moon had not yet risen. It was a dark winter's evening they would be riding into, along the tree-shrouded lanes they dignified here with the name of "road."

"My God," Marc said suddenly.

"What is it?"

"The horse has thrown a shoe."

"It couldn't have. You rode it in here okay."

"Of course I did. The shoe has to be somewhere around here."

The two men made what both knew would be a fruitless search through the straw inside and the drifts outside. No shoe was found.

"Well, you can walk him back to the mill without doin' any harm," Stebbins said cheerfully. "Shouldn't take you an hour."

Marc was already leading the animal into the stableyard.

"Hey, he's limpin' a bit," Stebbins said.

Marc swore, then bent down to examine the animal's right front hoof. "He's picked up a nail or something already. I'll have to dig it out and then walk him home very slowly."

Stebbins found a pair of pliers and handed Marc his jack-knife. "Worst comes to worst, you could walk him across to McMaster," he said. "Fancies himself a bit of a horse doctor, he does. Right now I gotta go. Got friends countin' on me."

Marc, angry and suspicious, decided on a single, direct gambit. "Where are you off to?"

"Oh, a small gatherin' of associates who enjoy rollin' the dice once in a blue moon." With that he left.

Marc waited for half a minute and then walked quickly out to the sideroad at the end of Stebbins's lane. From the tracks in the snow, Marc could make out that Azel had turned north and, when the road came to an end up beyond the Hislop place, had plunged into the bush on a line that would take him straight to Mad Annie's. Unless, of course, Stebbins was more subtle in his cunning than he had shown thus far. At any rate, Marc was without a mount and like a duck on ice when fitted out with snowshoes. All that remained was for him to tend to the horse and then trudge home in front of it. At least the roads were well trodden and passable to a desperate man on foot.

He had just removed the nail from the animal's hoof and noted with satisfaction that the cut was not deep when a cry from the house brought him to rapt attention.

"*Help! Somebody, help me!*"

Lydia Stebbins was standing in her doorway – screaming into the darkness.

Apparently a live splinter from the ebbing fire had been flung beyond the stone apron of the hearth and landed on a nearby pillow, setting it alight. By the time Marc arrived, rushing past a panicked Lydia, the pillow was merely smouldering. Oily ribbons of smoke snaked out of it, but under no circumstance would it have burst into flame or threatened the cabin. Marc picked it up gingerly, sprinted to the door, and tossed it into a snowbank.

Lydia was seated at the table, rocking her youngest in a bunting bag. The two-year-old remained unruffled in the loft. Lydia had made a remarkable recovery.

"Get me a drink of that rum, would you, Marc?"

Marc obliged, eyeing her intently.

"A lady don't drink alone," she said. "It ain't polite."

"I'll sit with you till you've gotten over your fright," Marc said as she sucked impolitely at her cupful of imported rum, courtesy no doubt of Messieurs Connors and O'Hurley. "Then I really must go. My horse has thrown a shoe and I've got to walk it home."

"That won't take you more'n an hour." She pouted prettily. "An' don't tell me a big grown-up gentleman like yerself has got to be in bed afore ten o'clock."

"A gentleman doesn't remain alone with another gentleman's wife without his knowledge or permission," Marc countered.

"Now that would depend on the nature of the gentleman, wouldn't it? And the lady." She drained her cup.

"I think it safe to assume your husband would not approve."

"Then he shouldn't go runnin' off an' leavin' me to fend fer myself three nights a week. Who am I supposed to talk to? Little Azel Junior?"

"Surely you exaggerate. Where would Azel go three nights a week in this township?"

She smiled and refilled her own cup. "So now you're interested. What's so goddamned attractive about my husband that you gotta give him so much attention? I'm a damn sight prettier'n he is!"

"All I'm saying, Mrs. Stebbins –"

"*Lydia.*"

"Lydia, is that I can't give credence to your statement."

"Christ, what a lingo! Where'n hell'd ya learn that? I bet you wouldn't say shit if ya had a mouthful."

"Azel told me he was going off to gamble," Marc said. He poured himself a cup of the contraband rum.

"And hooerin', fer all I know. He just goes off, I'm tellin' ya, an' leaves me here to talk to the walls."

"Well, you may talk to me – for an hour. I've been told I'm a good listener."

More than an hour later, Lydia Stebbins was still talking. Her dark curls billowed and fluttered as she grew more animated, and the round, black eyes took in less and less of the room and more and more of what they wanted to see.

"I grew up in that hotel. It had the grandest ballroom in Buffalo, in the whole western half of the state. We had dances an' card games that never ended. Two presidents stayed there. Dolly Madison was given my mother's bed fer the night. She sent us a china figurine. Every general and admiral in America passed through Buffalo an' not one of 'em but didn't stop to converse with my daddy, the Colonel. An' he weren't no country colonel neither. When I was eighteen he let me read parts of his war diary. You mayn't believe it, lookin' at me now, with these udders an' my bum bulgin' out, that my daddy sent me off to finishin' school in Rochester." She raised her rum cup like a proper lady, took a sip, and batted her black eyelashes. "I can even read French."

She surveyed the cabin skeptically, as if to emphasize the unlikelihood of ever finding a use for French in these quarters.

"In the year before Azel come ridin' up to sweep me away, my daddy was made president of the Loco Foco party in the Buffalo region, and I got to hear some of the most melodious speeches on local democracy ever given, an' that includes Tom Paine an' Mr. Jefferson himself."

Marc leaned forward. "What I don't understand is how you could give all that splendour up for a man who was already a farmer in a British colony opposed to democracy and who was likely to be more interested in yields per acre than the lofty sentiments of the preamble to the American Constitution?"

She stared across the table at him. "My word, you can talk just like them," she breathed.

"But Azel can't?"

"I don't need remindin' about Azel's foul mouth," she said irritably. Her expression changed as she added, "But the man was a stallion. An' when you're a girl of twenty and of a mind to disobey an' spite yer daddy, that's all that matters."

Marc flushed, and began to doubt the wisdom of having steered the *tête-à-tête* into this particular groove. But it seemed too late to turn back now. "Azel kept his nose to the plough, then? Stayed away from speeches and politicking?"

"Oh, he got himself in thick with the Reformers up here when they tried to take the farm from us just because we come from the States. But he soon got tired of all that."

"Still and all, he's a good farmer," Marc said, aiming for some respectable closure to a strange evening. "You're fortunate to have him." He started to get up.

"Enough of this palaver," Lydia said, a licentious sparkle in her eyes. "Take me to bed."

Marc dropped the jacket he was about to put on.

"You can't go plyin' me with wine an' sweet talk an' then just march out that door an' leave a lady in distress, now can you?"

"But your husband –"

"What he don't know or can't guess can't hurt him, can it?" She hunched nicely over until the rim of her dress slipped perilously close to the outer extremities of her breasts.

Marc realized, far too late, that he had drunk too much – here and earlier at Durfee's – than discretion or common sense or self-interest warranted. And it had been far too long since that brief, passionate encounter with Marianne Dodds in far-off Kent. And the room was overpoweringly warm and oddly reassuring, and the heady appeal of this wanton, bright, motherly, vulnerable vixen was not to be resisted.

She reached out for his hand, but it was he who led her towards the bed.

Marc was casting about for his other boot in the dark when Lydia rose up behind him and said, "I *told* ya, he never comes home before daylight, an' he's so stinkin' drunk he'd think you were Father Christmas or the Bogeyman." She threw her arms about his neck. They were both stark naked, having performed their feat of lovemaking in that pristine state beneath an engulfing comforter while the fire expired and the air cooled above them. Lydia's engorged nipples pressed into his back and mingling odours floated up from the warmth of their cocoon.

Marc had been prepared for some wanton, wild, or unco-ordinated coupling, with pent passions unleashed on either side. It was not so. It was measured and tender and playful. Which of them had initiated this mode and kept it going he could not say, nor did he want to. When she sighed against him, he was not sure whether she had climaxed or was simply expressing her pleasure in advance of the event. They rolled then side by side, still connected. She pressed his head between her swollen breasts in what was undoubtedly a maternal gesture, or so he interpreted it. He thought fleetingly of the mother he had never really known.

Just as Marc found his second boot and lined it up with the first one on the cold floor, the baby let out a hungry howl.

"Damn," Lydia said, releasing him and flinging herself naked from the bed into the shadows of the big room, illumined only by the full flood of moonlight through its narrow west windows. "Don't you move now," she sang sweetly, and seconds later the babe's cries gurgled out.

For a long time Marc lay back under the quilt, savouring his own nakedness and the sensation alive in every inch of his skin, and listening to the suckling sounds of the child. Finally Lydia crawled back in beside him. She shivered deliciously against him.

"I didn't let the little bugger have all of it," she laughed. "I saved a bit for you."

Hours later, it seemed, he fell into a blissful, dreamless sleep.

Marc was wakened either by the sensation of falling or the crack of both elbows on the floor. Whatever the cause, he was certainly awake and unmistakably sitting on his haunches in the dark beside his lover's bed. Lydia, delectably nude, was rubbing the glass of one of the windows at the front of the cabin and squinting out into the moonlight.

"Jesus, it's Azel!" she cried. "He'll shoot us both!"

Marc leapt into action like a recruit caught napping at reveille. He pulled his trousers halfway up, jammed a foot into each boot, and then, flailing at the bed and the floor beside it, snatched at linens, socks, belt, shirt, and frock coat.

"He's puttin' the horse away," Lydia called to him encouragingly. "He'll be a minute yet." She trotted across to the bedroom window and jerked back the gingham curtains. Moonlight poured innocently over their love nest.

"He'll see my horse in there!" Marc gasped as he stepped into the chamber pot and heard it crack once – like a gunshot.

The voice of little Azel Junior drifted down from the loft: "Da-da home?"

"He's too damn drunk," Lydia said. "It'll be okay, once we get you outta here." She was helping him bundle up the clothes he had had no time to put on. "Just pull yer big coat on when you get outside." She tossed it to him, then set about working her shift over the tousled mane of her hair.

"How the hell am I supposed to get out the front door without bumping straight into him?" Marc said as he rolled his uniform into his greatcoat.

Lydia grinned. "We got an emergency exit." Then she leaned over and kissed him gently on the forehead, like a mother sending her tot off to his first day at school. Taking his free hand, she led him across to the southwest corner of the cabin to the big woodbox beside the fireplace. "There's a hatch at the back so's Azel can stuff his chopped logs in without usin' the door."

"But it's half full of wood!"

She began yanking some of the split logs apart, and he soon joined her. In a minute or so they had managed to clear a wedge of space through which he had no choice but to wriggle fundament-first.

"You better hurry, I hear him shuttin' the barn door."

"Da-da home, Mummy?"

The Ensign's rear parts had reached the hatch in the wall. As his legs were pinned underneath him, the only way he could think to open it was to butt it severely. On the third butt the hatch fell. An icy wind took instant advantage. Marc heaved and squirmed and, with a clatter of wood, followed the hatch out into the snow.

Lydia reached down and thrust his bundled clothes after him. "I gotta hop right inta bed," she whispered. "He'll be expectin' to find me warm an' ready."

In more congenial circumstances, Marc might have appreciated the irony of his lover's remark, but the first shock of arctic air numbed everything but his brain. Sheer panic kept it functioning. Marc jammed the hatch back into place and leaned against the cabin wall to get his bearings. The moon had risen, and he could see that he was at the rear of the house. Twenty yards to the side lay the barn and outbuildings. Halfway between, the staggering figure of Azel Stebbins aimed itself at hearth and home – towards the front door, a route that would take him mercifully out of sight and allow Marc to sprint unseen to the barn. Even if he made the barn undetected, Marc would still have to pass dangerously close to the cabin to leave by the lane and through the opening onto the sideroad. The impossible alternative was to take his chances on the drifts in the field, where, in the morning, the tracks of his departure would be stamped for all to see and interpret. He took a deep breath and jerked his unsuspendered trousers up to his waist. Stifling a cry with one hand, he reached down with the other and drew a splinter, agonizingly, out of his left buttock.

Azel was carolling a familiar sea shanty with some improvised taproom lyrics as he disappeared along the far side of the cabin. Seconds later, a door slammed. Marc took off for the stables, having the presence of mind to keep to the trodden path between woodpile and barn – no strange bootprints to be found at dawn by a jealous husband with a harquebus. Luckily, the latter had left the barn doors ajar, so Marc was able to slip quickly inside, out of the wind. With teeth chattering, and in the gleam of a sliver of moonlight pouring through the crack in the doorway, Marc trembled and stubbed his way into his remaining clothes. He had just buckled his belt when he felt a tickle of hot breath on the nape of his neck.

Bracing for a savage blow or the plunge of a dagger, Marc instinctively reached down for the sword he had left at the mill. But nothing happened. Slowly Marc forced himself to turn around and face his ambusher. It was Azel's mare, unarmed and amorous.

Stebbins evidently had stumbled into the barn, flung the

saddle off, tossed a hasty blanket over his mount, and left it to fend for itself. If he had walked it down to its stall, he would not have missed seeing Marc's horse in the stall beside it. One nicker and the game would have been over.

Marc put his saddle loosely on his own horse, checked its shoeless hoof, and began leading it back towards the doorway. That's when he heard a floorboard creak somewhere above him in the region of the hayloft. This was followed by a kind of scritching sound, as if some nocturnal creature were hunkering down or squirming to get comfortable. A rat? A raccoon? A thwarted lover waiting his chance?

Slowly he made his way farther into the interior of the barn. He stopped and listened. There was nothing but the contented breathing of animals he could hear but not see. Then a floorboard creaked right over his head, heavily; it could only have been a man's footstep. Was someone up there hiding from Marc – or spying on him?

While he was trying to make up his mind whether to lie low or flush out the fellow, the decision was made for him. He heard the hayloft door swing open above him on the wall opposite. His man was on the run.

Marc moved silently along the dark corridor between the stalls. By the time he got outside and trotted around to the far side of the barn, all he could see was the hatch swinging on its hinges and a male figure disappearing into the woods fifty yards away. But he recognized the awkward gait: Ferris O'Hurley, without his donkey.

What would O'Hurley be doing hiding out in Azel Stebbins's barn? Marc was sure it had something to do with the smuggling operation. The Irishmen from the States and their compatriot, Stebbins, were up to their Yankee ears in contraband spirits. But was that all? Connors had been carrying a sackful of brand-new American dollars last Tuesday. And Stebbins was always off hunting without bringing home a deer or a grouse. If it was this gang that Jesse Smallman had been mixed up with last year, it mattered little whether they were smuggling spirits, muskets, or seed money for seditionists: they and the Smallmans were connected in some significant way. Of that he was certain. So, despite the debacle back there in the cabin, Marc felt he had not completely frittered away the evening – if what had taken place in Lydia's bed could be called frittering.

Marc peered over at the Stebbins household. It was dark and quiet. The moon had gone behind a cloud. A few flakes of camouflaging snow had begun to fall. Marc took a lung-chilling breath and began leading his horse along the regular path that led past the cabin and up the laneway to the sideroad. No musket boomed out behind him, no cuckold's cry hailed him back. And O'Hurley was long gone.

Once on the sideroad he was able to pick up the pace. His horse limped slightly but made no complaint. The snow thickened about them. Bruised, sated, dishevelled, splinter-riven, piss-splattered, he trudged homeward. As he turned eastward on the concession line, an ugly thought entered his head. Was it possible that he had been meant to remain in the Stebbins cabin? That Azel was not to be trailed under any circumstances? That someone had deliberately nobbled his horse? No. What had passed between him and Lydia could not have been faked.

Could it?

CHAPTER ELEVEN

M arc missed breakfast (and any speculative remarks on the reasons for his absence from the table), but after an improvised meal of dry cheese, lukewarm bread, and cold tea, he was joined in the parlour by Hatch. Both men lit their pipes, and Marc provided him with an expurgated account of the fiasco at the Stebbins place. Hatch mercifully refrained from comment, then said, "You'll have to fix on exactly what you're going to tell Hamish MacLachlan this afternoon. Our sheriff's a man who appreciates facts." He chuckled and added, "There's not much else he *can* appreciate."

"Well," Marc said, "we've got this much, I think: evidence of a note or message calling a respectable Tory gentleman out of his own house and away from his own New Year's celebration into a near blizzard. The gentleman seems pleased about the prospects he's being called to. 'I may have some news that could change our lives forever,' he tells his daughter-in-law, who swore to that under oath. The rendezvous with the summoner was to be at an isolated spot, but one we know now to have been a hideout or transfer point for smugglers, in particular two of their advance men, Connors and O'Hurley. Smallman dies in a freak accident on his way to the cave, said accident having been anticipated or, after the event, conveniently used to collude in the man's death. To wit: no assistance was offered and no report made to the constable of the township or the sheriff or magistrate of the county. Some evidence at the scene indicates that the summoner stood waiting for his victim only a few rods above the death trap."

"My goodness, lad, but you would have made a fine barrister. Perhaps your Uncle Jabez was right after all."

"Solicitor is what he had in mind, but I wasn't willing to wait five years while performing tasks an indentured servant would repudiate," Marc said quietly.

"Well, if you go using words that big with MacLachlan, he'll have you clapped in irons on the first charge he can pronounce!"

"I'll tone it down a bit," Marc said dryly, and carried on. "Having established a *prima facie* case for foul play, I'll lay out the two lines of enquiry we've been pursuing: the political and the contraband. All he needs to know is that radicals like Stebbins may have suspected that Joshua was an informer – given his past connections, recent arrival, and suspicious attendance at Reform rallies – or that he learned or surmised seditious information from his son while speculating on his activities and suicide."

"You're not going to tell him that Joshua *was* a spy?"

"Even in telling you, Erastus, I've broken one of Sir John's commandments to me."

"You'll have to tell the girl, sometime."

"But not yet." Marc relit his pipe. "The smuggling angle can be approached in a way similar to the political one. Physical evidence suggests young Jesse may have turned to smuggling to help stave off bankruptcy and the failure of his farm. Half the township appears to have purchased contraband spirits or acted as wholesalers, but only a few of these can be directly linked to Jesse – those who marched beside him at the protest rallies over the grievances and, in particular, those American immigrants whose property rights were endangered by the Alien Act. We can reasonably postulate that somehow Joshua came across information that threatened the smuggling operation. Some ruse was then used to lure him to his death, probably false hopes raised about the reasons for his son's self-destruction. Certainly, the locale points strongly to the latter theory."

"So far, all of this is circumstantial," Hatch said gently, "even though it's damn clever guesswork."

"At any rate, all I want to do is report formally to the Sheriff, show him Sir John's instructions to me, and alert him to the fact that I'm going to start using the Governor's authority to compel or cow certain suspects into telling something closer to the truth. I've been given full policing powers in the matter. I can hale these renegade farmers, and even old Elijah, before the Magistrate and interrogate them under oath. I've just about done with playing games."

"On the positive side," Hatch said, "most of your suspects'll be at the Township Hall in Cobourg later today to hear William Lyon Mackenzie rant and rave. You'll be able to watch 'em close up, stirring their own soup." He got up slowly and added, with the customary twinkle in his eye, "You can hardly see the mend in your trousers, but Winnie was wondering if you'd been reconnoitring grain in a sawmill."

Marc strolled up to Beth's place, not only because he needed some bracing air to clear his head, but because he wanted to convey to her personally the arrangements that had been made for the journey into Cobourg and to make sure she would agree to them. No persuasion was needed, however: Beth Smallman wasn't about to miss the opportunity to be roused once more by Mackenzie's fiery rhetoric, even when it meant accepting the charity of a ride with a neighbour and the company of a red-coated infantry officer from the Tory capital. The Durfees had offered the best seats in their cutter to Beth and her escort, Ensign Edwards. Erastus, Winnifred, Mary, and one of her sisters would be driven by Thomas Goodall in the miller's four-seater. Another of Mary's sisters would stay with Aaron.

"You don't need to chaperone me, you know," Beth said to Marc at the door. "Mr. Durfee will do nicely."

"Ah, but I *want* to," Marc said.

Hatch was not in the mill, but sometimes, Marc had learned, he could be found in the small office attached to it. Winnifred had gone down to Durfee's for the mail and a visit with Emma. Goodall was in the drive shed behind the barn making some minor repairs to the sleigh. The little window in the outer wall of the office was begrimed and frosted over, so Marc just pushed gently on the unlatched door and opened his lips to halloo the miller. No syllable emerged. Through the gap in the doorway, Marc saw a woman's oval face, eyes seized shut, cheeks inflamed with no maiden's blush.

Marc backed away. He didn't pause to close the door.

Ten minutes later, Hatch sat down opposite Marc in the parlour. He fiddled with his pipe but didn't bother poking the fire into life.

"It's not what you think, lad," he said.

Marc did not reply, but he was listening with intense expectation.

"I would never take advantage of a servant girl, whatever other sins I may be charged with before my Maker."

"You wouldn't be the first to do so," Marc said, remembering the rumours and whispered gossip that had titillated and scandalized the residents of Hartfield Downs.

"Two months ago she came to me. To my room. It took all my powers and the vow I'd made to my beloved Isobel to push her away. I'd not had a woman since Isobel passed on. I told Mary she didn't have to do this, that it was wrong, that I considered her to be a fine, chaste young woman who would marry soon and raise her own family. She wept, but she did go."

"Why do you think she came to you like that?"

"She was afraid I might send her home. You see, I have a niece in Kingston, and Winnifred's talked about bringing her here, for company and to help out with the chores."

"Mary could get other work, surely." Marc was thinking of the desperate need for decent servants in Toronto.

"Easily. But still, it would mean returning home, even for a little while."

"She was maltreated?"

Hatch grimaced. It was the first anger Marc had seen in the miller's jovial, kindly face. "The father's a drunken brute. He's been in the public stocks half a dozen times. Nothing short of a bullwhip could cure him."

"And if your niece did come, Mary would have to go?"

Hatch sighed. "She came to me again two nights later. This time she slipped in beside me, already . . . unclothed. I promised her she could stay on here as long as she wanted, or else see that she never had to go back to the brute that begot her."

"And?"

"I gave in to my urges. I know it was a terrible thing to do. A wicked thing. She's the same age as my own daughter. And the worse thing of all is, she really seems to like me. And now, though I pray every night for strength to resist, I've gradually, and alas gratefully, come to accept her . . . presence. She's a loving little thing." It took a great effort for him to hold back the tears that were threatening.

"Have you considered marrying her?" Marc knew full well that, in both the old world and the new, older men not nearly as robust and honourable as Hatch married girls half their age in their need for heirs or to satisfy the lusts that were expected to wane with age but didn't.

"I can't find the courage to." Hatch jabbed at the fire as if he might conjure in its flames some image of Isobel that would tender absolution. "And after all, Winnifred has devoted her life to me and our business since her mother died, giving up her own chances for happiness."

"She looks like a young woman who makes her own decisions, for her own reasons," Marc said.

Hatch sighed. "You know, lad, I've even prayed that Mary would get in the family way, then I'd *have* to find the courage, wouldn't I?"

That was a wish, Marc thought, that a benevolent Deity might easily grant.

Marc and Beth sat in the cutter's seat among buffalo robes, and James and Emma Durfee snuggled together on the driver's bench as the team of Belgians followed the familiar road to town more or less on their own. The afternoon was clear and cold, making the runners sing on the snow and sharpening the tinkle of the bells on the horses' harness. Emma Durfee had peremptorily refused to ride in the back with Beth, claiming, with just a hint of humour, that a woman's place was beside her man. Forty minutes of steady progress would see them in Cobourg.

"You've spent most of your time here firin' questions at me," Beth said, drawing one of her furs more closely about her throat, "but you haven't exactly told any of us your own life story."

"There isn't much to tell," Marc said. Their shoulders were touching fraternally through several layers of animal skin. "I was orphaned at five years and adopted by my father's . . . patron."

Beth looked puzzled by the word *patron* but continued to nod encouragingly.

"I soon learned to call him Uncle Jabez. He was unmarried, so I became the son he never had. I was raised on his modest estate in Kent, among gardens and hedgerows and thatched cottages. Next to us resided the shire's grandest squire, who befriended my uncle and me. Hartfield Downs was magnificent, both the Elizabethan house and the vast farmland surrounding it. I was permitted to play with the Trelawney children, who thought themselves the equivalent of princes and princesses."

"Which kept you humble," Beth said dryly.

"Uncle Jabez brought in private tutors who saw that I learned even when I didn't particularly want to."

"The distraction of all those princesses?"

"Horses, mainly. I loved to ride and be outdoors. I worshipped my Uncle Frederick, my adoptive father's younger brother. He was a retired army officer who had fought with Sir John Colborne and the 52nd on the Spanish Peninsula." When Beth made no response to this news, he continued. "Uncle Jabez had been a solicitor in London, but when he inherited his father's estate, he moved back to the country and took up the role of gentrified landowner. He sent me to London to article at law in the Inn of Chancery, which means six days a week with your head buried in conveyancing papers. But I spent all my free time at the Old Bailey envying the barristers in their grand wigs and robes – strutting about the court like tragedians on a stage."

"An' poor you with no horses to ride or foxes to assassinate?"

"More or less. What I secretly longed for was action, excitement, some challenge to the manly virtues I fancied I possessed in more than moderate measure."

"Your drudgery left you little time for dalliance, then?"

Marc tried to catch the look that underlined this remark, but failed. "I have seldom found women unattractive," he said.

Beth laughed. "Nor they you," she said.

Emma turned around and, for several minutes, engaged Beth in conversation about a proposed shopping venture and plans for a joint charity clothing drive among the Presbyterians, Congregationalists, Methodists, and, surprisingly, the Anglicans. This interlude gave Marc time to reflect on how he was going to reopen the interrogation of the woman sitting close enough that he could feel the heat of her breath.

"It must have been hard for an upright, honourable, and religious man like your Joshua to have accepted his son's suicide," he said as soon as Emma had turned back to her husband and the road ahead.

Beth shifted ever so slightly away from him. "Of course it was. He loved Jess, even though they weren't together much after we got married. An' Jess was no weaklin'. He was strong an' independent, or else he couldn't've left home like he did or started the farm without a lick of help from anybody."

"Did Joshua press you for answers? Reasons? Your own opinion of Jesse's state of mind before he died?"

"Not directly. That wasn't his way. But when I told him Jess was feelin' low, I also explained about the state of the farm an' what the future looked like to him back then. One day, Father just asked me to take him to one of the rallies. So I did. And he listened, as I already told you."

"He didn't hint in any way that he thought Jesse might have been tempted by more radical forms of action?"

"No."

"And you have no recollection of him remarking on anything unusual or suggestive that he might have found among Jesse's effects or heard about Jesse from some third party?"

"I was the one that sorted through my husband's effects."

"Still, it's difficult to believe that you and your father-in-law did not have, from time to time, some moments of severe disagreement. After all, he was accompanying you to Reform rallies, and presumably listening to their arguments, but, as you've pointed out, he remained a Tory and a supporter of the government you despise."

Beth didn't answer, but he could see she was deep in thought.

"Cobourg's just over the creek!" Durfee called out.

Marc's knowledge of the towns of Toronto, Hamilton, and London should have prepared him for the village of Cobourg, not yet confident enough to declare itself incorporated. There was a main thoroughfare – King Street, no less – with intersecting avenues and even, Beth told him, two or three concession roads running parallel to it farther north. But to one conditioned to expect cobbled roadways, brick buildings, gas lamps on every corner, tended gardens and stone fences, the rumble of hackney carriages, market wagons, and vegetable barrows, and the buzz and jostle of citizens on the go, Cobourg was a rude shock. The many log cabins and the few frame houses were largely obscured by clumps of untouched primeval forest. The roadbed was rutted solid from the last thaw and only somewhat smoothed out by packed snow. There were no sidewalks along the verges of King Street.

Marc's hosts vied with one another to point out to him the glories of the only stone church ("Presbyterian," Emma added, "up there on William Street"), the simple, frame-built Congregational church (vast enough to entertain two hundred of the faithful), and at the junction of King and Division (the lone treeless intersection) the first stop on their journey: Benjamin Throop's Emporium (a glorified general store). Kitty-corner to this squared-timber, two-storey commercial structure stood St. Peter's Anglican Church.

Hatch's sleigh pulled up behind them a minute later. The women were left to forage through the emporium and, afterwards, walk across to St. Peter's for their committee meeting. Goodall was to pick them up there at four o'clock and drive them up Division Street to the Township Hall for the political "picnic." Sandwiches and cake for afternoon tea had already been packed in wicker hampers, as if it were July and the occasion pastoral. In the meantime, Hatch had agreed to meet the Sheriff, not at the new courthouse and jail in Amherst just down the highway, but in the more commodious Cobourg Hotel.

In the Sheriff's "office," Marc was handed a mug of beer by the smaller of two constables and urged to tell his story. While the sheriff of the Newcastle District, Hamish MacLachlan, rocked back in a chair constructed for his considerable girth and backside, Marc recited his tale much as he had rehearsed it with Hatch (minus all but a dozen arguably necessary polysyllables). The young constables, part-time supernumeraries or deputies like the miller, were so awed they forgot to sample their complimentary beer. But the Sheriff himself showed no reaction beyond an occasional pull on his pipe.

"Well, what do you think, Hamish?" Hatch said when Marc had finished.

MacLachlan put out a boot to slow his rocking. "What you've got there, son, is one helluva bowl of beans – an' no fart."

Marc was not deflated by the Sheriff's summary judgment. Nor was the Sheriff offended by Marc's intrusion into local affairs. If Sir John and his successor wished to waste the time of an energetic young ensign on such a fool's errand, then it was no skin off his nose, especially if it meant no effort on his part. Besides, he was far too beset by immediate problems, like the potential firestorm out at the Township Hall.

"I could use another pair of strong arms out there," he said to Marc. "An' that flamin' red petticoat of yours won't be a hindrance either. Too bad ya didn't bring your sword, and a Brown Bess with a bayonet."

"He's exaggerating a tad," Hatch ventured.

"You know perfectly well, Hatch old man, there's lunatics on either fringe, and it's a bitch to try an' look over both yer shoulders at the same time."

"You're not anticipating a Tory riot?" Marc said with a glance at Hatch.

"No, but Ogle Gowan's Orange Lodgers have been spotted over in Durham County holdin' powwows, or whatever monarchist, anti-papist mumbo-jumbo they get up to when they're well liquored an' foamin' at the mouth."

"What about the Hunters' Lodges?" Marc said.

"Never heard of 'em, but they probably exist, if only to keep me from my good wife's bed. You fellas can take your cutter or ride with the constables here, but one way or t'other, I'm gonna need all of ya. I've outlawed all liquor in the hall and, of course, there'll be no weapons of any kind, not even a gardenin' trowel. Transgressors'll be bounced out pronto. I'm also gonna patrol the grounds an' privies, and empty every jug an' teapot I see."

When Marc looked skeptical, MacLachlan added: "You can be sure Mad Annie's brood'll be somewhere nearby. If you sight any one of them cretins – male, female, or otherwise – I want ya to latch on an' hold 'em down till I come with the irons." He took a lusty pull at his beer. "Philander Child's gonna be present to see the bylaws of the last quarter session are strictly enforced."

The young constables had finally noticed that their mugs were still full.

"All right, lads, finish your drinks an' be off. I'll trot down on Old Chestnut in a while." He winked. "My whistle ain't quite wetted."

Marc stood sentry on the porch of the Hamilton Township Hall, the largest secular structure in the village, and watched with growing amazement the arrival of the Reform party's adherents and detractors. They came by sled, sleigh, and cutter, pony and dray-horse, by shank's mare and snowshoe, toboggan and skid and Norwegian skis; in family groupings, couples, and fraternal cliques. That the backwoods could harbour so many sentient beings without advertising their presence was in itself astonishing, but that somehow these scattered and bush-bound castaways from Britain and elsewhere could discover the date and locale of this political gathering, could find the time to consider its significance, and then arrange for their simultaneous arrival within the hour appointed – this was truly cause for wonder.

For a few minutes Beth stood at Marc's side greeting one newcomer after another by name, many of whom, to Marc's consternation and concern, were women. "How did all these people find out about the rally?" Marc asked.

"Well, most of us can read," Beth said, "an' the *Cobourg Star* gives us some practice once a week."

At five o'clock the front doors were closed. A few torches had already been lit inside under the supervision of Magistrate Child and the fire warden. The brand-new Rochester Pumping Wagon stood at the ready on Division Street. At his own watch, Marc heard the commotion at the rear of the hall as a sleighful of dignitaries apparently drew up in a lane behind the building and entered it via a vestibule presided over by the Sheriff and the larger of the two constables. A raucous cheer, punctuated by hoots and catcalls, rose up. Marc hoped that Beth had kept her promise to stay close to the Durfees.

Before going inside to monitor the proceedings, Marc circled the grounds of the hall and checked the privies. All seemed quiet. He lifted each of the several dozen confiscated jugs and jars near the front door: all were now empty. Next to these lay a jumble of wooden handles from farm implements. The smaller constable was instructed to guard these rudimentary weapons, and keep an eye on traffic to and from the privies and the side door of the hall.

Marc made note of the arrival of Azel and Lydia Stebbins, Israel Wicks with his two sons, an unsteady Orville Hislop, and, to his mild surprise, Elijah, the hired man. How had he got himself to town? For the briefest second, Marc's eye caught Lydia's as she brushed past him. She looked quickly away, but not before offering him the hint of a smile – mocking or conspiratorial, he could not tell.

The fifteen or so women stood at the back of the hall near the double doors, not so much because their presence was considered inappropriate but because, in the event of a disturbance or fire, they could get out easily. James Durfee, though not officially deputized, stood watch for the women. Winnifred, Emma, and Beth were close beside him. Mary was with her sister – and many wives and children who had made the arduous trek with their husbands – a block away on King Street. Here, between the Cobourg Hotel and Throop's Emporium, there was much socializing around several bonfires and in the "open-air parlours" of the bigger sleighs.

Every one of the several hundred spectators inside the hall was standing, even though a number of benches were available on the periphery for the infirm or dyspeptic. The torches that lit the smoky, shadowed interior were set high on metal sconces on the walls. As Marc took up his assigned place between the podium and the side door, the first speaker was being introduced: Peter Perry, member of the Legislative Assembly for the nearby constituency of Lennox and Addington. A thunderous roar erupted as he stepped into an undulating pool of torchlight in the centre of the makeshift platform. His companions in the cause, four of them, were seated behind him, hidden in the oily darkness beyond the reach of torchlight.

The crowd's shouted approval rattled the windows and ricocheted into the rafters. Perry, a squat bulldog of a man stripped to his shirtsleeves and in fighting trim, began his speech at full throttle and cranked it upwards from there in carefully calibrated degrees of vehemence and mockery. His target was Sir John Colborne and the news that, in the final days of his regime, he had secretly signed a bill creating fifty-seven additional rectories for the Established Church, thereby adding a thousand or more acres to the already corrupt and bloated glebe lands of the Clergy Reserves.

The crowd roared its disapproval as one. It cheered each note and jab of Perry's defiance. The occasional dissenting "Nay" or "Shame" was drowned out instantly or used by Perry to goad the faithful to further indignation. The heat in the hall – the heat of exhaled rage, of bodies sweating in winter gear, of anticipation – was growing unbearable as Perry soared to the peak of his impassioned flight.

"We shall no longer tolerate the insolence of high office, the flouting of His Majesty's will by petty appointees of the Colonial Secretary, the hauteur of Rector John Strachan and his Anglican cronies, the daily repudiation of bills passed by the people's duly elected Assembly! We will march through every village and town in this province and tear these ill-got rectories down, board by arrogant board!"

During the tidal wave of applause that pursued Perry to his

seat, Marc slipped out the side door. He breathed in several draughts of cold, fresh air and set about on the first of his half-hourly rounds. It was completely dark now. Marc studied the steady stream of men moving from hall door to privy and back. The glazed excitement in their eyes, like a flame under liquid wax, was not wholly due to the effects of the fiery rhetoric from the platform. Many, he suspected, would have concealed flasks to draw inspiration from as occasion demanded, but such a limited source could not account for the extent of the weaving and yawing in front of him.

Half an hour later, after the third speaker, a failed Reform candidate from Kingston, had finished, Marc noticed a pronounced increase in the level of inebriation. The crowd, somewhat more subdued during the two speeches following Perry's opening salvo, was pacing itself no doubt for the feature attraction yet to come. At the current rate of imbibing, Marc hoped it would come soon.

"Where in Sam Hill are they getting the stuff?" Hatch said to him outside.

"Damned if I can figure it." The two men stared at the three privies carefully. They had been erected in such a way that they were set into a hedge-like row of cedars: to mute their vulgar presence perhaps, or to provide in the cedar fringe a ready alternative for male relief. Only some of the men here bothered to use a privy, but they were the ones for the most part doing the weaving and muttering. Marc took a quick look into each cubicle and in the near-dark could see nothing unusual. No jugs littered the floor or bench.

As he turned back towards the hall, Marc heard a shout that he imagined might have risen from the Highlanders on their first charge at Culloden or King Billy's crusaders at the Battle of the Boyne.

William Lyon Mackenzie was centre stage, the spot marked out for him by Destiny – God's or the Devil's, depending on your politics. The heat and stink of the room was overpowering, but the audience pressed forward so tightly that anyone fainting would remain upright and unnoticed. The double doors were open, the principal effect of which was to have the torches shudder more ominously in their tin calyxes and throw a less reliable light on the crowd below. Marc stood on a bench to better monitor the proceedings.

Mackenzie, the Scots firebrand whose name Marc's superiors had never uttered except in contempt, was surprisingly small. Even though he was swaddled in two greatcoats (of different colours), the thinness of his frame and fragility of his bones was evident – in the delicacy of his fingers, which probed and struck the air in rhetorical bursts, and in the dancer's nimbleness of his feet, which hopped and paused in concert with his words. His head was absurdly large for such a body, as if it had been fashioned solely for the passion of public speech. His blue eyes blazed continuous outrage yet still found moments to dart and judge, or confer brief benediction on those few apostles positioned near enough to receive it. During the first minutes of his jeremiad, the crowd, even those who had been jeering bravely, went quiet, as if some stupefying awe had taken hold. Their messiah did not disappoint.

He reviewed for them the long and sorrowful history of their attempts to gain a legitimate voice in those affairs of state that most affected their lives and the future of their children. There was no need to remind anyone in the room, he said, of the sacrifice already made by a populace comprised almost entirely of outcasts, voluntary exiles, and the dispossessed: ordinary men and women who, like their courageous counterparts in France and the United States, were to be numbered among those first generations of humankind who, in the simplicity of their conviction, said no to tyranny, laid their bodies naked before it, and proclaimed to all oppressed peoples of the Earth: "It shall not pass!"

A rustling thrum and a sustained murmur began to resonate through the hall, wordless but nonetheless coordinated and edged with threat. Marc glanced anxiously towards the big doors but could see no one that mattered. A few souls – exhausted, drunk, or frightened – were slipping out into the night.

The firebrand moved on to catalogue the most recent outrages, pausing between tirades for roars of approval and working the crowd like a seasoned tent-preacher, while his orange-red hair flared about his face like a demonic halo. The throng hooted and participated in his derision of Chief Justice Robinson and Attorney General Boulton and other charter members of the Family Compact who had three times had him expelled from the parliament to which he had been elected and defiantly re-elected. They laughed wildly when he recounted, with apt mimicry, the stunned response of said worthies when, unable to assume his lawful seat in the House, he had subsequently been elected the first mayor of the new city of Toronto. He paused, took a swig of water from a pitcher, ran his fingers through the shock of his hair, and glared out over the crowd as if seeing, beyond them, their common tormentors.

He changed to the subject raised by his fellow legislator, Peter Perry: the fate of the *Seventh Report on Grievances*. One by one, and in a voice now more terrible for its calculated restraint, he touched on the particular wounds that festered and burned amongst them: the Clergy Reserves, the ruinous lending policies of the Bank of Upper Canada, the rejection by the *appointed* Legislative Council of bill after bill that would alleviate their suffering, the graft and bumbling of the Welland Canal Company, the low prices of grain manipulated for the benefit of the Mother Country and its coddled emissaries here among the ruling clique, the greed and venality of district magistrates more arrogant than English squires or the absentee landlords of Scotland and Ireland.

A chant now rose up from the throng, softening whenever Mackenzie hammered home a point and swelling to occupy even the briefest pause: "No more! No more! No more!"

The rage had become contagious. The parishioners were slowly metamorphosing into a mob, with a mob's unreasoned and overfocused hate, its craving for a scapegoat. Suddenly Marc realized that this kind of collective outrage was potent enough to propel one of its participants to murder, to a sort of political execution whose sole purpose might be release for pent-up anger. The choice of victim could be arbitrary, as long as he represented the party of oppression. Even someone like Joshua Smallman might well do, particularly if he were behaving like a paid agent of the "enemy."

Mackenzie had not quite finished. Having stirred their passions and gained their full attention, he began explaining to them, in moderated tones and with didactic earnestness, the importance of their recent success in getting the *Report on Grievances* a fair hearing in the British Cabinet, of their unequivocal victory in the alien question, of their current control of the Assembly and its bills of supply, and, no mean feat, of the Family Compact's acute embarrassment over the abrupt recall of the meddling John Colborne. Indeed, a new governor – a man with no military experience to hobble him, a man of letters who penned travel books and poems – was en route from Montreal to Toronto at this very moment. Now was not the time for precipitate or thoughtless action. The recent and sterling example provided by Jacksonian democracy in the republic to the south proved that, with patience and unceasing pressure and petition, the voice of the people even in remote regions would be heard and would prevail.

A reverent hush once again gripped the faithful. Hope, however feeble, had been resuscitated.

"What about *my* rights?" The voice from the crowd was a high-pitched, irreverent cackle.

Mackenzie halted in mid clause. Instantly his gaze fixed the woman twenty feet from him who had spoken. He smiled and, with a twinkle in his eye, said, "And what rights have we not yet addressed, madam?"

Heads craned and feet shuffled.

"I wanta know when the land I've been squattin' on fer twenty-five years is gonna be deeded to me an' my young'uns."

"But squatters' rights have always been protected, ma'am – unless you're perched upon a bishop's birthright!"

The crowd roared its approval of this quip, but not before one phrase tittered through it, lip to lip: "It's Mad Annie!"

From his position Marc could see the portly Sheriff trying to force his bulk across the room towards the citizen of his county he admired the least.

"Then why won't the arsehole callin' himself our magistrate assign me the deed?"

"Have you improved the property according to regulations?" Mackenzie said patiently to Mad Annie over the derisory howls of the men around her.

"If plantin' whisky trees an' harvestin' a bastard a year are improvements, you shoulda had that piece of swamp years ago!" a neighbourly wag suggested.

"You shut yer fuckin' face, Hislop!"

"Madam, there are ladies in the hall –"

"Fuck the ladies! I want my rights! What kinda dickless wonder are you anyways?"

The Sheriff and a brace of constables were closing in.

"We got trouble outside," Hatch said to Marc, drawing him through the side door and away from the low comedy. At least Mad Annie had redirected the crowd's attention, and, with Mackenzie's own unexpected shift at the end of his speech, Marc felt certain that the evening would conclude without a riot.

"Behind the privies," Hatch said, hurrying towards an opening in the trees to the right of the outhouses. "Young Farley spilled the beans to me inside."

Marc followed Hatch, and the two soon emerged into the clearing behind the privies. A few yards farther into the bush, they heard a commotion: low cursing, hissed commands, and a clatter of wood and crockery.

"Damn!" Hatch cried. "Somebody's tipped them off!"

By the time he and Marc reached the scene of the crime, Mad Annie's enterprising progeny had scurried into the trees, lugging their paraphernalia with them. Pursuit was unthinkable.

"Well, I suppose the Sheriff will appreciate us confiscating what's left." Hatch chuckled as he held up one of the dozen or so clay jugs that remained unbroken.

They walked back to the privies, noting a well-trodden path between the improvised outdoor shebeen and one of the toilets. "How in blazes did they get the rotgut to the customer?" Hatch mused aloud.

"This way," Marc said. He was pointing to a Dutch door cut into the upper half of the back wall of the middle privy. "Not everyone came here to do his business."

"Jesus," Hatch said, "and I bet the ruckus Mad Annie created in there was a diversion while her lads dismantled the operation and hightailed it home."

Hatch went back into the hall through the side door, but Marc decided to go around to the front door for a final check. He remembered that the shorter constable had left his post there to assist the Sheriff in his pincer movement against Mad

Annie. The uproar inside appeared to have escalated a decibel or two, and Marc hoped the crowd had not begun to view the hapless Annie Pringle as its scapegoat. As far as he could tell, the pile of potential weapons had not been reduced. Six or seven of the women had wisely come outside (Beth was not among them), and several were standing on alert beside their family sleighs. The Reform rally was nearing its end.

Marc stepped through the double doors – into bedlam.

"I'm gettin' the ladies out!" Durfee shouted at him. "Try to get to the platform if you can!"

In front of him Marc could see only a seething tangle of arms, legs, and contorted faces, the arms ending with fists, and not a few of them wielding stout sticks or cricket bats. As the weapons came crashing down, the thud and crack of wood upon clothed bone or vulnerable skull reverberated above the cries, curses, and howls of pain. A full-scale donnybrook was in progress. But who was fighting whom? And where had the weapons come from?

Marc plunged in. A berserk fellow was indiscriminately swinging a hobnailed stick at a group of farmers in desperate, jumbled retreat.

"We're gonna bust the heads of every one of you republican arseholes!" the attacker screamed, and he lashed out, striking one of his victims on the shoulder and knocking him sideways. Marc leaped ahead and put both hands on the stick before it could be raised again, ripped it out of the lunatic's grip, and clipped him on the jaw. He dropped in his tracks.

The victim groaned. It was Angus Farley, one of the American immigrants Marc had visited late Thursday afternoon. "Who are these hooligans?" he said, helping Farley to his feet.

"Orangemen from Toronto," Farley rasped. His left arm was hanging limply at his side. "We gotta get to the platform. It's Mackenzie they're after!"

"He'll get out the back way," Marc said.

"They'll be waitin' for him. You don't know these people!"

There was no way that Marc, even armed with a hobnailed bat, could push through to the platform. From the scuffling and scrambling about him, he got the impression that the invaders were fighting a holding action while the main thrust of the attack lay elsewhere. He dashed to the double doors, where a score of bleeding and battered men were staggering onto the street, picked up a dozen hoe handles, and tossed them back into the fray. At least the odds could be narrowed a bit. Then he sprinted through the snow towards the rear of the hall. And stopped.

Mackenzie's sleigh was occupied by three bat-wielding thugs, lying in wait. Two more commanded the side exit. The honourable members of the Reform party were still trapped inside.

Suddenly the rear door burst open. Six burly men emerged, strung out like pallbearers, and wriggling frantically in their grip was William Lyon Mackenzie.

This outrage, Marc knew, if carried off successfully, would wreak such havoc on the body politic of Upper Canada that the mere murder of a retired dry goods merchant would seem but a mote in a maelstrom.

CHAPTER TWELVE

T he stableboy bringing the Sheriff's horse, Old Chestnut, from the livery on Division Street did not recognize the soldierly figure who leapt into its saddle, dug his heels into the horse's ribs, and galloped away towards the rear of the Township Hall in a furious blur of scarlet and grey.

Marc bore down upon his quarry with only the vaguest of rescue plans in mind. Fortunately, the abductors had chosen to indulge in a bit of boyish fun before settling down to their more serious business. To raucous cheers from their three bat-wielding companions on the sleigh, they formed a ragged circle, lifted the helpless Mackenzie above their heads, and began spinning him counter-clockwise – with the intention, it seemed, of concluding the game with a bravura flourish that would see him tossed like a beanbag onto the floor of the getaway vehicle.

"Hurry up, lads," a burly fellow cried from his perch on the sleigh. "We got the tar hot an' the feathers itchin'!"

Marc drove the Sheriff's horse hard between the sleigh and the abductors, reached down with his right hand, grabbed a thick handful of overcoat, and drew Mackenzie up across the horse's withers. As he charged back towards the road, cries of dismay trailed away behind him. He didn't pause to see whether or not he was being pursued, but he did catch a sideways glimpse of a huddle of astonished women just before he wheeled and galloped south to King Street, with the bundled bones of William Lyon Mackenzie bouncing unceremoniously in front of him.

Marc hurried eastward on the main road, cantered across a bridge over a small creek, and pulled up in front of the Newcastle Court House and Jail. He dismounted, then reached back up and tipped Mackenzie upright. The little Scot slithered down the horse's flank and landed on both feet. He was gasping for breath and struggling unsuccessfully to utter some word appropriate to the occasion.

"We'd better get inside, sir. I am not armed and I have no way of knowing how far those men will go to get you back."

Mackenzie let out a wheeze that resembled a "Yes," which Marc took for consent. Holding his prize by the elbow, he led him into what appeared to be the Sheriff's office and anteroom to the jail. A rotund woman of indeterminate age sat snoozing beside a candle-lantern.

"Mrs. MacLachlan!" Marc shouted. "Does your husband keep a pistol here?"

The woman's eyes popped open, and then popped wide open. "Jiminy," she cried, "I ain't Miz MacLachlan, an' who in blazes are you?"

Mrs. Timmerman, the charlady, stirred the fire in the stove, got some water boiling, made the tea, and helped Mr. Mackenzie wrestle out of his two mismatched overcoats and adjust the orange-red wig that had come askew. While Marc stood vigil by the window, she poured two dollops of Jamaican rum into Mackenzie's tea. He drank it down like a parched Bedouin at the last oasis. His fingers trembled as he held out the cup for more.

"Are you going to turn around, young man, so I can see your face and thank you properly?"

Marc obliged. "I'm Ensign Edwards, sir, from the 24th Regiment at Fort York."

"The latter I've been able to deduce, Ensign Edwards," Mackenzie said dryly, thrusting out his ungloved hand. His blue eyes glittered with intelligence and unshakable purpose. Only the cold sweat that glistened on his craggy face indicated the extent of his fright and the shock of its aftermath. "I am Willie Mackenzie."

"I deduced that," Marc said, smiling.

Mackenzie smiled back. "You realize, Ensign, how this will look when the Tory newspapers get hold of the story: radical Reformer saved from a tar-and-feathering he well deserved by one of His Majesty's own house-guards."

"They won't hear about it from me, sir."

Mackenzie eyed him closely. "No, I don't believe they will," he said, and he wiped the sweat from his brow with his sleeve. "Tell me, though, why did you do it? You are unarmed. Those lunatics would have broken your skull as soon as look at you. And I find it difficult to believe that you adhere to many of the sentiments I expressed in the hall tonight."

"I'm a soldier, sir. I know my duty."

Mackenzie smiled again; there was no mockery in it. "This province would be a better place for all of us if every man in it did his duty."

They were interrupted by a commotion outside. Marc opened the door in time to see Hatch at the helm of a cutter drawing up to the jail. Several figures spilled out of it. Sheriff MacLachlan and his two constables pulled a resisting body out of the cutter and began dragging it, kicking and spewing obscenities, across the snow towards the cells at the back of the building.

"Lord in Heaven," Mackenzie said, "that's a woman they're abusing."

"That's no woman," Hatch said, coming up to them and grinning, "that's Mad Annie."

The jail's anteroom was almost as crowded as the hall had been – with constables, combatants itching for a rematch, and assorted well-wishers and town gossip-mongers – but space was quickly made for Magistrate Philander Child and his estate manager cum bodyguard, John Collins, who wore a pistol in his belt. Mad Annie's protestations of innocence could still be heard through the stone partition, like howls under water.

Child went right to the seated Mackenzie. "I am happy to say, sir, that none of your colleagues has been injured, and, even now, they are on their way here to retrieve you."

"And I, sir, am happy to report that I am unscathed, except for the wound to my dignity, which is likely to heal in due course."

Child looked relieved, then said with some vehemence, "I am embarrassed, outraged, and indeed mortified by what happened back there. I am a justice of the peace, and the peace of my jurisdiction was broken tonight in a most reprehensible manner. I realize, sir, that there are those amongst your supporters who will conclude that the attack on them and upon the safety of their leader was instigated by the authorities in Toronto, or that, in the least, they turned a blind eye to it."

"I am not among them," Mackenzie said. "I know who did this, and why."

"I believe that," Child said. An anger he was struggling to contain made his cheeks flame and the pupils of his eyes dilate dangerously. "For my part I do not condone public violence of any kind. My forebears have served as magistrates and squires to every king since Henry the Eighth. One of my grandfathers stood with the Royalists against the Antichrist Cromwell. We have taken pride in meting out justice according to its rules, sparing not even ourselves. Hence, I do not condone the barbaric behaviours of the Orange Order or those acting under its direction. They may profess the same cause I do, but he is neither friend nor ally who perverts my cause by committing outrages in its name."

"Well spoken, sir," Mackenzie said. "And I commend this young ensign here. He has loyalties and a sense of duty as powerful as your own."

Child acknowledged Marc with a slight nod. "I will arrange an escort for you," he said to Mackenzie.

"No need," Mackenzie said, pulling on one of his coats. "I hear my fellows coming for me now."

Outside, several sleighs had drawn into the yard, the largest and nearest one filled with cheering Reform supporters, now armed with sticks and clubs. Some of them sported bandaged heads or slings supporting battered limbs. Mackenzie quickly disappeared into their midst, and they drove off, as cheerful as if they had just won the Battle of Lundy's Lane. In one of the other sleighs, Marc thought he saw Beth.

Behind him, in the smoky, sweaty anteroom, Child had switched from lofty anger to infantile tantrum. "None of this would've happened if that travesty of a woman, that whore of Babylon back there, hadn't primed the crowd with her rotgut liquor and then had the temerity to spew out such malodorous drivel and create the confusion that allowed those maniacs to *waltz in through the front door!*" He fixed the smaller of the two constables with an Old Testament stare.

"My man left his post only to come to my assistance," MacLachlan snapped. "An' we did get the bitch! By God, Child, we got the old harlot in chains after all these years!"

"I say it's time we cleared out the whole rotten mess of them!" Child cried, and he banged on the desk with a fist as heavy as a mace. Mackenzie's teacup shivered.

A dozen heads swivelled and froze. The Magistrate's countenance, governed usually by civility and the courtesy of office, was now swollen with a wrath as venomous as Jehovah's before the sins of Jeroboam. His voice was hollow, sepulchral. "I will take away the remnant of that house as a man taketh away dung."

"Mad Annie's, ya mean," the Sheriff said helpfully.

Child cast his eyes over the motley crowd in the room. "Yes," he said more calmly, but with no lessening of purpose. "I am hereby authorizing a raid on that squatter's pigsty tonight. We'll go in there with guns and torches and purge every last one of that bastard brood!"

Within minutes, the Magistrate's enthusiasm (and legal warrant) had galvanized those in the room and in the courtyard beyond. A tactical plan of action rapidly evolved. A score of stalwarts from the town would be deputized as supernumerary constables. Four sleighs and teams would be officially commandeered. They would leave town at ten o'clock, proceed along the frozen ribbon of Cobourg Creek to the point where it intersected with Crawford Creek in the thick cedar-and-birch bush immediately north of Mad Annie's squattery. From there they would march on snowshoes through the woods to unleash a lightning assault on its unprotected (and unbooby-trapped) rear. With Madame Tarantula in leg irons, the broodlings would panic and scatter. A discreet torch touched here and there, and Mad Annie's seraglio would no longer offend the public eye, ear, or sensibility.

"I've got to go with MacLachlan," Hatch said wearily to Marc. "I'll do my best to see that no one gets hurt out there. Folks are mightily stirred up tonight."

"I'm going back with James," Marc said. "I'm exhausted,

and I've got some hard thinking to do." Pieces of the puzzle were now flinging themselves up faster than he could catch and examine them.

"Good," Hatch said. "The women'll need an escort. We didn't nab a single one of Ogle's loonies, so the woods and back roads could be full of 'em. Thomas is gonna drive the Huggan girls and a couple who live farther west along the highway. You could follow them, if you wouldn't mind."

"What about Winnifred?"

"She's helping Dr. Barnaby with the injured. They're setting up a hospital in the Common School. He'll bring her home, tonight or in the morning."

Emma Durfee was yoo-hooing them from the driver's bench of the cutter. A light snow was beginning to fall.

"By the by," Hatch said, "I do have some happier news."

"Oh?"

"One of the speakers at the rally told me they'd stopped for refreshment at Perry's Corners on the way down, and the constable there had an Irishman in manacles." Hatch laughed. "And one unhappy donkey."

"So how did you persuade Uncle Jabez to let you quit lawyerin' an' head off to military school?" Beth asked.

"I didn't. I persuaded Uncle Frederick and he persuaded Uncle Jabez."

Beth laughed as if she were now part of that happy conspiracy. A snowflake chose the tip of her nose on which to alight, glisten in filigree, and turn invisible. Emma and James Durfee, wrapped together in a single buffalo robe on the driver's seat, were humming an ancient air suited to the occasion and their feelings and letting the Belgians lead them home.

Although still windless, the evening had grown much colder, and the soft, drifting snow gave only an illusion of coziness.

Beth drew the buffalo robe off her shoulders and then did likewise with Marc's. She lifted the separate furs that were shielding their thighs and legs and looped them over one another. Then she leaned in against Marc – shoulder to shoulder, hip to hip – and arranged the upper robes to form a continuous, cozy canopy.

"It's called bundlin'," she explained. (How he loved the teasing lilt of her voice, with its exotic accent.) "You're allowed," she said, "even if your intentions aren't honourable." She placed her fur-capped head on his shoulder. He could feel her breathing.

"You'd still need money to buy a commission, wouldn't you?" she murmured.

"Uncle Frederick helped. He also wrote to Sir John Colborne on my behalf, and paid my passage to Montreal."

"It must be nice to have friends in high places."

"I've been lucky all my life," Marc said, sliding his right arm around her shoulder and drawing her closer. There was no resistance.

"I haven't told you everythin' about Father," she said after awhile, moving only her lips. "I did accept from the very first that you were in earnest an' that you could probably be trusted to keep anythin' I told you to yourself. Still, I couldn't tell you all of it, not then. But when I saw what you did back there at the hall, the last of my doubts vanished."

Marc wanted to speak, but he kept very quiet, and very still.

"So much of what you needed to know was painful to me. I save my weepin' for the dead of night, but it still comes and it still hurts. But so does the not knowing. It's so much like the grief I felt for Jess: not knowing why – really, really why – he went out there an' hanged himself for me to find him. Why didn't he give me a chance to talk him out of it? Why didn't it occur to him that I might've wanted to join him? I felt alone an' betrayed. My love was not enough. An' because I didn't really know, I couldn't grieve the way other widows do – an' there're plenty of them around here. What was worse, my grievin' didn't seem to have any end to it. Every reminder of Jess brought all that pain back instantly. If Joshua hadn't come, if Mr. Child hadn't given us a mortgage, if Elijah hadn't taken on so much of the daily burden, and if dear, sweet Aaron didn't need me to survive, I'd never have made it through the summer."

"You don't *have* to tell me all this," Marc whispered, brushing her hair below her hat with his lips.

"Then Father was killed. And again I had the not knowing. No one at the inquest believed there ever was a mysterious note calling him away. But, of course, I knew things I couldn't say to them, that I'm gonna tell you now. Joshua was *obsessed* with Jess's death. Every ounce of energy left over from helpin' us save the farm was given over to quizzin' me – oh, ever so gently, for he was a kind, kind man – about Jess's last days. He rummaged through every note an' letter Jess ever wrote an' searched the house an' barn for more. After a while I could tell he'd finally quit blamin' me. After that we became truly fond of each other, an' then we both needed to know why. So he went along to the Reform rallies with me to hear an' see for himself what his son had seen an' heard the year before. He knew firsthand from the drought last July what the Clergy Reserves fight was all about, what'd made his son mad an' drove him to choose death over disloyalty. Then, by the end of October, a strange thing had happened."

Marc withdrew his lips.

"Father began to understand an' feel the way his son had, an' then he began to believe in the cause itself. Tory though he was, through an' through, he came slowly to see that the injustices were unthinkingly or callously caused – an' by the very people he so looked up to an' revered as the pillars an' mainstays of the province. An' that they could be cured without the collapse of the state an' the ruination of the worthies in the capital."

"He must have felt the conflict terribly."

"He did. He started neglectin' his friends. Then he started skippin' Wednesdays at the Georgian Club. The day before Christmas he walked over an' told Mr. Child he couldn't come any more."

She had finished. Marc drew her face up to his. She pulled away, reluctantly – or so it seemed to him.

Durfee was about to point the horses north onto the Miller Sideroad when instead he drew them to a sudden halt. "Christ," he said, "the door to the inn's wide open!"

Marc and Durfee leapt from the cutter and rushed into the saloon area of the inn. The door to the inner office hung by one hinge. Durfee found a match, lit a candle, and the two men went in cautiously. The unbreakable safe lay sideways in the middle of the room. Axe marks and dents from a sledge marred every inch of it, the rage and frustration of the perpetrator appallingly evident. In a final fit of frenzy, he had taken his axe to Durfee's desk and cupboard and chopped them to pieces. Papers and spilled ink were everywhere.

"What kinda madman would do a thing like this?" Durfee sighed, leaning against the wall to steady himself.

"Only two men knew what was in that safe," Marc said.

"Connors and O'Hurley?"

"Who else? Except for those Yankee peddlers, only you, me, and Hatch knew the money was here."

Durfee knelt down to the safe, and moments later he withdrew a wad of American banknotes. "Well, they didn't get it, did they?" He riffled through it with some satisfaction.

A slip of paper, not a banknote, fluttered out.

Durfee held the candle while Marc examined the paper. It

was about four by five inches and, judging from the torn edges, had been ripped from a larger document.

"Are you all right, James?" It was Emma, in the taproom.

"Stay out there, ladies. We'll be right out."

"It looks like a list of their customers," Marc said.

"For tinware, or somethin' more potable?"

"Can't tell. All we got here is a list of names. The rest of the sheet is missing."

"That paper looks awfully old."

"True. But the writing is similar to that on a whisky list Hatch and I found out at the cave by Bass Cove."

"Ya don't say. Then it's rum-runnin' we're lookin' at for sure."

Marc did not hear this remark. He was staring at a name near the bottom of the list.

"What is it?" Durfee said.

"There's a J. Smallman listed here. And the name's been crossed out."

"An old list for sure, then. You think young Jesse was involved in this business?"

"I don't know, James. But there is one thing I do know for certain. Everything about the death of his father points to smugglers and their doings. It's been about rum-running all along. I should have seen that before now."

"The keg of liquor Hatch said you found in Jesse's barn?"

"Yes. And there's only one place a fugitive rum-runner could hide without fear of discovery."

"Mad Annie's."

"I've got to get there and find Connors before the Sheriff and his posse flush him out. And when I find him, I'll *thrash* the answers out of him."

"You can't go out there into the bush in *that* costume," Beth said to Marc in the taproom as the men prepared for their mission.

"The lass is right," Emma said. "They'll see you comin' for miles."

"An' there may be shootin'," Beth said.

"I'll pick up my pistol and sabre at the mill," Marc said.

"Come to my place first, then. Jess's clothes'll fit you fine."

Half an hour later Marc and Durfee were on their way up Crawford Creek in the cutter. A fresh team borrowed from Barnaby's place next door moved in sprightly fashion over the powdered snow on the creek ice. Marc was dressed in a coonskin cap, grey ribbed wool sweater, plaid Mackinaw, corduroy breeches, and woodcutter's boots.

Marc thought that, with luck, they might arrive at the junction of the two creeks before the Magistrate and his deputies. What exactly they would do after that Marc had not worked out yet. But Connors held the key to Joshua's death. Marc recalled with a shudder the viciousness of the blow that had been meant to send him to his Maker last Monday night. Connors had even said to O'Hurley, "It's your turn." How naive, and arrogant, he had been in dismissing out of hand a pair of would-be murderers and boasting of where they could find their saddlebag if they had the gumption to come and get it! Well, if he didn't unearth Connors, he'd ride thirty miles to Perry's Corners and have a run at O'Hurley and the donkey.

"They've beat us to the trough!" Durfee cried.

Four sleighs loomed out of the light snow that still descended peacefully, indifferently upon the countryside.

"Welcome to the show, lads!" MacLachlan boomed as they pulled up.

Philander Child was standing beside him on the driver's bench. "All right, gentlemen. Mr. Collins here, who knows these woods well, is going to lead us through to Mad Annie's. The strategy is to fan out and surround the place. Fire your pistols only in the air. I want no one shot. If they are armed and fire back, well, that will be another story. But I doubt that will happen. At heart, these hooligans are cowards and turncoats. They'll run like rabbits into our trap and then fall over each other trying to play innocent and cast blame anywhere but on themselves. They are the dregs of civilization. Let's clean 'em out!"

The deputized lawmen jumped down and began snowshoeing into the woods behind the energetic stepping of Philander Child and his man, John Collins. Durfee and Hatch walked with Marc, offering earnest but contradictory bits of advice on the subtle art of manipulating raquettes. Twenty minutes later, they chuffed up behind the vanguard and peered into the clearing that separated the posse and the wretched cabins of Mad Annie's menagerie.

Marc and Durfee were instructed to follow the Sheriff and several constables to the right, while the others shuffled to the left. They stuck close to the verge of the woods for cover, but little activity was visible in the main cabin ahead or the half dozen huts teetering around it. A pathetic droop of smoke from its chimney indicated a near-dead fire. If the Pringles were expecting trouble, or were wide awake anguishing over the capture of their matriarch, they were doing so quietly. By the same token, no constable or magistrate had ever before come within two hundred yards of the main cabin: the booby-trapped swamp and a general public indifference had kept the Pringles secure for a generation. And, Marc was thinking, what safer haven for a murderer on the run?

The vigilantes spread out silently, then crouched down, awaiting the signal. Five minutes later, John Collins fired his pistol into the air, and each man strode determinedly forward. The only escape route for the besieged would be the frozen swamp to the southeast, and in the dark its leg-hold traps would be as deadly as a bullet in the back.

Several more shots were fired, but the first one had produced the effect the Magistrate was hoping for. Half-dressed or nude figures spilled out of every door and hatch of the several hovels – at first shrieking in blind terror, then scrambling in bewilderment and shock as the ring of armed men marched closer and cried out for their surrender.

In front of Marc a naked male Pringle dropped abjectly to his knees in the snow and proceeded to grovel. "Don't shoot! Don't shoot!" he wailed in the singsong chant of a petrified child. Behind him, a girl not unlike Agnes was darting about in ever-smaller circles, her shift shredded by her own hand, her bare feet pounding the snow, her shrieks piteous and animal-like. It was clear that the Pringles thought they had awakened in the middle of a collective nightmare, with no mother to comfort them.

One of the constables stepped up to the girl and cuffed her smartly on the neck. He grabbed her frail arm and dragged her like a carcass to the periphery, where he pointed a pistol at her head, then returned for another victim.

Marc felt sick to his stomach. He found himself kneeling beside the fellow who had dropped into the snow before him. He might have been fifteen or forty, it was impossible to tell. He was skin and bone, his stare goitred, and his face crawling with scabs and pustules. Fear had turned his pleas into babble. Marc lifted him tenderly up and carried him towards a coop of some sort. He glanced around. It was chaos everywhere: shouts, wails, frantic dashing and collision, sporadic gunfire. Marc opened the hatch to the coop. Animal heat radiated from within.

"Slip in there," he said, "and don't make a sound. You'll be all right."

As he swung back towards the woods, Marc noticed two things: several torches had been lit on the far side of the enclosing circle, and a fully clothed male had just popped out of one of the huts. Agnes came tumbling out naked in his wake. Hatch was beside Agnes in a wink, but Marc was already plodding madly after Connors.

Despite his uncertainty on raquettes, Marc easily gained on Connors, who sank to his knees at every step and quickly exhausted himself. A few feet into the woods, he gasped like a spent horse and slumped down.

A triumphant huzzah rose behind them, and Marc arched around to see what it was all about. One of the chicken coops – not the one concealing the wretch Marc had pardoned – had been set ablaze. The inquisitors were virtuously cheering the conflagration. But something stopped the celebration in its tracks. Even Connors, panting and searching for a curse to fling at the ungrateful gods, looked on, speechless. A dozen hens scrabbled and tottered and attempted flight out of the fireball of their roost, their feathers in flames. Then one by one they fluttered, faltered, and expired, like crepe-paper baubles. The snow hissed at their demise.

The vigilantes stared, awed by the consequence of their own righteousness. Without a word or sign they doused their torches. There would be no more burning. To men for whom the erection even of a log cabin in the bush represented the triumph of the will over a cruel and dispassionate Nature, the deliberate destruction of any beast nurtured by his care and sweat was deeply reprehensible. Philander Child did nothing to urge them further. Three or four of the better-fed Pringles took advantage of the lull and slipped into the bush.

Connors had gotten back to his feet but was still too weary to skulk anywhere. His face was obscenely bloated. He was hatless. His flies flopped open. All the bravado had gone out of him. He stared at the pistol in Marc's belt and the sabre in its scabbard, then looked directly into Marc's eyes. Suddenly he paled and threw both hands in the air.

"Don't shoot me," he rasped. "I wasn't gonna kill ya, honest."

"Your partner was in Stebbins's barn, wasn't he?" Marc said, one hand on the pistol butt.

"We only took the horse's shoe off, I swear to God! He stepped on that nail by himself. Stebbins didn't want ya trackin' us here." Connors took one step towards Marc, bringing his hands down slowly as he did so but holding them well away from his body, as if readying them for the manacles.

So, Connors, O'Hurley, and Stebbins had conspired to keep him from leaving the farm that night. And Lydia had ensured that he was nicely distracted for the duration. What an ass he had made of himself!

"I'm taking you in to jail," Marc said with deep satisfaction.

There was a sharp report and Connors' face widened with astonishment. He opened his mouth to speak, but a bubble of blood flicked out. Then he pitched forward into the snow.

"Jesus!" Hatch cried just behind Marc.

They both turned to see John Collins, pale as a ghost, standing a few yards away at the edge of the woods with a smoking pistol in his right hand.

"I didn't mean to kill him," he stammered. "I thought he was pointin' a gun at you."

"It's all right, John," Hatch said. "You probably saved us the cost of a rope."

Marc had already turned Connors over. Blood was leaping out of a hole in his chest. His eyes were still open. They stared up at Marc in mute appeal. "Father, give me the sacrament . . . please."

"I'm not a priest," Marc said, pressing his fur cap uselessly into the spouting wound.

"I've a confession to make." Connors's voice was a desperate whisper. "Please. I can't go out like this."

Marc leaned closer. "I'm not your confessor, Mr. Connors."

"I killed a man."

Hatch was now at Marc's side.

Blood surged out of Connors's mouth. He choked, coughed, gasped in pain.

"Who did you kill?" Marc said, willing the villain to speak.

The voice was less than a whisper now. "Smallman."

Marc's heart jumped in his chest. He tried to quell the foolish elation, the almost childish sense of triumph rippling through him.

"Joshua?" he said, and waited.

The final two syllables uttered by Ninian T. Connors in this life were crystal clear:

"Jes-se."

CHAPTER THIRTEEN

Marc showed Erastus Hatch the list of names on the torn document he had found in Durfee's office. Both men were exhausted, but too much had happened for either of them to entertain the possibility of sleep. The miller's house at midnight was quiet and growing cold. The women were home and safely in bed. Mad Annie and five of her offspring were gracing the cells of the district jail. The cadaver of Ninian T. Connors had been wrapped in a horse blanket and carted off to Cobourg.

"I've seen plenty of lists like this over the years," Hatch said. "Could be customers or potential retailers for the rum. This is definitely an old list: Jesse's name must've been crossed off after he was . . . murdered." Hatch stifled a yawn. "Still, I'd feel a lot better if we had the missing half of this paper. A string of names isn't much in the way of proof."

Marc sighed. "True. Which leaves us with a confessed murderer but no clear or provable motive."

"We have to figure it had something to do with a falling-out over the smuggling business."

"Whatever the exact motive, it's conceivable that Joshua

found something among Jesse's papers, either about the rum-running or perhaps even the apparent suicide, and tried to confront Connors or one of his cronies."

"There's still O'Hurley," Hatch said between yawns. "He may be the only one alive who can tell us what really happened in that barn a year ago."

"I've got to tell Beth, of course. The one good thing to come out of all this so far is that her husband did not take his own life. You can't imagine the relief it'll be to her."

"She'll have to know something about the ugly circumstances, though."

Marc sighed again. "I know."

"Anyways, O'Hurley should be safe under lock and key. MacLachlan's sending a courier up to Perry's Corners and another to Toronto. In fact, there'll be couriers galloping up and down the province all night."

"Well, sir, I'm too tired to think straight," Marc said, getting up.

"I quit *thinking* an hour ago," Hatch replied.

Marc had willed himself to wake at dawn, and he almost did so. Certainly it was no later than seven o'clock when he slipped into Jesse's clothes and padded out to the main room. Mary had the stove going and was humming some Gaelic ditty. In the hearth in the parlour, a fire was starting to warm the air.

"We're to let the mistress stay abed," Mary said. "She worked her fingers to the bone at the hospital. And such a ruckus, eh, among Christian men who oughta know better." The apostasy of Christian males did little to dampen the girl's spirits, as she resumed her ditty with scarcely a missed beat.

Just as Marc finished a hasty meal of bread and cheese, Hatch opened the front door and came in. He set down an armful of parcels on the writing table and brushed the snow off his coat. He and Mary exchanged glances, the latter blushing nicely.

"I got some unsettling news," he said to Marc. "Durfee tells me one of the couriers sent back in the night from Perry's Corners reported that O'Hurley got away."

"Damn!"

Mary giggled.

"It seems his jailer got overly interested in some of O'Hurley's liquid wares. O'Hurley got clean away. But he left the donkey behind."

"They'll never get him," Marc said. "He'll be in Lewiston by noon."

"There's worse news," Hatch said, with a very unserious twinkle in his eye. "Durfee says MacLachlan's constables come riding up at daybreak and rousted him out of his wife's arms to tell him that Mad Annie and her litter broke out of the escape-proof jail."

"I wish them well," Marc said.

"You heading over to Beth's?"

"Right away."

"But it's the Sabbath, she'll –"

"I don't want any of this news to reach her before I do."

"Didn't see any smoke up that way."

Marc pulled on Jesse's Mackinaw and the fur cap, still encrusted with Connors's blood. "I'll be back soon. We both have a lot of deep thinking to do." He paused at the writing table. "What are these parcels?"

"The big ones are clothing for the Hislop children. Winnifred collected them at the church yesterday. She's going to drive the cutter out to Buffaloville after the service this morning to deliver them. The others are letters for some of the folks out that way. Durfee gets Winnifred to take them along whenever she can."

Marc was staring, incredulous, at one of the letters. It was addressed to Miss Lydia Connors, Crawford's Corners, Upper Canada.

"Lydia Stebbins . . . is a Connors?"

Hatch's face lit up, then turned a slow, rosy red. "By God, that's right. I remember Winnie telling me something about that last year, but as usual I was only half paying attention. Something about Lydia's mother down in Buffalo refusing to admit the girl had gone and married a fool like Stebbins."

Without a thank-you or farewell, Marc whirled and left the house.

He ran along the path beside the creek and into the rear of the Smallman farm. No one was up or about. Several cows were lowing, as if in distress. Elijah's cabin was sealed and smokeless. Marc hurried by and, rapping once on the summer-kitchen door to announce his arrival, he stumbled inside.

At the door to the big room stood Aaron, surprised and still rubbing sleep out of his eyes. The house was as cold as a tomb.

Ten minutes later Beth emerged in a nightshirt and shawl. Her eyes were wide with expectation. Marc had seized the opportunity to change back into his uniform, which Beth had brushed and laid out for him.

"It's all right, I've brought good news," he said immediately to quell the rising anxiety in her face.

"Then we'll have time to make a fire an' have a decent cup of tea."

After the tea had been poured, and Aaron had left to split wood in the summer kitchen, Marc sat down beside Beth and tactfully recounted the remarkable events of the evening past.

"Murdered?" she whispered, as if the word itself were tantamount to the deed. "But I saw him there in the barn – alone.

I'd watched him grow more troubled an' heartsick every day. No one, not even me, thought it was anythin' other than what it seemed to be."

"I understand. You hadn't the slightest cause to think anyone would want to murder your husband. But Hatch and I heard a dying man's confession. He mistook me for his priest, remember. There can be no doubt about it. And when we find O'Hurley, we'll know all the facts."

Beth said nothing for a long time. Marc watched her intently, wanting so much to lay a comforting hand over hers, but knowing there were more questions to come, brutal ones that had to be answered.

It was Beth who finally reached out and folded both of his hands in hers. "You don't know what solace you've brought me this mornin'." Her eyes filled with tears. "I can get on with my grievin' for Jess now." She squeezed his hands fiercely, but he knew the passion in the gesture was not meant for him. "An' then maybe I'll be able to get on with my own life." A fresh thought seemed to strike her. "I'm only twenty-three years old."

Marc went over to the fireplace and poured more hot water into the teapot. He gave Aaron a salute through the open doorway, and walked back to Beth.

"I think I know why Jesse was murdered," he said. "And it may also help me to find your father-in-law's killer."

She looked up politely, her mind elsewhere.

"You *will* need to know why, won't you?" Marc said.

"Yes. I think I will."

"It may be painful."

She smiled ruefully. "I'm growin' used to that."

"I'm convinced that Jesse had some kind of dealings with his murderer in the weeks before his death. We know that Connors and O'Hurley were peddlers of rum and possibly other contraband from New York State. We found Jesse's name on what we're assuming to be one of their lists."

Seizing on the word *assume*, she said, "Could there be some mistake?"

Marc placed his hand very lightly upon her wrist and looked straight into her eyes. "Please tell me: could Jesse, in his desperation to save the farm and show his father he could make it on his own, have thrown in with smugglers to get the money he needed to keep up the mortgage?"

Beth did not turn away, but she dropped her eyes as she said, "Yes."

"Did you suspect anything like that at the time?"

"Only that he started behavin' rather odd, comin' an' goin' at all hours. He told me he was doin' carpentry work out on the Pringle Sideroad. I asked him about the cask in the barn, and he said Hislop or somebody'd given it to him as payment for a corncrib he built. But why would they want to murder him over a bit of smuggled rum?"

"I'm not sure they did."

"What do you mean?"

"I was told on Wednesday evening that sometimes these peddlers are used as couriers and go-betweens for seditious activities. A secret society called the Hunters' Lodges may have been imported here from the United States, with a view to providing support for Mackenzie's more radical proposals, maybe even insurrection or an invasion in aid of one."

"That's just talk," Beth said. "I've heard nonsense like that for years. Nobody really believes it. You heard what Mr. Mackenzie said at the end of his speech last night."

"If Jesse were even toying with the notion of linking up with these lodges, he could have learned vital and dangerous information. He may even have discovered it inadvertently while participating in rum-running, since the two activities are often combined."

"How long have you been listenin'?" Beth was staring anxiously at Aaron, who was standing by the woodbox with an armful of split logs.

"I just co-co-come in," he said, dropping the wood helter-skelter at his feet.

Beth looked relieved. "It's all right, Aaron. I'm not mad at you."

Marc suddenly had an idea. "Did anyone question Aaron about the night of Joshua's death?"

Beth grimaced. "MacLachlan an' Mr. Hatch, both of 'em – in my presence. He was out back for a few minutes an' saw Father walkin' past towards the front of the house. He saw no one else."

Marc looked at Aaron, who was following the conversation closely. "Son," he said, "would you think back to the night when Mr. Smallman rode out into the blizzard?"

"I reme-me-member," Aaron said.

Beth couldn't bear to see her brother distressed. She turned to Marc. "Please –"

"I've got to," Marc said. "Think carefully, Aaron. When you saw Mr. Smallman pass you on his way from the barn to the front door of the house, was he carrying anything in his hand or did you see anything sticking out of his pockets?"

Aaron smiled and said without hesitation, "He had a le-letter."

Aaron stood placidly amidst the scattered wood, but Beth leapt up. "Why didn't you tell that to Mr. Hatch?" she said as gently as she could.

"He di-di-didn't ask me."

"Don't you see what this means, Beth?" Marc said as soon as they were alone. "You were right all along. There *was* a written message calling him out there on some pretext. It *was* a rendezvous. There *was* foul play. And we *must* pursue his killer until we find him!"

"Calm yourself. You'll have a fit."

"I'm having more than that! I know who killed Joshua."

Beth's face betrayed her skepticism. "You do?"

"First of all, the motive behind the murder was Joshua somehow discovering among Jesse's effects evidence related to his dealings with Connors and O'Hurley. You said last night that Joshua became obsessed with Jesse's suicide. He may have deduced that Jesse was rum-running. He could have bumped into Connors anywhere about here last fall. He might have learned, from Winnifred or Durfee, that Mrs. Stebbins was Connors's sister and –"

"What?"

"When I left the mill," Marc said breathlessly, his heart racing as fast as his mind, "I saw a letter from Lydia Stebbins's mother in Buffalo: it was addressed to Lydia *Connors*."

"She was a *Connors*?"

"That's right. And her father was a bigwig in the Loco Foco wing of the Democratic Party, a group of fanatics who hate centralized government and big banks and go about rattling sabres everywhere. The Hunters' Lodges could easily be an offshoot. And Connors's mate O'Hurley was hiding out at Stebbins's place the day I went there. He hobbled my horse so I couldn't trail Stebbins to some secret meeting out past Mad Annie's."

Beth leaned back, a bit overwhelmed by Marc's fervid narrative. "But I heard he's a gambler an' dicer," she offered.

"He tells his wife and everybody else he's going *hunting*!"

"Most of the farmers hunt –"

"Don't you see, *hunting* is the code word. And he's never come back with a deer that anybody's actually seen. Gambling at Mad Annie's was just another cover story, like the hunting. Somewhere out in the bush there were secret and dangerous meetings going on."

"But how did Father –?"

"Joshua would've found out from you that Jesse was out in Buffaloville doing carpentry work most of the summer and fall before he died. My hunch is that your father went out to Stebbins's place to confront him with whatever he thought he knew. Remember that Joshua must've had mainly suspicions at this point. If he had had hard evidence, he would have gone immediately to Philander Child with it."

"Come to think of it," Beth said, "Father did go out that way – once – sometime in October, to look at some pigs."

Marc scarcely heard. "As it was, he was probably relying on surprise and conviction. We'll likely never know exactly what Joshua thought he knew: whether it was suspicion that Jesse was a rum-runner whose death could have been linked to those outlaws, or something more sinister, like secret societies and vendettas against turncoats."

"Turncoats?"

"Well, if Jesse joined the Hunters even nominally and then got cold feet, they would have considered him to be a turncoat. In that case, either Connors forced him to hang himself, or he and O'Hurley did it for him."

Beth shuddered. "So you're sayin' that if Connors didn't kill father, then Stebbins did?"

"It could have been any one of the Hunters," Marc said. "Stebbins no doubt denied all the accusations, and, without proof, being an honourable man, Joshua told no one for the moment. But I'm certain he had not given up. Nevertheless, the wind was up among the conspirators. My guess is that on New Year's Eve one of their lesser lights delivered a message to Joshua. The bait would have been information related to Jesse's death. It might well have hinted that somebody knew something to suggest it had not been suicide after all. That would have drawn your father out in a blizzard on any night. It would also have sealed his own silence in the interim. Likely he was instructed to tear up the note and scatter the pieces, or his killer callously came down from the cave and removed it."

Beth was having difficulty with the pace and fever of Marc's monologue as well as with what he was saying. For a moment she had an image of this man in the thick of some battle, eyes ablaze, sword raised in righteousness. "But Azel an' Jess were good friends," she said. "We went to rallies together."

"Not everyone is what he seems," Marc said, and the sudden deflation of his voice and demeanour caused her to glance at him in alarm.

Marc took a deep breath. "I should have told you this right at the outset," he said quietly. "You must believe me when I say it was not because I mistrusted you. I trusted you right away, and I've had no cause to regret it."

"What is it?" Beth appeared incapable of bracing herself for more news, good or bad.

"I didn't want to tell you unless it became a necessary part of the investigation. I think now that it is." After the briefest of pauses he said, "Joshua Smallman was a commissioned informant for Sir John Colborne. He sent back monthly reports on suspected incendiaries in this district."

Beth sighed, not with disappointment but relief. "I've known all along."

"You have!"

"Oh, he never told me. But I knew all the same."

"But you took him to Reform rallies, to party meetings!"

"I told you that first day: he was the most honourable an' decent man I ever met." Something in her glance intimated that she could easily have added "until now." "You see, I knew he would report the truth. An' the truth's always been that the farmers of this township are simply fightin' for their rights an' their livelihood by electin' members who'll represent their interests. It's not been *us* who've twisted the laws for our own ends."

Marc wisely refrained from mentioning contraband rum and bat-wielding rallymen. "I've got the last report he ever wrote in my saddlebag," Marc said. "When you get to read it, you'll see that your faith in him was justified."

"But why is this important now?"

"If the Hunters, or whoever they really are, suspected your father was an informant or even a personal friend of Sir John's, they would be even *more* desperate to silence him, and to do it quickly."

Beth took that in. Then she said, "But what are you goin' to do about Stebbins? You've got no more proof than Father had."

"Maybe not – not until we run O'Hurley to ground anyway. But I don't intend to wait for that to happen. If Stebbins himself didn't kill your father-in-law, then he knows who did. The answers lie somewhere in Buffaloville. And, Sabbath or not, I'm riding out there as soon as I can get the horse saddled. I'm going to shake the truth out of that conniving weasel and then haul him before the Magistrate!"

At the door Beth said, "Be careful. There's been too much death around here lately."

Marc had just finished saddling the Colonel's horse – which showed no sign of lameness, thanks to a temporary shoe and the ministrations of Thomas Goodall – when Hatch came puffing up to him. He had a piece of paper in his hand, but before he could comment on it, Marc launched into a sustained narrative of his theory of the murders of Jesse and Joshua Smallman. Thomas and Erastus stood wide-eyed and open-mouthed.

"So you see," Marc concluded his tale, "it's been about rum *and* politics all along. I'm going to tell Stebbins that you and I witnessed Connors's deathbed confession, and that he admitted to Jesse's murder and complicity in Joshua's. That ought to shake him up!"

"My God, but you're a devious fellow for one so young." Hatch laughed. "I reckon you'll be pleased then to see what I've dug up for you." He held out the quarto-sized sheet of paper he had brought with him.

"What's that?"

"All this talk about smuggling reminded me of one of them lists we found back in December. In fact, it's the one we mentioned to you Wednesday night. I took it from Isaac Duffy before we packed him off to Kingston for smuggling. This one's got names, places, and the kind and amount of booze as well. It was enough to nail the bugger in court."

Marc was scrutinizing the information. It covered the full page. Under headings for "Rum: Jamaican" and "Bourbon: Charleston" appeared lists of names and what seemed to be townships or locales.

"It's J. Smallman again," Hatch prompted, with evident satisfaction. "And it's been crossed out – real faint, mind you, but crossed out just the same. We saw it there in December, but with Jesse dead a year, I paid it no heed."

When Marc continued to pore silently over the document, Hatch decided to press on unaided. "Don't you see, lad? Jesse was definitely up to his ears in this sordid business. And Joshua found out! There's the connection we've been looking for, eh?"

Marc was staring, transfixed, at the heading under which "J. Smallman, Crawford's Cnrs. – 6 casks" had been set and then very lightly crossed out: "Hunting Sherry." The word *hunting* had been underlined. And the two names just below it were Nathaniel Boyle and Jefferson Boyle, the Yankee smugglers Hatch and Child had driven from the county.

Every ounce of blood drained from Marc's face. "My God," he whispered. "This is the second list I've seen with J. Smallman on it. I've had it wrong from the beginning."

"Had *what* wrong?" Hatch said.

"Thomas, do you know Elijah's last name?"

Goodall, who was unused to being abruptly included in an ongoing conversation, was caught off guard by the question, but he managed to give Marc an answer that shocked even the imperturbable Hatch.

"Where're you off to?" the bewildered miller said, watching Marc climb slowly onto his horse as if in a trance.

"To flush out a murderer," Marc said.

CHAPTER FOURTEEN

Marc's first stop was Elijah's cabin. He knew that he would not find the hired man in it, now or ever. He also had a pretty good idea where the old devil would turn up. But for the moment, it was the contents of the cabin itself he needed to examine, something he should have done long before this.

The door opened easily enough. The signs of a hasty departure were everywhere, and it was such haste that Marc was counting on. The table had been cleared of the incriminating newspapers with their religiously underlined accounts of the radical activities in the Cobourg area and beyond. Marc now knew the real reason why they had been singled out, and again chastised himself for having missed the obvious on his first visit here. But the clutter of spilled tobacco, broken quill pens, and pieces of clay pipe remained just as he had noticed them earlier in the week. In less than a minute he had found what he was looking for.

Not wishing to disturb Beth again (it didn't appear as if she were going to ride into Cobourg to church with the Durfees),

Marc walked the horse back to the path beside the creek, rode down to the mill and then across the road into the bush that surrounded Deer Park estate. He would have to walk the last few yards, as he intended to approach the grand house from the rear. It was the Magistrate's cook he had to see next.

Marc left Ruby Marsden in tears, but Philander Child's servant had told him what he needed to know, breaking down rapidly under his quick and intimidating interrogation. He walked around the stone house from the servants' quarters to the porticoed entrance at the front with the confident stride of a young man who has the truth in his pocket.

Squire Child's cutter stood beside the porch. As Marc strode up to it, the great man himself came down the steps and boomed a hearty "Good morning" to the sleigh's driver.

"Off to church, are you?" Marc said, coming up.

"Do you wish to ride with me?" Child said, unconcerned, friendly as ever.

"I wish to talk to you in the privacy of your study, sir, about a matter of some importance."

"Indeed?" Child showed only mild suspicion. "But you can see, young fellow, I am about to set off for St. Peter's."

"The service will have to wait, then."

Child, who had taken one step up into the cutter, halted. He turned a severe face towards the rudeness offered him, the kind he had occasion to practise often on the bench and at the quarter sessions, where his unappealable decisions could make or break a man and his family. "I beg your pardon?" The driver had dropped the reins and was looking on with amazed interest.

"I wish to speak to you, alone and immediately, about the death of Joshua Smallman. I know who killed him."

Child blinked once. "Well, then, we had better find a warm place to sit."

Coggins was haled from his mid-morning nap to stir the fire and coax coffee out of a distraught cook. When he closed the door of the study discreetly behind him, Child poured out two snifters of brandy next to the coffee cups and raised his glass to Marc.

"To the truth," he said. Then, "Well, don't give me a long rigmarole about it, tell me what it is you have to say to me about poor Joshua's accident that's important enough to keep me from the Reverend Sinclair's sermon."

"Murder, sir. Joshua Smallman, like his son, was murdered."

"Yes, Hatch told me about Connors's confession. Puzzling business, that, but I've sat on the bench for twenty years and I still can't fathom the serpentine convolutions of the criminal mind."

"Joshua Smallman was also murdered," Marc persisted and, eyeing Child intently, added, "by you."

Child's coffee cup paused almost imperceptibly, then continued up to his lips. He sipped contemplatively. His brows arched as he said, "Me? Well, then, it's *quite* a tale you have to tell me." He eased his bulk back into the leather folds of his chair. "If you don't mind, I'll just sit here and listen. It's one of the things I do best."

Marc was somewhat nonplussed at the calm response he was getting, but then he realized he had not laid out any of the pieces of the puzzle that, with Ruby's admission and what he had found in Elijah's cabin, now formed a complete pattern in his mind.

"The tale, as you like to call it, begins with motive. I surmised long before I arrived here that I would have to discover the motive for Joshua's murder before anything else could come clear. I have already explained to you, on Wednesday evening, how I thought the killing took place that night –"

"And a plausible bit of deduction that was. Though highly improbable. But I interrupt – please continue."

"You decided that Joshua must be killed because you concluded he was a turncoat and because his death would be personally convenient and profitable to you."

Child smiled. "The man was a Tory. When he cut himself he bled blue."

"Quite so. When he came back to Crawford's Corners, you took him into the Georgian Club. You attended the same church. You became his solicitor. More than that, you had already taken an interest in the property of his son and daughter-in-law. You arranged a mortgage on their farm for them so they could build a barn, buy cattle, and diversify, likely using your contacts with the Bank of Upper Canada, which routinely refuses loans to impecunious farmers."

"You've learned a lot about us in eight short months."

"Not enough, I fear. But I suspect you coveted Jess's farm because it borders on the Clergy Reserves section. Given your status and influence with those in high places, you planned to purchase that protected property, a very valuable piece of real estate that would eventually yield a handsome profit."

"It is not against the law to make a profit."

"But you knew that Jesse Smallman was not likely to make a go of his farm –"

"Then why would I be foolish enough to bail him out with a mortgage?"

"You had to get him in deep enough to ensure his complete financial failure, and to have the land revert to you as the mortgage holder. You must have been pleased when he took his own life, as you and everyone else thought at the time."

"It wasn't I who manufactured the drought. Nor did I sit in the Legislature that enacted the Clergy Reserves statute. Even so, I fail to see what this putative bit of melodrama has to do with Jesse's father or cold-blooded murder."

"Following Jesse's death, Joshua Smallman surprised himself and you by packing up and leaving Toronto to come to the aid of his daughter-in-law. He paid off the mortgage, thwarting your designs on the property. Still, with the drought and no government action on the Clergy Reserves, the farm remained a doubtful prospect for the Smallmans. I believe you befriended Joshua not only because he was a conservative businessman but because you hoped you might persuade him to give the farm up as a losing proposition and take his in-laws back to Toronto or over to Cobourg."

"You are employing a surfeit of 'suspectings' and 'believings,' are you not?"

Child appeared to be enjoying himself. Certainly Marc could see no sign that his mounting assault was having any disquieting impact on the Magistrate.

"I also *suspect*," Child continued with a smile, "that you eliminated me as murderer because I happened to have spent New Year's Eve from eight o'clock till two in the morning in this very room with a score of the district's most law-abiding citizens. But do continue. I'm eager to hear how I killed a man I admired while I was several miles from the site."

Marc took a deep breath. "I believe you watched with growing unease as Joshua Smallman began to attend Reform rallies with his daughter-in-law, ostensibly as her chaperone. Every Wednesday evening you and your Tory acquaintances talked a bit of politics between bouts of whist, and it became apparent that the Reform propaganda was having a serious effect on Joshua. I imagine he nodded his head in assent less and less as the summer wore on. I'll wager he began to stay on after the others had left to voice his concerns to a man of some power and authority in the district, and indirectly in the councils of the Family Compact in the capital. He would have been discreet at first, ambivalent even, not knowing himself what was happening to him. I think he found it nearly impossible to accept the dawning truth that the Tories themselves were ultimately responsible for the economic mess the province was falling into, and not the rebellious farmers with their legitimate grievances."

"You can't be a true believer without periods of doubt," Child said.

"But *was* Joshua Smallman still a true believer? That was the question that tormented you. Beth has told me that her father-in-law started missing the Wednesday soirees in the fall. By early December you two had had a serious falling out. All your subtle attempts to persuade him to sell the farm had failed. Moreover, Joshua's increasing sympathy for the Reform cause seemed to guarantee that he would never sell his son's land – as a matter of principle. I suggest that you quarrelled openly after the others had gone one evening. He may have hinted to you that his own son might have been driven to break the law, and later to take his own life, by the injustices inflicted upon him. However he worded his withdrawal on that day, he left you with the shattering conclusion that he had turned Reformer."

"Good reason for losing a friend, I should think, but hardly provocation for murder." Child poured himself another brandy. The man seemed to be pleased that this droll young ensign had provided him with a ready excuse to miss the scourge of an Anglican sermon.

"Agreed. But it is one thing to turn one's political colours – many gentlemen have done so in the mother Parliament – and quite another when those colours belong to a nation."

"As our own United Empire Loyalists did in the eyes of the American revolutionaries?"

"I'm talking about treasonous activity, sedition, casting your lot in with your own country's enemies."

"You are not implying that Joshua Smallman was a traitor, a turncoat?"

"No, but I know for a fact that you yourself thought so."

"Indeed. Do you read minds in addition to your military duties?"

"Just before Christmas, Constable Hatch apprehended a peddler named Isaac Duffy and brought him promptly to you. You soon discovered he was up to his Yankee eyebrows in rum-running. On the document Hatch had removed from him, you caught sight of the names of a couple of notorious villains you'd been trying for years to get evidence against: Jefferson and Nathaniel Boyle. The two of you rode straight out to their farms, but they'd already fled back to the States or gone into deep hiding."

"I fail to see where this is going," Child said, but he made no move to rise.

"You took special note of their names, but you also took note of the name just below the Boyles' on that incriminating document: J. Smallman. A very faint line had been drawn through it, so faint that Hatch only noticed it this morning upon close examination. Since the list seemed to be a current one, *you* assumed that the 'J' referred to Joshua. Hatch assumed it was Jesse and ignored it: what good would it do to speak ill of the dead? But you were so shocked you said nothing. Instead, you went along with Hatch in search of the Boyles. But you couldn't get it out of your mind that Joshua Smallman's name was listed under the words 'Hunting Sherry.' You likely knew from your own sources at Government House that there were serious allegations being made concerning the existence and operations of an insurrectionist group of American immigrants calling themselves the Hunters' Lodges – even though you showed only nominal interest in the subject on Wednesday evening. To you, it fitted the pattern you had observed in Joshua's life over the preceding months." Marc leaned forward in his chair. "I submit, sir, that by Christmas Day you had reached the sad conclusion that Joshua Smallman, in his grief over his son's horrific death and the bitterness he felt at the collapse of his lifelong beliefs, had gone over to the enemy and that, using the smuggling operation as a cover, he was actively supporting the Hunters." Marc practically hissed the next sentence. "And you yourself said to me in this very room that the people you despised most in the world were smugglers and traitors."

"It sounds as though you're well into the second act of this tawdry little tragicomedy," Child said affably. "Or should it be called a fairy tale?"

Marc ignored the jibe. "When you gave that heartfelt speech in front of Mr. Mackenzie last night, I realized just how fanatically you felt about loyalty and about playing by the rules. Your family has served eight or nine kings through thick and thin, dispensing justice and upholding laws even when they didn't agree with them. You can't be half a patriot any more than you can be half human."

"This is not even news, let alone evidence."

"I also got a glimpse into the depth and vindictiveness of your temper when, after tolerating the peccadilloes of Mad Annie for years, you incited a herd of vigilantes to burn her out. It's also possible that you got wind of Connors and O'Hurley operating hereabouts again. It wouldn't do to have one of them blabbing on about Joshua's involvement in smuggling – raising questions you wanted left alone – so you decided to eradicate the whole lot of them at one fell swoop, despite the dubious legality of the operation."

Child looked abruptly up at Marc, held his eye, and said, "I imagine murder might be viewed in some circles as legally dubious."

"Yes, surely. But not when it comes to the treatment of seditionists or spies, not in circumstances where authority feels itself besieged or in a state of apprehended insurrection. The unobtrusive removal of a dangerous turncoat becomes a kind of noble service to the state, to be sanctioned – lauded even – after the event, should it ever become public knowledge. And when that 'noble' act eliminated a man who stood in the way of your gaining his property, then it was doubly serendipitous."

"You seem to have forgotten that Mrs. Smallman would inherit her father-in-law's estate. If so, why would she sell, eh?"

"But I have not forgotten that you were the man's solicitor. You knew he had no will, and that there were possibly relatives in the States with a claim on the estate."

"The chances of finding them would be slim."

"True, but as a lawyer, you knew you could delay the probate until Beth Smallman was forced to sell her farm – to you."

Child smiled cryptically, poured himself another brandy, and said, "Why did you ever abandon the bar, young man?"

"Words are no substitute for action."

"Agreed. Well, you've established a plausible motive for me, but I must say that I'm still unable to envision my leading a friend-turned-enemy into a deadfall trap while sitting in this chair sipping brandy, much as I am now. Did I have a three-mile-long piece of string to trigger the trap or a siren song only poor Joshua could hear?"

Like the accomplished barristers he had seen in high flight at the Old Bailey, Marc decided it was time to prick the complacency of the witness in the box by playing the first of his trump cards. "I have just come from interviewing Miss Marsden. It didn't take long for her to break down and admit that she lied to the Sheriff when she swore that Elijah Chown spent the whole of New Year's Eve with her."

A corner of Child's left eye twitched once – that was all. "You had no authority to trespass on my property and intimidate my servant," he said, but it seemed more a *pro forma* objection than righteous umbrage.

"I have Sir John's warrant authorizing this investigation, along with his detailed memorandum of instructions," Marc said, tapping the pocket of his frock coat. "And when Miss Marsden saw the Governor's seal, she soon decided to tell me the truth."

"If that is so, then I advise you to interrogate Elijah, not me. I fail to perceive what motive that deranged soul might have had to waylay and murder the man he worked for, whose daughter-in-law he protected as if she were his own child. In any case, Elijah is no concern of mine."

"Ah, but he is. He is in every way *your* man. It was you who brought him here from Toronto, ostensibly to help Jesse and Beth to survive on their farm."

"Indeed it was. He was the relative of a friend in the capital, addled but good-hearted, and knowledgeable in farming here. It was an arrangement that suited everyone involved."

"And I have no doubt that your motives were less than altruistic. You needed someone you could control close to that scene, and such a gesture would be sure to disguise your true motive. And if need be, Elijah could be persuaded to be *unhelpful*."

"You are inordinately cynical for so young and inexperienced a gentleman. But remember, when Jesse couldn't pay

Elijah's wages, I did so," Child said with serene detachment. "That is, until Beth found out. When Joshua came, she was able to pay the man properly."

"Yes, and by then Elijah had become attached to Mrs. Smallman. But when you needed to, you made sure he realized where his loyalties lay. He owed his living to you. He took a shine to your cook. He spent more and more of his free time over here. Furthermore, I'm certain you have some more tenacious or threatening hold over him, something so compelling that he would do your bidding even if it entailed murdering Beth's father-in-law."

"And precisely how were such an improbable duo able to execute a scheme to assassinate a harmless dry goods merchant?" Child was looking relaxed and bemused again. No hint of a twitch. "Your fantasies are far more entertaining than Holy Communion at St. Peter's."

"I can only speculate on the details, but from the evidence available, I've been able to set your scheme reliably in outline. What I surmise happened that night was this. You decided that Joshua must be confronted and your suspicions put to him – man to man. Even if he could successfully dispute them, you likely intended to pressure him into selling the farm to you by threatening to ruin his reputation with vicious innuendo. After all, he couldn't *prove* that the 'J. Smallman' on the smugglers' list you confiscated was not him."

"But why then did I not merely summon him here into my magisterial presence and have it out in this very room?"

"You did not do so because you had already determined that if he could *not* satisfy you of his innocence of sedition, you would execute him on behalf of the Crown – for its sake and to satisfy your own greed. That is why the double motive here and the explosive nature of your character are so relevant. For you, nothing could absolve a turncoat or exculpate a Guy

Fawkes with a grenade in his fist. And your lust for land and status is without bounds."

"And this Elijah chap is supposed to have joined me in my murderous crusade. Just like that?"

"I think you decided to confront Joshua in a secluded spot, interrogate him, and then, if necessary, have Elijah dispatch him – out where no one would think to look. Oh, they'd find his horse, all right, miles from the deadfall, but I believe the body would have been dragged along the lake ice and dumped into the snow half a township away. The bears and wolves would scatter the bones. They might never have been found, or identified."

"You do have a florid imagination. You should take up novel writing: the three-volume Gothic variety."

"As it turned out, you didn't need to do any of that. Elijah established his alibi with your besotted cook, then slipped out and rode one of your horses to the smugglers' cave at Bass Cove, a place you'd likely heard about from Durfee or one of the other longtime residents of the area. His instructions were to wait there for Joshua's arrival, and then to keep him there, by force if necessary, until you came yourself to begin the inquisition. Elijah may appear old and addled, but he's neither. He's a muscular farmhand who can and does read. A knife or pitchfork would be all the weapon required to intimidate the older and weaker man."

"I was in this room until two hours past midnight."

"I'm sure you were, with many worthies to testify so. Your plan was to make some plausible excuse to retire early – a touch of indigestion perhaps – and then sneak out and ride undetected up the lakeshore to the cove at the foot of the ridge. But you did not have to. When you 'stepped out for some air,' say, around ten o'clock, Elijah himself was waiting for you in the stables. He told you that Joshua Smallman had indeed been lured out to Bass Cove but had never reached the cave. The God who anoints and protects monarchs had steered the turn-coat into a deadfall trap meant for deer or bear, and thus meted out His own brand of retribution. And that's most likely how you viewed what happened out there, though I strongly suspect that Elijah directed Joshua into the deadfall trap or, in the least, deliberately left him there to die. A personal trial of the man's honour out there would have pleased you perhaps, but it was not to be. Higher powers had intervened and done the dastardly work for you."

"The Lord moves in mysterious ways His wonders to perform?" Child said with deliberate irony.

Marc didn't notice, for he was riding the crest of a rhetorical adrenaline rush, soaring along on the wings of his own argument. "At first I thought Joshua had been tempted out there by a note from one of the political radicals suggesting knowledge about Jesse's apparent suicide."

Child was fussing nonchalantly with his snuffbox.

"But that was wishful thinking. Joshua may have been obsessed with his son's inexplicable death, but I don't believe now that he would have been foolhardy enough to venture up there in a blizzard unless he recognized the handwriting on the note delivered to him – by one of your servants, who doubtless thought he was the bearer of an invitation, perhaps a peace-offering – and found it to be that of a man he had no reason to fear, even if he did quarrel with him over politics and land acquisition. After all, this man was a justice of the peace. What you put in that note I do not know, because the note was destroyed by Joshua or, more likely, removed from his body by Elijah after the fact. Joshua was knocked unconscious: alive but dying. Leaving a man to die and not reporting it is tantamount to murder. And those who seduced him out there under false pretenses are equally guilty. In the least, you were an accessory after the fact."

"At the inquest, as I recall, even Beth could not swear to the existence of a note."

"But her brother Aaron will."

A minor twitch of the left eyelid. "I see. So you've been browbeating helpless cretins, have you?"

"The boy is as sharp as you or me. His testimony will stand up in court."

"Perhaps. But you have nothing but a falsified alibi for evidence. You could not bring this within a mile of any court."

Time to play his second trump card, Marc decided. "At this moment, I have your accomplice incarcerated in the miller's office. He has confessed to the salient details as I've outlined them. Moreover, he has implicated *you*." This devastating fabrication was delivered with such élan that Marc almost believed it himself.

Child rocked back, but not from shock or the onset of fear. He was laughing. "Well now, this time you've been too clever by half," he roared. "For a second there you had me damn near convinced that you knew what the hell you were talking about. You might even have swayed a gullible jury envious of the gentry's innate superiority."

"My duty is to report everything I find to Sir John or his successor."

"It'll have to be to Francis Head, I'm afraid. Your mentor and protector is on his merry way to Montreal and obscurity." He let a chuckle ripple to a halt, heaved his bulk forward in his chair, and fixed Marc with a look that blended contempt, complacency, and aristocratic anger. "You are a brilliant fool," he said, "a meddling tyro whose vanity is exceeded only by his vocabulary. You do not have the hired hand in custody at Hatch's. You appear not even to know his last name."

"What do you mean?" Marc snapped.

"Elijah *Gowan* left the district right after the donnybrook last night, with his own kind." The Magistrate smiled his patronizing, judiciary smile. "The man is second cousin to Ogle Gowan, Grand Master of the Loyal Orange Lodge, whose lunatic apostles broke up the rally last night and tried to tar and feather the leading light of the Reform party. Elijah's a more fanatic Orangeman than his notorious cousin. He can track republican sentiment like a hound on the spoor. The Orange Order see any suggestion of annexation or democratization as tantamount to treason against the British Crown, which in turn they revere as a bulwark against popery."

Marc was momentarily thrown off stride by the sudden failure of his trump trick, but he quickly regained his momentum. "I didn't know until this morning that Elijah's name was Gowan, not Chown, and I readily admit that I do not have him in custody. However, he will not be very far from his cousin; we'll have him apprehended within a day." Marc did not feel obliged to admit that he had inferred from Elijah's obsessive interest in radical newspapers that he was a sympathizer, not an implacable opponent.

"We shall see, shan't we?" Was there a flicker of doubt before the resurgence of confidence? "Anyway, Elijah Gowan is long gone from Crawford's Corners. And I have good reason to believe he will be found only if he wants to be found. You've played your bluff, I'm afraid, without a deuce to support it." The smugness in Child's face was galling, to say the least.

"We'll find him. And when we do, he'll talk. In fact, I see now that you did not really have to have a hold on the man. All you had to do was convince him that Joshua Smallman was a turncoat who had thrown in with Hunters' Lodges and arch-republicans. He would have throttled Joshua in his own bed."

"That is quite true. But even if you should somehow find him, he'll never say a word against me or any other loyalist. You could put him on the rack and crack every rib and he would remain steadfastly silent. You see, for fanatics like Elijah, this isn't a game of politics or conflict of ideologies, it's a holy war, a crusade carried forth with God's own connivance."

"And what does that make the man who uses such fanaticism for his own ends?"

"It depends on the ends, doesn't it?"

Time now for the ace up his sleeve. "I think he'll talk," Marc said, "because I have irrefutable evidence that places him outside that cave in a position that gave him an unobstructed view of, and snowshoe access to, the deadfall trap."

Child maintained the smug expression he had no doubt cultivated on the bench and in the counting house, but his gaze was fixed on Marc as he reached into his jacket pocket and drew out two halves of a clay pipe.

"Hatch and I found this bit of stem on a ledge near the cave. I picked up this other piece a few minutes ago in Elijah Gowan's cabin. As you can see, they are a perfect fit. This evidence and his fabricated alibi will be enough to loosen his tongue. He won't fancy hanging or rotting in prison for a man whose motives had as much to do with greed and personal power as political sentiment and loyalty to the Crown."

"You have no direct proof of my involvement." Child's voice had gone cold.

"But I do have a case: a motive, a plausible scheme of events, a suborned servant, a man in flight without explanation, testimony that a message was received by the victim, and a summary of this conversation."

"You would take all that rubbish to Francis Head?"

"I intend to. Without delay."

Child uttered a world-weary sigh and sat back in his chair. "You are a sterling young man, Ensign Edwards. You showed us incredible courage and a selfless devotion to duty yester-evening when you rescued Mackenzie from that lunatic lot. You are a credit to your regiment. Your actions could well earn you promotion, even in these post-Napoleonic doldrums when such preferment is hard to come by. I observed your kindness out there at Mad Annie's, and the calm and solicitous way in which you dealt with the dying Connors."

"My God," Marc said suddenly, "it was *your* man who shot Connors. Would you stoop so low to protect your own hide as to involve John Collins in your crimes?"

Child ignored the remark. "My point is this: why are you going to the fruitless trouble of concocting such a report and presenting it, with all its flaws showing, to a lieutenant-governor who will have been in office for less than a week?"

"Until Elijah Gowan is caught and offers up his confession, I may not have proof enough to satisfy a court," Marc said, with more spite than he had intended, "but the evidence I do have, at the very least in these politically sensitive times, will throw serious doubt upon your character and on your probity as a justice of the peace. You are finished as a magistrate and as a pillar of this community."

"Francis Head will laugh you out of his office," Child said, straining now to maintain his air of unconcern and suppress his rising anger.

"I have no alternative but to do my duty," Marc said stiffly.

"Then you truly *are* a fool," Child said.

Marc rose. He reached into his pocket and withdrew two letters. "I may know little of politics, sir, but of one thing I am absolutely certain. Joshua Smallman was no turncoat. I doubt even that he was a committed Reformer. What you didn't know, and what you would have learned if you had not been obsessed with seizing control of his farm and had given the gentleman the courtesy of an interview, is that he was a commissioned informant for Sir John Colborne, the Governor's personal friend and a trusted confidant."

Philander Child desperately tried to look amused. "Another bluff, Mr. Edwards?"

"Why don't you take a moment after I've left to peruse the last report he ever sent to Sir John? I had it from the Governor's own hand, along with this detailed memorandum outlining the reasons why Sir John himself suspected foul play and chose me to come down here to investigate."

Marc dropped the letters on the table beside Child. It took all the moral courage he could muster not to turn at the door and watch the Magistrate as he read through the documents – whey-faced, stunned, all the pomp and pride leaching out of him as the contents of each successive page burned itself into his heart.

CHAPTER FIFTEEN

Marc was almost at the end of the winding lane that linked Philander Child's estate to the Kingston Road when he heard sleigh bells. He brought the Colonel's horse to a halt and waited. Seconds later, Erastus Hatch's Sunday cutter passed by the entrance to Deer Park on its way to Cobourg, where the rituals and ceremonies of the Sabbath would be played out as they had for generations of millers and other ordinary day-labourers. Thomas Goodall manned the driver's bench, cracking his whip above the ears of the horses and trying not to over-notice the erect and proper, but not unhandsome, figure of Winnifred Hatch seated at his side and looking quite ready to take the reins should he unexpectedly falter in his duty. Seated serenely in the sleigh itself, cheek by jowl, were the stout constable of Crawford Township and his one-time scullion, Mary Huggan.

Marc waved but they did not see him.

Well, he thought, there was at least one truly happy outcome of his week in Crawford's Corners. Father and daughter had found someone besides each other to cherish and build a life with.

Marc left a brief note on the table for Erastus, took a last, fond look around, and left the house. He threw his bedroll and pack over the horse, secured them, checked the saddlebags, and mounted. He nudged the animal around to the mill, then trotted up to the rear of Beth's place. A casual observer might have thought that the Ensign, dressed for Sunday parade, was enjoying a leisurely morning ride along Crawford Creek. Not so. Marc's mind had raced and seethed since the confrontation with Philander Child. There was much to sift, assess, decide.

As he led the horse up to the house, Beth appeared at the back door. She ran towards him, hugging a sweater to her small body. "Elijah's gone," she cried. "He never come home last night. I'm worried sick."

Marc took her hand. "He's gone for good," he said. "Let's go inside. I've got a lot to tell you."

How much to tell Beth, and how, had occupied a good portion of Marc's thoughts since he had left Child. Even now, as they sat sipping tea, Marc was only half certain of what he needed to say. He had been brought up to believe that women were weaker than men, but more delicate, refined, and sensitive – and hence more vulnerable to poetry, music, art, the graces that make the world bearable. But the price of such sensibility was, alas, intrinsic frailty, the constant spectre of psychological disintegration. Here before him was a woman only two weeks into mourning the loss of a "father"; the shocks she had borne over the past year and those rude revelations of the last two days ought to have crushed her, left her emotionally maimed, utterly exhausted, dependent upon the strength of some consoling, masculine arm. And yet here she sat with a teacup on her knee, waiting patiently for Marc to say what she knew could not be kept from her, whatever her own wishes might be. (And, of course, though it would be much later when he had time and the predisposition to ponder the more eccentric aspects of his week in Crawford's Corners, he would be forced to admit that few of the women he had encountered here – Winnifred, Lydia, Bella, Agnes, Mad Annie – fitted the comfortable cameo of womanhood presented to him by dear Uncle Jabez.)

Marc began. "After I left here this morning, I went straight over to Hatch's and told him my theory. But before I could set off for Stebbins's place, Erastus showed me a document that completely altered my view of what happened to your father-in-law and why. I'm sorry to say that it pointed a finger at Elijah."

"That can't be so. He's worked here without pay. He's been kind to me an' especially to Aaron." She looked truly bewildered for the first time since Marc had met her.

He swallowed hard. "I found a Bible in his cabin. It had his name in it: Elijah Gowan."

"Gowan?" She drew out the syllables of the name slowly, as light dawned in her eyes. "Not like Ogle Gowan?"

"He's a second cousin, yes. And an –"

"– an Orangeman."

"Apparently he believed that your father-in-law was about to throw his lot in with the annexationists. And to many Orangemen, that is an anti-monarchist act, an act of high treason."

"But how?"

"How and why he came to believe Joshua had gone that far we'll only know when we catch him."

She nodded, still perplexed. Marc told her about the matching pieces of clay pipe.

Beth sat very still, as if absorbing more than words. "Elijah couldn't have got Father out there in that blizzard," she said.

"Yes, that is true. And that's why I'm convinced that a second person was deeply involved in Joshua's death. I believe Elijah was to be made the instrument of murder, but someone a lot more clever and knowledgeable planned it, with cold premeditation."

"Who?"

"I've identified the culprit," Marc said, releasing each word carefully, "but so far I don't have enough evidence, and until I do I am honour-bound to keep the name to myself."

"I understand," she said, implying more than mere agreement.

"But as soon as Elijah is arrested, we'll have the means to establish the whole truth, and justice will be fully served. Joshua's murderers will not go unpunished."

Beth smiled wryly, the hurt hidden in the humour: "It's been some time in this province since justice has been served."

Marc could find no words to deny it.

Putting a hand on his wrist, she said, "It's not *your* fault – the bush, the politics, the mess we're in. You've done me a great service, so great that nothin' I can do or say will ever be enough to repay you."

Marc knew this was not so, but offered no suggestions.

"You've given me answers to questions that would've plagued me – perhaps for the whole of my life. You've given me back the Father I loved more than any other, a man who did not wander foolishly to his death in a blizzard but died for what he was, what he stood for. An' you've given me back a husband I can mourn an' remember as I ought to."

"I did my duty," Marc said, "that is all."

For the moment they both accepted the lie.

Marc shook hands with Aaron, and Beth accompanied him to the back door, where the Colonel's horse waited.

"I'll write Erastus and James in detail as soon as I can, but I'd be obliged if you would, in the meantime, extend my sincere thanks to them for their many kindnesses."

"They'll want to know about Elijah."

"Yes. You may tell them anything I've revealed to you."

"Still, they'll be disappointed not seeing you off."

"Yes. I've grown quite fond of them. I have never made friends quickly, but this week has been like no other in my life."

"Your long and interestin' life."

"My short and boring life."

"Till now," she said, smiling.

"You won't be able to run this farm on your own," he said softly.

"I know. But we'll be all right just the same."

"You could come to Toronto. Open up a shop."

"You mustn't talk like that. We're only allowed one hope at a time. *You* must go back to your regiment. *I* need time to grieve, an' reacquaint myself with God after our recent quarrel, an' be a mother to Aaron, who's never had one."

"I understand," Marc said, though he didn't. "But I'll come back, just the same."

"Hush," she said, laying a finger on his lips. "Don't make promises you may regret havin' to keep."

And before he had a chance to argue his case, she eased the door shut.

He waited for the latch to click into place before he took three reluctant steps to Colonel Margison's second-best horse, which was already dancing with traitorous thoughts of an open road and the company of its own kind somewhere at the end of it.

EPILOGUE

E lijah Gowan was apprehended a week later, cowering and bewildered in a pantry off the summer kitchen of his cousin's house. He was eager – proud even – to make a full confession, viewing his actions as righteous and necessary. Moreover, he readily implicated Philander Child. In fact, he had kept the note he had removed from Joshua's body (telling Child that he had destroyed it) – the one in the Magistrate's own handwriting. His trust in his benefactor, it seemed, had not been total: the note was his insurance against betrayal. Child was arrested and bound over at Kingston to the spring assizes.

Marc's own actions and his subsequent report to Sir John Colborne (who forwarded it to Sir Francis Head, the newly arrived lieutenant-governor) had two immediate consequences for the young ensign, one happy and one not. Marc was promoted to lieutenant on Sir John's enthusiastic recommendation, for which he was more than grateful, but that gentleman also suggested that Sir Francis put him in charge of security for Government House and make him his aide-de-camp. Both of these honours were regarded as promotions and were the cause of much envy among his fellow officers. Marc, however, saw the new posting as an insuperable obstacle to his being transferred to Quebec, where rebellion and true military action were thought to be imminent.

Ferris O'Hurley, the escaped peddler, never reached the border. He had unwisely decided to circle back to Perry's Corners and liberate his donkey, still in the hands of its captors, and was caught trying – unsuccessfully – to persuade it to accompany him home. O'Hurley soon confessed to having "witnessed" Ninian T. Connors as he "assisted" Jesse Smallman to hang himself in his barn, following a violent quarrel over the spoils of their rum-running business. And while he admitted that he was aware of the hundred dollars that Marc had impounded, he maintained that all he was ever told was that it had come from the Hunters' Lodge in New York State and that Connors was taking it to a group of Upper Canadians to aid them in their ongoing struggle against tyranny. Only Connors knew who the contact person was, and that secret died with him.

As Marc sat at his desk pondering these matters, he could not help feeling that his week in Crawford's Corners had been somewhat more than an adventure. He had carried out a successful murder investigation. He had learned much about this odd colony and its extraordinary citizens. He had made some friends. He had met a woman to whom he was preparing to write a long and, he hoped, persuasive letter.

He picked up his pen and began to write.

Now read the opening pages of *Solemn Vows,*
the next mystery in the Marc Edwards series

Solemn Vows

Chapter One

June 1836

Marc Edwards wiped the sweat off his brow with the sleeve of his tunic, but not before a rivulet of it had slid into his left eye and two greasy drops had plopped on the shako-cap cupped between his knees. The afternoon sun of a cloudless June day was pouring a relentless, shimmering heat down on the hustings and its well-fed, overdressed, inebriated occupants. Surely, Marc thought, the grandees of Danby's Crossing (or pompous old Danby himself) could have erected the rickety scaffolding within the shade of the maple trees he could see drooping at the north-west corner of the square, or at least close enough to Danby's Inn for its two-storey verandah to provide some shelter. Such was not the case, however – here or anywhere else in the backwater province of Upper Canada, where, it seemed, elections were considered life-and-death affairs, and high seriousness and bodily suffering prime virtues. And such sufferings invariably included a shaky platform groaning with dignitaries, each of whom contrived to "say a few words" in as many sentences as possible.

At the moment, Garfield Danby, the self-appointed chairman of the day's proceedings, was droning away with his introduction of the guest speaker, Sir Francis Bond Head, lieutenant-governor of the province, who was seated directly behind the podium and next to Marc. As Marc gazed out at the dusty square and the several hundred people gathered there on a sweltering Tuesday afternoon in the middle of the haying season, he marvelled at their perseverance, their dogged insistence on hearing every word uttered, as if words themselves might somehow right their many grievances against the King's representatives, grievances that had bedevilled the colony for half a generation.

Not two days ago, many of these same folk – farmers, shopkeepers, draymen, often accompanied by their wives or sweethearts – had stood in this same spot to listen to platitudes from politicians of both parties, the Constitutionists (as the right-wing Tories were now styling themselves) and the left-wing Reformers. And today they had laid down their tools and come back to hear the most powerful man in the province, King William's surrogate in this far corner of his realm. They came to listen and, from what Marc had learned about them in the twelve months since his arrival in Toronto, to judge. Hence their willingness to stand quietly in their place and tolerate the ill-grammared maundering of Mr. Danby. Sir Francis *would* speak, eventually – if the heat didn't liquify them all first.

Marc could hear the governor shuffling the several pages of notes he had prepared with the help of his military secretary, old Major Burns, and Marc, now his principal aide-de-camp, even though this speech, like all the others over the past week, would simply be a reconfiguration of his constant themes: public order before any redress of acknowledged grievances; a stable government to assure justice and to effect lasting reforms; a purging of extremists of both left and right (Sir Francis being, after all, a Whig appointment in a Tory domain); reiteration of His Majesty's implacable opposition to republicanism and the

"American party" led by William Lyon Mackenzie; and a direct appeal to the moderate, pragmatic common sense of the stout yeomanry who peopled the colony and whose roots reached deep into the fostering soil of the motherland. With Major Burns's rheumatism acting up more frequently and incapacitating him ever more grievously, Sir Francis had been calling more and more upon Marc, whose days as a law student had left him proficient in the King's English, to assist him in speech-writing and, on occasion, to compose from notes official letters to the colonial secretary in London, Lord Glenelg.

While Marc had chosen the action of the army over the tedium of the law, he was not too dispirited by these tasks because he found himself by and large in agreement with both the sentiments and the strategy of his superior. Marc was now certain that ordinary citizens had genuine grievances, mainly as a result of the winter weeks he had spent at Crawford's Corners and Cobourg, where he had carried out his first investigative assignment. However, he now felt, as did Sir Francis, that because these grievances were of long standing and had been exacerbated by the violence of local politics and by the sudden influx of "republican" immigrants from the United States, the first priority was to calm the waters, reassert the King's authority with a firm and fair hand, and then one by one deal with the people's complaints in an atmosphere free of partisan rant and rhetoric. This message seemed to be having a positive effect on the electorate. (That the lieutenant-governor was by tradition supposed to be a neutral in election campaigns was a forgivable lapse of protocol.)

On the bench directly behind the governor, Langford Moncreiff – the newly appointed member of the Executive Council – slumbered noisily. Above the low murmuring of the crowd and the rush of a sudden breeze through the maple trees, the councillor's snores rose as loud as any hog's. Sir Francis shuffled his papers again: Mr. Danby appeared to be running out of inspiration. The victims of his wordiness shuffled in anticipation.

Reminded of why he was here on the hustings platform – to ensure the governor's safety – Marc put his shako back on, leaned forward and scanned the village square. Just behind the hustings, where the path south began its meandering through the woods, two junior officers, he knew, stood watch, their horses tethered nearby. Marc swept his eyes over the Danby Inn to his left, where the governor's entourage had arrived mid morning with flags flying. Ensign Rick Hilliard, fresh-faced and keen to please, stood stiffly at the door, gripping his Brown Bess musket tightly. The platform dignitaries – including three merchants, a brace of lawyers, and a rotund banker – were less than twenty yards from the balustrade of the inn's upper verandah. Hilliard gave Marc the briefest of nods. Beyond the inn, the wide corduroy road that led west to Yonge Street was fringed with tall maple trees, now rustling in the breeze. Marc could see the bare legs and feet of the dozen youngsters who had climbed the branches to "get a gander" at the governor or simply to make a happy nuisance of themselves. Opposite the hustings, the general store and the sprawling livery stables merited only a cursory glance. On the east, the smithy was fireless and quiet, and in front of the harness shop next to it, the proprietor and his family stood in the sunshine, smiling at the penultimate phrases of Mr. Danby's windy introduction. Above the harness shop, Marc could see the glass windows and calico curtains of the second-storey apartment and, higher still, a gabled garret.

Half-throttled by his own snores, Councillor Moncreiff let out a gasp, but apparently did not jar himself awake, for the snorting started up again. How many of the other self-invited platform guests were also dozing, Marc could only speculate.

It was not yet three o'clock, but everyone here had already put in a full day. For those travelling in the governor's retinue, the morning had begun at nine o'clock outside the garrison at Fort York, and had included a lurching ride up dusty Yonge Street, past Blue Hill, Deer Park, Montgomery's tavern at Eglinton and a quarter-mile east to Danby's Crossing.

Once there, with as much of the grime removed as possible, Sir Francis and the Toronto worthies had been greeted by the local gentry and their ladies (from as far away as Newmarket), several of whom had got into the madeira sometime earlier. Danby had laid on a stultifying midday dinner (as it was quaintly termed in the colonies), replete with wine, several desserts, and cigars. If Sir Francis had been shocked by the presence of women throughout the meal, by the ingratiating speeches of welcome, or by the port-and-cigar aftermath, he was too well mannered to show it. Marc and his second-in-command, Colin Willoughby, had led their troop into a back room where a more modest meal awaited them.

Willoughby had given Marc a look that said quite plainly, "Did we really leave England for *this*?" Marc had grinned. He liked Willoughby a lot. The young man had arrived with the governor in January, suffering terribly, it seemed, from a luckless love affair. Sir Francis had taken Colin under his wing and had looked to Marc to assist him. Marc found it easy to sympathize with the pain of unrequited love, as his own attempts to win over Beth Smallman in Cobourg had met with little success. None of his letters had been answered.

At the moment, though, they both had more serious matters to attend to here at Danby's Crossing. The place was not an official village yet. Its "commons" had been laid out and surrounded by lots severed from the property of landowner-merchant Garfield Danby with a view to its becoming eventually, as the province matured, an official town, whose chief magistrate and beneficiary would be the man who had had the foresight to envision it all. In the interim, the rents from the tradesmen and income from the Danby Inn would suffice. None of this escaped the notice of the farmers and woodsmen who patronized Danby's businesses and suffered the tedium of his *noblesse oblige*: like so many others in the province, they observed, judged, and waited for the polls to open. It was to these citizens, not to the avaricious Danbys of the Family Compact and its ruling clique, that Sir Francis was about to make his appeal for common sense and old-fashioned loyalty.

Marc glanced down at Willoughby, whose watch upon those gathered in the square in front of him was as keen as Marc's had been upon the peripheral buildings. Willoughby nodded reassuringly and turned to scrutinize the crowd once more. Danby's audience was now audibly shuffling about in a vain attempt to get comfortable before Sir Francis rose to speak.

"Ladies and gentlemen," boomed Danby at last, "I present to you this afternoon, Lieutenant-Governor Sir Francis Bond Head!"

Without warning a gust of wind swept across the platform. One of the sheets of notes fluttered out of the governor's hand just as he was about to step up. He reached down to retrieve it before it reached the floor, as did Marc. There was an embarrassing collision of heads, followed by a loud cracking sound somewhere beyond them, a muted thud close behind them, then silence, as if all those assembled had drawn their breath in as one astonished person. Marc turned partway around in time to see Councillor Moncreiff sit bolt upright and flick open both eyes – eyes that saw nothing. The old gentleman was already dead, his blood and lungs beginning to ooze through the gap in his waistcoat.